Ann McMillan is the author of *Dead March*, *Angel Trumpet*, and *Civil Blood*, the first three book in this series. A native of Georgia, she lives in Richmond, Virginia.

CHICKAHOMINY FEVER

FEVER

A Civil War Mystery

Ann McMillan

PENGUIN BOOKS

PENGUIN BOOKS

Published by the Penguin Group

Penguin Group (USA) Inc., 375 Hudson Street, New York, New York 10014, U.S.A.

Penguin Books Ltd, 80 Strand, London WC2R 0RL, England

Penguin Books Australia Ltd, 250 Camberwell Road, Camberwell, Victoria 3124, Australia

Penguin Books Canada Ltd, 10 Alcorn Avenue, Toronto, Ontario, Canada M4V 3B2

Penguin Books India (P) Ltd, 11 Community Centre, Panchsheel Park, New Delhi–110 017, India

Penguin Group (NZ), cnr Airborne and Rosedale Roads, Albany, Auckland 1310, New Zealand

Penguin Books (South Africa) (Pty) Ltd, 24 Sturdee Avenue,

Rosebank, Johannesburg 2196, South Africa

Penguin Books Ltd, Registered Offices: 80 Strand, London WC2R 0RL, England

First published in the United States of America by Viking 2003
Published in Penguin Books 2004

10 9 8 7 6 5 4 3 2 1

W. Eugene Ferslew, *Map of the city of Richmond, Henrico County, Virginia. Prepared from actual
surveys, and published expressly for subscribers to the Richmond directory, 1859, W. Gillespie, Sc. S.A.
Sandys, Printers, Baltimore. Reprinted by The Virginia Guardsman, 1935.* Map Collection (755.44,
1859, 1935), Archives Research Services, The Library of Virginia, Richmond, VA.

PUBLISHER'S NOTE

This is a work of fiction. Names, characters, places, and incidents either are the product
of the author's imagination or are used fictitiously, and any resemblance to actual persons,
living or dead, business establishments, events, or locales is entirely coincidental.

THE LIBRARY OF CONGRESS HAS CATALOGUED THE HARDCOVER EDITION AS FOLLOWS:
McMillan, Ann, date.
Chickahominy fever : a Civil War mystery / Ann McMillan.
p.   cm.
ISBN 0-670-03107-0
ISBN 0 14 20.0456 1
1. Powers, Narcissa (Fictitious characters)—Fiction. 2. Daniel, Judah (Fictitious character)—
Fiction. 3. Richmond (Va.)—History—Civil War, 1861–1865—Fiction. 4. African American
women healers—Fiction. 5. Female friendship—Fiction. 6. Race relations—Fiction.
7. Nurses—Fiction. I. Title.
PS3563.C38657 C48   2003
813'.54—dc21   2002074061

Printed in the United States of America

To Ruth and Phil Hallman—welcome back to Virginia.

ACKNOWLEDGMENTS

While confessing any errors as my own, I want to thank the following individuals for their generous gifts of time and expertise: Colleen Callahan, Carolyn Carlson, the Conference for Women and the Civil War, Ruth Ann Coski, Gertrude Jacinta Fraser, Robert Kenzer, Gregg Kimball, Jodi Koste, Robert E. L. Krick, Estelle Porter, Teresa Roane, Lucia Watson, T. Adrian Wheat, and Nancy Yost. Thanks to H. Alex Wise Jr., president of the Tredegar National Civil War Center Foundation, for sharing his knowledge of his great-great-grandfather Governor Henry Wise—one of the most interesting figures in Virginia history. Special thanks, as always, to Randy and Hunter.

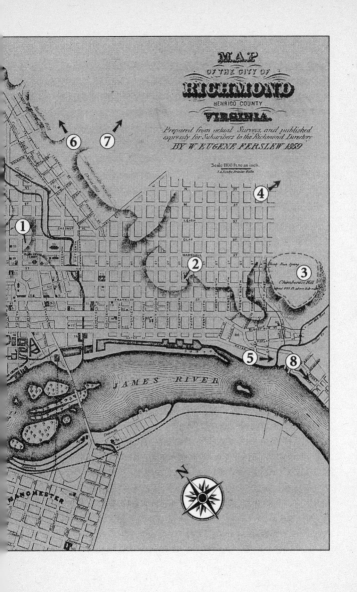

CHICKAHOMINY
FEVER

✦✦✦

CHAPTER ONE

Richmond, Virginia
SUNDAY, JUNE 22, 1862

The gas lamp threw a circle of light on the desk. A single piece of paper covered most of the desk's surface. Vines grew on the paper, black on white. Some branched from a thick trunk that meandered downward from the left margin to the right—the James. The lesser vines bore different labels: the South Anna and the North Anna; the Pamunkey; the Chickahominy. Within this tangle of snaking curves some careful hand had placed a rule and drawn a pattern of lines that formed an elongated checkerboard about ten inches across: Richmond. A few of these lines extended farther, trailing off to the edges of the paper in all directions, running straight and true for the most part, but curving or angling here and there as if the snaking movement of the vines had jostled the draftsman's hand: the Mechanicsville Turnpike, the Petersburg Turnpike, the Darbytown Road.

Jefferson Davis squeezed his eyes shut, then opened them. To his good eye, the black marks seemed to wriggle and jump. The man's stern, bony face was strong-willed, but his eyes were disobedient servants. At last he brought his hand up and held them shut.

"President Davis?"

The man behind the desk drew his hand away and looked up at the speaker.

"Brigadier General Wise to see you, sir."

Davis sighed. Here was an interview he would give much to avoid. Wise openly expressed his contempt for the Confederate president—not caring, apparently, that his words would be reported to the man himself. Officers gossiped worse than women, and tattlers were everywhere. One despised the tattlers, of course, but the seeds of their gossip could not help but lodge in the brain. It wasn't that he didn't understand Wise's anger. But it was wrong of Wise to blame him. And given the bulldog stubbornness of the man, nothing Davis could say would ever soften that anger or deflect that blame.

The young man prompted gently, "Shall I see what he wants?"

Davis placed both hands on the map and pushed himself up to stand. "I know what he wants. What he always wants. I can't give it to him. But he's a hero—not just a former governor of Virginia, but the governor who hanged John Brown. I have to see him, Burton. Give us ten minutes, and if he's still here, interrupt me for an urgent message." Davis's thin lips curved in a slight smile. Burton Harrison nodded and hurried off down the stairs.

Out in the kitchen of the Davis house, Susy Reynolds got word that the president was asking for cold tea served. There was no ice, that was understood; any ice that had survived the weeks of hot weather had gone to the hospitals. But pitchers of brewed tea were waiting in the cellar, cool enough to provide relief on this hot, moist night. She fetched one of them, dried its wet surface with a towel, and set it on a tray with the glasses, sugar bowl, napkins, and spoons. Then she walked, quietly and carefully, up the stairs to the second-floor office.

Henry Wise ignored the horsehair sofa opposite the president's desk and was standing, holding forth in his orator's voice despite the fact that he had but one listener, and that one obviously pained by headache. "I can't but think you do not know what I have been asked to do. I have three thin regiments—fifteen hundred men, roughly. That paltry force, stretched between the Williamsburg Road and the James, is all that stands between this city and its enemies." Wise bent over the desk and stabbed at the map with his forefinger. "I am expected to dig rifle pits at Chaffin's Bluff, *here,* nearly two miles from my headquarters, as well as *here*"—the finger jabbed again, a little lower down—"a mile downstream, where we trust a damned pile of refuse thrown into the water to keep out the Federal gunboats. I am guarding the bridge, *here,* four miles from my headquarters. My infantry is picketing the Varina Road and the New Market Road, separated from one another by a distance of *five miles.*" The finger sketched a triangle. "General Magruder is impressing slaves to dig fortifications, but I don't have enough men to keep the slaves from running off. Meanwhile, it's been three weeks since our forces have engaged the enemy; three weeks in which your generals have allowed McClellan to bring up his men and his tents and his beeves and his asses and his God damned sheep."

Leviticus, thought Davis.

Wise took a breath, then went on. "The whole of my cavalry was sent to Stuart. Those men volunteered to serve under *me.* Just over twelve hundred men healthy I have now, and who knows how long they'll stay healthy, digging in the mud all day and sleeping in the rain for lack of tents, breathing the bad air from the swamps. Three hundred of my men are already sick, most with the Chickahominy fever. It saps their strength; it saps their spirit."

Wise stopped, looked away. When he spoke again, his voice was low. "Just four months ago we were at Roanoke Island, given three thousand men and asked to hold an indefensible position against a Union force of five times that number. I wrote to Huger, I wrote to Benjamin, pleading—but no, they could not spare the men. My son was a martyr to their cold hearts. So now I am coming to you."

President Davis rubbed his temple and waited, letting Wise spend his ammunition.

Wise reached into his uniform jacket and drew out an envelope sealed with red wax. "I've written it all out, my assessment of the danger we are in and the reinforcements I need to do what I've been asked to do. If things turn out as I expect, let no one say I did not try to make it otherwise."

Davis took the sealed envelope. Wise lowered his long, bony frame onto the sofa as if to wait while the letter was read, but Davis made no move to open it.

A discreet knock sounded on the other side of the door. In a moment the door opened and the maid Susy walked into the room, her eyes fixed upon the heavy silver tray she carried as if she feared with every step to drop it. She nodded to the men, crossed between them, and placed the tray on the round table. She picked up the silver pitcher and, holding the towel just under the spout, poured the tea into the glasses. She handed a napkin and a glass to each man, then made an awkward little bow and left the room, closing the door behind her.

Henry Wise dampened his napkin on the cool glass, then held the napkin to his forehead. Wise was a strong-featured man who shaved the wiry white beard from his cheeks and cleft chin but left it like a ruff under his jaw. In this weather, it looked as hot as a fur collar.

"I wish General Johnston could take the field." Davis seemed to be talking to himself. Wise grew still. "Of course, General Lee has my complete trust. But at a time like this, experience . . ." Davis's words trailed off.

Wise put down his glass. "Give me hope, sir," he

prompted. "Tell me we have reinforcements coming. Tell me Lee plans to attack."

Davis nodded, his face solemn. "It's a bold notion, and a great gamble." He placed the envelope containing Wise's letter on top of the map. Then he picked up a silver pencil and, holding the envelope flat, began to draw on it— the James, and above it the Chickahominy; the Williamsburg Road running southeast out of Richmond, and above it the Mechanicsville Turnpike running north. He paused and looked up at Wise, who had come around to stand at his shoulder.

Davis spoke, gesturing with his pencil. "If we let McClellan bring up his siege guns, we'll have no choice but to abandon Richmond. For the present, McClellan's army is cut in two by the Chickahominy. It's not much of a river, but with all the rain we've been having, it makes quite a swamp. Lee is concentrating all our force, as much as can be spared, against FitzJohn Porter above the Chickahominy. Reinforcements are expected." He spoke those three words with deliberation, letting Wise know that was all that would be said upon the subject. "Meanwhile Lee is taking a risk, here." Davis drew an arc from the Williamsburg Road south to the James. "We are betting everything that *your* force, thin and battered though it is, can hold the line and fight off any incursions until Lee is ready to strike. When he does strike . . . well, we can but hope it will be a decisive blow."

Davis stood, and the two men faced each other. "I am sorry I have no more troops to give you, General."

Wise straightened his shoulders and drew in a breath that expanded his chest. "My men and I will fight—and die, if we must—for Virginia." The fire in his eyes made his meaning clear: *Not for your Confederacy; for Virginia.*

Davis let the challenge pass. "I need not tell you that this information must be kept secret, even from your junior officers." He extended his right hand to Wise, who grasped it briefly, then turned and left the room.

Jefferson Davis stood listening to Wise's boot heels on the stairs. He raised his hand again to his temple and probed the vein there. He was thinking about his new commander in chief. "Granny Lee," the newspapers called him, and "the King of Spades," because he was having the men dig fortifications around the city when they would rather go and fight. But though they did not know it yet—those carpers at the newspapers, and in the streets—Lee had had enough of caution. He was determined to attack. If McClellan should discover the thin spot in Richmond's defenses, though, Union troops could take the city in a matter of hours. Lee was making a dangerous wager, putting Richmond at stake.

At last Davis picked up Wise's letter, its seal still unbroken, and dropped it into the low-banked fire that was kept going in all weather for just such a purpose. He watched for a moment as the edge caught, then left the room through a different door, the one that led to his bedchamber.

Susy Reynolds passed on silent, felt-shod feet into the office where Davis and Wise had conferred. She took two steps toward the silver pitcher, then hesitated, turned, and looked into the fire. In a moment she was kneeling by the grate. She drew out the letter, laid it on the hearth, and put her foot on it, just hard enough to snuff out the pinpricks of flame that still glowed along the blackened edge. Then she took it up and thrust it into the pocket of her apron, wiped the ashes from the hearth, and stirred up the fire to a stronger flame.

Ward 27 at Chimborazo Hospital was allotted to hopeless cases. Not that there were not plenty of hopeless cases throughout the other wards—but the concentration here was absolute. If any man walked out of Ward 27, the surgeons—not normally modest men—would acknowledge divine intervention.

"Sergeant Robert G. Smith received a bullet wound to the thigh on June seventh, while on picket duty on the Williamsburg Road."

Dr. Cameron Archer was addressing the three young men gathered around the bed of the patient. Smith's was the next to last in a row of twenty beds. Two such rows lined the whitewashed walls of the pine-plank building, with one long aisle running between the rows. The young men were medical students preparing for examination and commissioning as assistant surgeons. They would not spend much time here, among the hopeless cases. Nor would a skilled surgeon: Archer would pause over an interesting case or two, then hurry on, leaving Dr. Wright, the contract surgeon, or Dr. Coster, a newly commissioned assistant surgeon, in charge. Wright was on duty now. He was standing a little behind the students, frowning with exaggerated attention, but his eyes wandered, and he plucked at his scraggly beard.

Though Archer habitually spoke in the low and languid tones of the Tidewater gentry, his voice carried clearly to where Narcissa Powers was sitting near the door of the long building. Narcissa wondered if it depressed the patients' spirits to hear their injuries and illnesses announced by the doctors. Archer had developed his teaching style as demonstrator of anatomy at the medical college, where the subjects under his knife had been, of course, dead.

Sergeant Smith would not complain: his jaws were locked together with tetanus. But if he understood the surgeon's words, he knew he had cause to fear. The disease caused convulsions so strong as to sometimes break the back of the sufferer, and was almost invariably fatal.

Narcissa shivered a little, imagining what Smith might feel. Perspiration had soaked her underclothes. For weeks, it seemed, a damp heat had hung over the city, building to thunderstorms that rumbled in the distance like artillery fire before they broke and poured down rain. Someday— today? tomorrow?—man-made thunder would blast across the earth again, shaking the city, leaving more broken men. This was the calm within the eye of the storm.

Narcissa focused her attention on the penknife and the quill in her hands. She was preparing the quill, smoothing the narrow end so that, after Dr. Archer and the students had passed by, she could use it to feed Sergeant Smith, filling the tiny cavity with a few drops of nourishing beef tea or milk punch, then guiding it through his lips and holding it there until he was able to swallow.

"The following day," Archer continued, "his right thigh was amputated, the lower part of the upper third, by a circular operation. He was being nursed in a private home until four days ago, when symptoms of tetanus appeared. At admission, the tetanus was marked: no tetanic convulsions, but the lower maxilla fixed, the posterior muscles of the neck also rigid, perspiration profuse, pulse one hundred and ten. The stump was in an unhealthy condition, with a large slough some three inches deep, separating on the external side; bone protruding about an inch, and a fungus growth from the medullary canal."

Had Sergeant Smith heard this description of his own thighbone, corrupted like a bad piece of meat? A shiver ran through her, so strong she had to put her hands in her lap for a moment.

"The wound was cleaned," Archer continued, "and drawn together with adhesive plaster. Citrate of iron and morphine are being given to ensure rest. Note the tetanic grin: the lips are drawn back to reveal the clenched teeth. Milk punch, soup, eggs, et cetera, can be taken through a quill—such as Mrs. Powers is now fashioning."

So I'm not invisible, after all. But he had said it kindly. After all, it was Archer who had suggested to Narcissa that she come up to Chimborazo to work with some more challenging cases; Archer who had pointed her in the direction of the tetanus victim. *If the patient does not eat, the gangrene does.* That was the doctors' wisdom, and Archer had said it might hold true for lockjaw as well.

Narcissa looked up at the surgeon's smiling face. He looked handsome, his beard shaved cleanly away from his cheeks into a neat Van Dyke. He had not looked so dandified in the days after Williamsburg and Seven Pines. Weeks had passed since those engagements. Many of the wounded had died; some had recovered; others, like Sergeant Smith, lingered on. Now only a few were coming in wounded, the victims of sharpshooters or skirmishes between patrols. Of course, life in the camps claimed its own casualties, and now the hospitals were admitting victims of diarrhea, dysentery, and various types of fever. There was time, for now at least, to spend on a tetanus patient who had little chance to live.

Archer turned away and led the medical students down the aisle, Wright following behind. Narcissa rose from the camp stool on which she had been sitting and looked over at Smith. Only his glossy brown hair showed him to be a young man. His face was gaunt, and his bearded chin jutted toward the ceiling, drawn up by the stiffened tendons in the back of his neck. She could see the shape of his mutilated body under the sheet—the skeletal ribs, the decaying stump. In the battle between life and death, Sergeant Smith was disputed territory.

Narcissa moved the camp stool over beside Sergeant Smith's bed. There was just enough space for it between his and the next bed, the last in line, occupied by a man whom head injury had plunged into coma. She dipped the little quill into the tepid beef tea, put her finger over the opening at the top, then carried the quill carefully to the sergeant's mouth. Slowly, carefully, she worked the quill between his teeth, then moved her finger away to release the liquid so that the few drops thus transferred could trickle into his mouth. Then she took the quill quickly away; if his teeth sank into it as he swallowed, the delicate tube might be crushed. She sat back, waving away the flies. Smith swallowed. She could see his whole body tense with effort—and, she feared, with pain. When he relaxed, she repeated the process.

At last the sergeant signaled with a little shake of his head that he had had enough. Soon a dose of morphine would ease Sergeant Smith into sleep. She put down the quill, wrung out a clean rag in cool water, and blotted the perspiration from his face and neck. And she looked up to see another woman, the first she had seen that day— tending to a patient several beds down from Smith. The patient's head was bandaged down to his eyebrows, and his eyes were closed. The black-dressed woman was talking to him as she bathed his face and arms—or praying, perhaps; her voice was too low for Narcissa to hear what she was saying.

As if feeling Narcissa's eyes on her, the woman looked up. She gathered up the bowl and cloth, crossed over to Narcissa, and nodded a greeting. Then she said, "It's good of you to come, ma'am. I been the only woman here these last two days."

"Is he—your loved one?" Narcissa asked the woman. So little of the wounded man was showing that she could not tell whether he was of an age to be this woman's son or her brother or husband. He was lying very still; only the faint rise and fall of his chest showed there was life in him. She guessed his injury to be severe—after all, he'd been given a bed among the hopeless. And there was no question that the woman tending to him had suffered a terrible loss. She was brittle with it.

"No, ma'am," the woman answered. "This here's Private Devlin. They say he can't hear what I'm saying, but I talk to him. I got no one else to talk to. Both my husband and my son died at Seven Pines. So I come here, most days."

"I'm sorry." Narcissa put her hand on the woman's shoulder. The thin shoulder blades were prominent through the well-worn cotton cloth. "Have we met before? I'm Narcissa Powers."

"Annie Yates. Pleased to make your acquaintance, ma'am."

That smile again—less of a smile than a wince, really. Every time she tells someone, she feels it all over again—the pain of her loss. "Tell me about them," Narcissa said gently. "Your husband and your son."

Annie looked blank for a moment. Perhaps no one had cared enough to ask her before. "They was both killed," Annie said again. "I went every day to where they had the names posted, and I—I took a paper that the chaplain writ for me." Annie felt in her apron pocket and drew out a grimy, much-folded piece of paper. She held it up for Narcissa to see. It had two lines printed on it: "John Yates, Private, Twenty-fourth Virginia Infantry," and "James Yates, Private, Twenty-fourth Virginia Infantry." "I checked to see if there was any writing on the list that looked like this." Annie refolded the paper carefully and put it back in her pocket.

Oh—of course. How would you learn if your loved one was killed or injured if his regimental chaplain didn't know his fate and you couldn't read?

"Both of their names was on the list." Annie Yates made

the statement in a flat voice, looking away from Narcissa, frowning as if the light hurt her eyes. Narcissa felt the strength of her determination not to cry, and she knew how Annie must feel—that if those pent-up tears were allowed to fall just once, they would never stop. She touched Annie's shoulder again. Annie turned toward her, acknowledging the gesture, then gathered her skirts and walked away, leaving Narcissa wondering if her overture, though kindly meant, had done more harm than good.

Archer had been waiting for a word alone. "You're bearing up well, Mrs. Powers. Not many women could stand it." He couldn't help comparing her to the wives of the other doctors who worked around him. Matthew Lester's wife wouldn't have set foot in here, even before she'd fled the siege and its deprivations. Thomas Wright's wife—if the rumors were true, she'd not want to go anywhere her husband was, hospital ward or not. Douglas Coster was courting a young lady whose mother likely would have locked her up sooner than have her come here. Of all the doctors he knew, only old Stedman had a wife anything the equal of Narcissa, and she was old enough to be Narcissa's mother.

"What do you mean, Dr. Archer?" she replied with a slight smile.

"Most young ladies would find it depressing to be among these men. I merely mean that you are courageous."

"Oh—no. It's a privilege."

"We surgeons don't always find it so. These are our failures."

"You are doing all that can be done—all anyone could do," protested Narcissa.

Archer shrugged. "If they were in a state to know it,

they'd likely resent the ragtag bunch assigned to their care—Wright, who's a drunk; and Coster, who'd never amputated more than a hangnail before he walked in here as a newly minted surgeon. I walk through once or twice a day with students, and Lester comes through about as often, since he has thirty wards—the whole Sixth Division—to oversee."

Narcissa's smile quirked at the corners. "And yet, a year ago, you were among those who questioned whether ladies should be allowed in the hospitals."

Why, Archer asked himself angrily, do I persist in lowering my defenses? "And there are some who still question it."

"I would imagine," Narcissa went on, "the surgeons and the patients differ in their opinion of the hospitals. You see a model of efficiency, compared to the old notion of a hospital as an almshouse for the sick, where no one would go except out of desperation. But your patients compare the hospital to their own homes, where they were tended by their loving mothers and wives."

"No doubt you are right," Archer agreed, repressing a sigh.

Among free blacks as well as slaves, it was bad luck to name a baby too early, before it had lived a few weeks in the world. Elda Chapman had been careful to hold off naming her second son, but he had died anyway, so she had given him a name to be buried with: Tyler, after her husband, who had gone over to the Yankees. Might be Elda's husband would return someday to lift his name out of the grave. But for now, the name linked two losses.

Judah Daniel untied the strings that fastened Elda's nightdress at the throat. Elda's breasts were hot and hard under Judah Daniel's gently probing fingers. Sometimes Elda would agree to express the milk; other times she refused, though she never put up a fight, just turned her head away. To express her milk sometimes but not others was keeping her sick, and Judah Daniel told her, but Elda didn't seem to hear, or didn't care. Judah Daniel pulled the throat of Elda's nightdress back up to cover her breasts but didn't retie the ties. "I'm making up a poultice—just warm mullein leaves. You get comfortable, now, and I'll be back."

Young John came running, looking back over his shoulder and giggling at Darcy, who was hurrying to catch him. Young John—the older and now, again, the only son of Elda—was almost two, walking and talking and getting into everything. Judah Daniel stood still and let him run into her skirts. He looked up into her face, bright-eyed and laughing, as she caught him up in her arms. "Watch where you going, young'un," she mock-scolded, looking over his ringleted head to see Elda smile at her son. That was a hopeful sign—but Judah Daniel had seen those smiles come and go before.

Judah Daniel lowered Young John into Elda's arms and went on out the back of the house to the kitchen. On the brick hearth, warmed by the cooking fire, lay a little bundle. With a gingerly touch Judah Daniel pulled it to her and unwrapped layers of hot, damp cloth to reveal the contents—a dozen leaves, silvered green and soft, each one roughly ten inches long and a few inches wide. She lifted the bundle up to her face, feeling the leaves velvet against her cheek. In such lowly things as weeds, the Lord sent healing—lowly, but beautiful to those who did not despise them, like the slave women, the doctoresses, who had learned the use of such weeds from the Indians and brought their own knowledge from the distant lands of Africa. She had grown up among them, learned from them, and won her freedom with the knowledge.

Sure enough, when Judah Daniel returned to Elda's room a few minutes later, Young John was struggling in

Darcy's arms, turning his head away from her so as to see his mother. Elda was lying back, face slack and eyes shuttered. Darcy cajoled Young John with talk of a play-pretty, and his sobs died down to whimpers, but he looked back at Elda until the door closed behind them.

Judah Daniel bared Elda's breasts, then unwrapped the warmed mullein leaves and laid them next to Elda's skin. Elda shuddered at the heat coming from the furry leaves, but she didn't protest, and in a moment she seemed to relax a little. Judah Daniel fastened the nightdress over the leaf poultice, then fixed the quilt so that it covered Elda up to the chin. "Now don't fidget," she cautioned Elda, "let them stay on there till I come take them off."

Elda lay there, limp as a rag, saying nothing.

Narcissa stood at the door of Ward 27, umbrella in hand. The heavy clouds had erased the sun, and darkness was falling early. She would have to hurry to get across town while there was still enough light to see her way.

She heard a step behind her and turned to see Annie Yates. Annie had pulled a shawl over her head and shoulders and was clutching a small bundle—her apron, Narcissa thought. "Are you leaving?" she asked Annie. "Would you like to share my umbrella?"

Annie took a half-step back. "Oh, no, ma'am, I—the rain don't bother me none."

"Come on." Narcissa held out her hand. At last Annie stepped forward, and they walked out together, Narcissa fumbling with the umbrella to hold it over both their heads. The rain, gentle but insistent, tapped on the stretched cloth. Narcissa thought, sneaking a glance sideways, that Annie had the look of one whom the rain had washed many times, leaching the youthful color from her hair and lips, the walnut dye from her black dress. The most womanly thing about her was her sorrow.

They headed north toward Marshall Street. "Where's your home?" Narcissa asked, fearing Annie would allow herself to be led far out of her way rather than speak up.

"We come from Floyd County, in the mountains," Annie answered in a flat voice.

"I meant, where are you staying here in Richmond?"

"Oh . . . I got me a little house near here."

Narcissa wondered at this—was Annie more prosperous than she appeared, to afford a whole house when so many were sharing rooms?

"But I ain't going there," Annie went on, speaking quickly as if to avoid questions. "I go up to Oakwood Cemetery most days, to visit John's grave. My husband."

"Is your son buried there as well?"

Annie stumbled a little. Narcissa reached out and took her arm. "No, ma'am, he ain't. I reckon they buried him quick, near the place where he fell. I don't reckon I'll ever find his grave."

With her hand on Annie's arm, Narcissa could feel the sob she was holding in. "Couldn't any of the doctors help you? There may be a record somewhere—"

"No, ma'am. They's hundreds of boys buried in unmarked graves." Annie's face in profile was set in lines of resignation. "But I don't dwell on it. God meant him for a better place, I reckon."

Brit Wallace passed through the crowded lobby of the Exchange Hotel, his eyes and ears on the alert for many-tongued Rumor. There, that little knot of a half-dozen men in civilian dress, grouped around a lieutenant—a government functionary, by his immaculate uniform and supercilious manner, and very young. Brit edged closer. One of the civilians, a man named Peters, welcomed him into the circle with a "How d'ye do, Wallace?" Others nodded recognition, but no one said much, apparently too eager for the next pronouncement from the lieutenant, who was pink-faced with a transparent fuzz of white-blond hair, like a week-old piglet. He was holding forth while the others listened, mouths agape. "They say Jackson's foot cavalry is threatening Washington City." The piglet winked broadly at his listeners. "Well, no doubt that's what Stonewall wants them to think! He's a fox, though—chances are, if that's what *they* think, the truth is quite the opposite."

"Stonewall's on his way here, do you think, Ownby?" a plaid-suited civilian asked eagerly.

The lieutenant made a shushing motion with his hand. "Now, I don't say that!"

"What about Beauregard? Is he coming to relieve Richmond?" another civilian asked.

Ownby laughed satirically. "Beauregard! It's ludicrous. Some ignorant darky sees a few hundred men on the march north through the city and thinks it's Beauregard! We don't need the little Napoleon, when we have our Prince John."

Magruder, Brit thought, as the men laughed. Something on his face drew Ownby's attention, then Peters's. "Oh, don't you know each other? Lieutenant Ownby, may I present Mr. Wallace. He's a correspondent for one of the British papers. Mr. Wallace, what do *you* think is afoot?"

The men shook hands, Brit watching with some concern as the pink of Ownby's face deepened to magenta. Was Ownby angry about the transfer of attention from himself, or embarrassed at having his indiscretion observed by a reporter? "Well, you know," Brit temporized, "no one reads the *Weekly Argus* for news of the war. My readers are interested in what is going on behind the scenes—the more sentimental, the better. They've been fed a steady diet of Dickens, after all." Some of the other men smiled and nodded, but Ownby's expression did not soften. He took his leave rather abruptly, and the little group dispersed.

Brit went up to his room. The crowd at the Exchange had dwindled somewhat with the threatened fall of the city. Nevertheless, his share of what had once been a comfortable suite of rooms now consisted of a bed, chair, and table. His fine, once-fashionable clothes were packed away under the bed, victims to the ridicule of the soldiers. The chair and table were both covered with books and papers. He sat down on the bed. *Magruder . . . here, involved in the defense of Richmond . . . and men marching northward through the city. . . .* Brit lay back, arms behind his head, and thought.

Susy Reynolds slumped, eyes downcast, arms at her sides. Mattie, the Davises' cook, was standing, hands on hips, glaring at her.

"Look at this mess! What you doing, making such a mess in my kitchen?" Mattie leaned forward, giving emphasis to her words.

"I'm sorry—" Susy pronounced the words carefully: *Ah'm sahry.* She had to be as careful around the servants as the masters; more careful, really, since they noticed more. "I just wanted to make some biscuits."

Mattie ruffled like an angry hen. "What call you got to go making biscuits? Don't you know we gets our biscuits from Chapman's? All the best families gets their biscuits from Chapman's. Yours won't be fit to eat. And now I got to clean this up."

Susy cringed, making herself the picture of misery. In truth, the operation of making biscuits—which she had observed numerous times, though not performed herself, at least in the last twenty years—was more difficult than she'd thought. "Oh, no, Mattie, I'll clean it up."

"You get on out of here." Mattie flicked her apron in

Susy's direction, but she was smiling now. "And don't let nobody see you till you get washed up. All that flour on your face, you look like you done turned white!" Mattie picked up a rag and began to tackle the mess of flour, eggs, and butter that had somehow spread itself around the room. "Them biscuits won't be fit to eat." The cook's scolding followed Susy out the door.

Mirrie's little mixed-breed spaniel, Friday, welcomed Narcissa at the door of the Powerses' house and trotted before her into the dining room. Mirrie was sitting at the table, apparently trying to read a newspaper by the dim and flickering light of a tallow candle. She got to her feet with a jump, gave Narcissa a quick embrace, and then frowned over her spectacles. "You are so late! I was beginning to worry. What was it like up at Chimborazo? Much different from the medical college, I expect. Hurry and get your supper. You must be famished."

A short while later Mirrie placed the big rose-patterned tureen in front of Narcissa and lifted the cover. "I made it myself." Mirrie was smiling, and Narcissa thought how pretty she looked, face flushed and pale hair curling into tendrils from the damp heat. But to tell Mirrie, even in jest, that such housewifery became her—that would never do.

Narcissa ladled the soup—a weak broth of chicken with potatoes and carrots, plus a little something green—into the bowl left for her. She had been hungry; but now, the sight and smell of it made her throat close. She sat back, away from the steam, then picked up her spoon and began to stir the broth. It was just the heat of the soup, probably, after the heat of the day . . . surely she could eat it once it cooled. To leave it untouched would hurt Mirrie's feelings, though they joked between themselves that Mirrie, who could follow the directions of a chemistry demonstration to an exactitude, seemed incapable of boiling an egg.

Rather than eat, Narcissa forced herself to talk. "Chimborazo *is* very different. There are dozens of wards, and each one holds almost as many men as the college hospital. And they are so very sick." She told Mirrie about Sergeant Smith. Meanwhile her spoon stirred the soup in slow circles, setting the dark specks whirling, but even though she felt Mirrie's eyes on her, she could not bring herself to eat any of it.

"But you do plan to go back there tomorrow?" asked Mirrie.

Narcissa wondered a bit at her interest. "Yes."

"Good! Then we will go up to Church Hill together. Louisa Ferncliff has invited me to visit her, and she plans to send the carriage for me. I will go early, Louisa and I will have a nice long visit, and then you and I can come back here together in the evening. Though it would not hurt you to make a shorter day, Narcissa. You look exhausted."

"Louisa Ferncliff! Oh, Mirrie—what will people think?"

The moment the words were out of her mouth, Narcissa wished she could recall them. An appeal to convention was the worst approach to take with Mirrie. Sure enough, the eager tension in Mirrie's face hardened into irritation.

"What *should* people think if I choose to visit an old friend? And why should I care? She's an abolitionist—so am I. She hates disunion—so do I."

"I hear she does more than that," Narcissa replied, provoked in spite of herself.

"People talk about me, as well—you know they do. And yet you do not abandon me."

"Oh, Mirrie, it's not the same! You and Professor Powers are my closest family, as well as my dearest friends. You are the family I have chosen," she added quickly, lest Mirrie pretend to misunderstand. Of course her two sisters and half brother were blood relations. Mirrie had become her sister when Narcissa married Rives—Mirrie's brother, Professor Powers's son. "In all the time I've lived here, you've hardly spoken of her." *And then*, she added to herself, *not in the most flattering of terms.*

Mirrie shrugged. "It was a foolish misunderstanding. We were both stubborn. She has apologized. She *is* my friend." She scowled at Narcissa as if daring her to say more.

Narcissa remembered the time they had crossed paths with Louisa Ferncliff at Cohen Brothers' dry goods shop. Louisa had swept past with barely a nod in their direction, but Narcissa had gotten the impression of a small, thin, beaky woman, eyes bright with malice under carefully arranged dark hair. Louisa's wealth and status showed in her dress and even more in her imperious manner, yet her passion was for freeing the slaves. On the surface, it would seem that Louisa and Mirrie would have much in common: both unmarried women of the age to be classified as spinsters, both educated in the North, both committed abolitionists. But though Mirrie would not back down from an argument, Louisa seemed to go out of her way to sow discord. Louisa's visits to Union prisoners often attracted the notice of the newspaper editors, who stopped short of naming her but not of implying that she was disloyal. "Does Louisa know you are engaged to Major Cohen?"

Mirrie looked away. "Yes—she knows." Was Narcissa imagining that Mirrie looked embarrassed? Then Mirrie sighed. "Sometimes I think it would be the best thing for me to act upon Mr. Cohen's offer to join him in Paris or London. But—can you really see me, a Confederate diplomat's wife? Do you think I could keep quiet about what I believe? I'd hate to marry him and then get him hanged as a traitor!"

"Mirrie, you are opposed to slavery. Many southerners are. It might do our cause good in foreign capitals to put forth the point of view that many southerners do see slavery as a problem—but one that we must resolve in our own way."

Mirrie turned back to meet Narcissa's eyes. "And in our own time? I'm not sure how long that excuse will pass muster."

Narcissa felt exhaustion rising in her. Perhaps it would come to her tomorrow, what she ought to say to Mirrie. The idea of a carriage ride across town to Church Hill was appealing. But now, she wanted more than anything to take off these hot, damp clothes, to lie down. . . .

"Are you feeling ill?" Mirrie's voice sounded gentler now.

"Just tired," Narcissa said again. "The heat is so oppressive. I believe I will make an early night."

Mirrie picked up the bowl and put it on the floor. Friday, tail wagging with frantic enthusiasm, began lapping up the soup. Mirrie made a wry face. "At least someone appreciates my cooking."

Narcissa went down the hall to the professor's room—he had been moved to the ground floor when he could no longer manage the stairs—and knocked softly, then entered.

Professor Powers was in bed, a thick leather-bound book propped up on his knees. He looked up at her and smiled over his spectacles. "There you are, my dear. I'm afraid I've already had my dinner." Then he frowned a little. "I hope you will be getting to bed soon. You look exhausted."

Narcissa came over and took his hand. Under the thin

skin the veins showed blue, ropy, so tangled in places it seemed a wonder the blood could get through. She leaned over and gave him a kiss on the cheek. "I'm going now."

As Narcissa was leaving the room, Beulah entered, carrying a glass with the professor's medicine. She and Narcissa exchanged greetings.

Thank goodness for Beulah. It occurred to Narcissa as she prepared for bed that hardly a day passed that one of them—the professor, Mirrie, or Narcissa herself—didn't make that comment. The free black woman was living in the house now in order to care for the professor—a sacrifice made easier by the fact that her husband, Will, the Powerses' coachman, had been impressed by the Confederate government to work on the fortifications. Without Beulah, the weight of Professor Powers's care would have fallen on Mirrie, who, though devoted to her father, was not temperamentally suited to be a nurse; or on Narcissa, who would have had to give up her nursing of the soldiers. Beulah seemed the answer to their prayers.

But Beulah and Will might themselves be praying for something quite different. Did they want things to return to the way they were, before the war? Or did they have a vision of the future that she could not imagine? And what kind of future did she herself imagine, come to that? It was strange, praying for something to be over, with no clear picture in mind of what might take its place. Leave us to solve our own problems: that's what she would say to Abraham Lincoln, George McClellan, all of those who were now determined to force submission on the part of Virginia and the South. Don't turn *us* into a replica of *you*, with your poor crowded into factories and tenements. But Mirrie would ask—and she herself would not be able to answer—where was the will to change, to free the slaves and give them the education and responsibility that for generations now had been withheld? Those questions could not be answered when the minds and hearts of all the southern leaders were focused on the war. And so Narcissa's thoughts would circle back to the war, unable to look beyond it, however much she might pray for its end.

CHAPTER TWO

JUNE 23

For the past ten years his son Tyler had done the job. Now John Chapman was driving the bakery wagon again. He liked it, in a way. After the hard, hot work of baking, he could move at the slow pace set by the old horse, Raven. He could watch the sun rise and the city come alive, just as he had in his youth.

But this was not the Richmond he remembered. It was full of strangers now, men and women who spoke with the accents of Georgia and Mississippi and puffed themselves out like toads because their masters held positions in the Confederate government. He spoke to them pleasantly, bantered with them if they invited it. He didn't make a point of the difference between them and himself, the fact that he had been born and had raised his family in freedom and had property to pass down. He didn't know if they knew, and it didn't matter really, but he would be glad when they all packed their bags and went back where they came from.

Even the smell of the city had changed. Gone was the odor of curing tobacco that used to flavor the smoke from the foundries and railroads. The blockade had strangled the business of tobacco almost to death. Now, after the rain of yesterday, the air had the sour tang of churned-up clay. He breathed it in and frowned. This was what the country smelled like, he reckoned—earth and the sweat of field hands.

Raven stopped by long habit at the trade entrance of the Spotswood Hotel. Chapman got down and lifted out a tray of biscuits, two hundred of them, covered with a white cloth. He handed the tray to the boy who came to the door, then went back to the wagon for a second tray. As he was handing it to the boy, one of the hotel cooks came to the door. "Morning, Lucinda," he greeted her.

"Morning, John. How's Elda doing?" The low tremble in the woman's voice carried her sympathy. She knew the answer wouldn't be good.

"Well as can be expected, I reckon," Chapman answered. "She be all right. She got the older boy, you know, Young John, and she set great store by him."

Lucinda smiled sadly. "I know she do." The boy came out again, carrying the trays, now emptied, that Chapman had left there the day before. As Chapman remounted the wagon, Lucinda called out, "You tell her I asked after her."

"I'll do that," he called back as Raven pulled the wagon away from the door.

The wagon traveled along Main to Fourteenth Street, where it turned north. At the end of the block were the Ballard House and the Exchange Hotel. They were good customers, buying as many biscuits as the Chapman family had to sell—today, three trays of them; later on, he would deliver the pies and cakes that his sisters and nieces were baking now. Behind the Exchange three young white men were lounging. They wore civilian clothing, but their muskets were leaning up against the wall. He knew them to belong to the ranks of the Home Guard. And they knew him. He nodded to them and got down from the wagon. He didn't like to turn his back on them, but he had to get the trays.

As he turned, bracing the load, one of them drawled, "Heard anything from that son of yours lately?"

"No, sir, I ain't," John replied, keeping his head bowed over the tray.

"You thinking about joining him? Having the easy life out there with the Yankees?" The speaker giggled, and his friends echoed the scornful sound.

John looked up, not in the face of any one of them—they would take that as an affront—but straight ahead. "I reckon he got what he asked for. Got them Yankees working him like a field hand. I told him not to do it, and he done it anyway. Now I got to do his work and mine too."

The guardsmen laughed and spat out a few obscenities directed at Tyler. At last their attention drifted away, so that John Chapman could go on about his business. The church bells tolled six o'clock. Might be Tyler was in one of the Union camps, close by—close enough to hear the church bell toll. But there was no way to get a message to one of those the Yankees called "contraband of war." When would Tyler learn that Elda's baby—their second son—had died? How would he feel? Would he wish that he had stayed in Richmond, tended to his own business, and let the white men fight their war?

From the Exchange Hotel, Chapman used a firmer hand on the reins. Raven was not accustomed to the new route up Twelfth Street to Clay. When President Jefferson Davis moved out of the Spotswood Hotel back in the fall, the Davises' cook had suggested that John Chapman continue to supply some baked goods to the family. Mattie still worked for the Davises, but now a different servant met him, one who'd been with the household only a few weeks. Her name was Susy Reynolds.

Try as he might, John couldn't keep his heart from beating faster when he came near the gray mansion set on the crest of Shockoe Hill. He had seen famous generals go in and out, and the president—a man most himself when around his wife and children, otherwise tense and squinty-eyed, as if something important were happening a long way off, and he could see it. When McClellan's troops closed on Richmond, Davis had sent his family away. The Richmonders who'd stayed resented that, but Chapman understood. It's what he'd have done himself.

John walked Raven around back, near the kitchen, and tied him so that he could drink from the trough. Then he picked up a tray, smaller and lighter than the others had been, and went with it along the path that skirted the garden and down the stairs to the little door, beneath ground level, where Susy would be waiting. At least, he hoped she would be. Every time he came, he held his breath.

Peering through the open door, he saw her. Her modest servant's dress, dark cotton with a clean white apron and headcloth, couldn't hide her womanly roundness. The tight bands around his heart eased a little. They weren't sweethearts, but that was the effect she had on him. She made him feel like a hero going around in a poor man's clothes. He'd never been a man who romanced women, either before he'd married his wife or after her death, but he thought this must be what it felt like. If anyone found out about them, his life would fall apart, and he would lose everything that was dear to him. But that didn't matter . . . so long as no one found out.

Susy came closer, and his heart froze again. There was something in her face that hadn't been there before—a very serious look, a warning. She took the tray from him and gave him another in its place. It was the tray he had left the day before, but it wasn't empty. He peeked under the napkin. There were biscuits already on the tray—poor, thin ones to his eye, probably as tough as the soldiers' hardtack—but they were there to conceal something: something she wanted him to carry from the home of the Confederate president to the home of the Unionist Ferncliff. She held it out to him, insistent. At last he wrapped his fingers around the handles, but he didn't take the weight of the tray. They stood, holding the tray between them. Her brown eyes looked up into his. Electricity seemed to move through the tray to his fingers, up his arms, so that he could hold on to it only with an effort. "Go on, take it," she insisted, her eyes locked on his. "Like we said."

What had they said? Not much. Just that he would meet her every morning with a tray of biscuits, and that his next stop after would be at Louisa Ferncliff's. All that lay behind these few words had been unspoken.

Would he be a hero in her eyes? This was the time to decide. He took the tray.

The last stage of his route was the longest, down Shockoe Valley and up Church Hill to another mansion, more imposing even than Davis's. A low iron fence set off the small yard from the street on this side. Only here, in all his rounds, had he been instructed to walk up to the front door instead of to the kitchen. He guessed the abolitionist Miss Ferncliff enjoyed provoking her neighbors with this sin against custom.

His hands hovered over the tray he had filled that morning with freshly baked biscuits, then moved to the tray Susy Reynolds had handed him. It was that tray he picked up and carried to the door. Selah McRae met him at the door. Did he imagine it, or was she more alert, more watchful, than before?

"Be careful now," he said quietly. "It's a mite heavier than usual."

Selah's eyes flicked over him. With her left hand, she braced the trays against her meatless hip; with her right hand, she closed the door.

John Chapman walked away, feeling let down. What had he expected, that she would bring out whatever it was that was hidden there and show it to him? It wasn't for

him, after all, or for her, come to that—it was for Louisa
Ferncliff.

-+>-<+-

In Louisa Ferncliff's carriage, Narcissa and Mirrie had
conversed like distant acquaintances. But Narcissa was
still feeling tired, and the comfortable ride was welcome,
whatever the source. Louisa's driver had taken Narcissa to
the extreme northwest edge of the Chimborazo grounds,
then turned around to drive Mirrie back to the Ferncliff
house less than a quarter mile away.

Narcissa arrived at Ward 27 in time to feed Sergeant
Smith his breakfast. He didn't swallow much of the un-
palatable mixture, the chief ingredient of which was
tasteless arrowroot. But she resisted taking this as a bad
sign, since the men who could talk invariably grumbled
about having to eat it. This morning, she was grateful
that the arrowroot had no more odor than taste. Her
nausea of the night before had left a sort of tender spot
in her stomach.

The ward was bustling with morning activity, but she
didn't see Annie Yates. Annie's sad story had been much
on her mind. The more she thought on it, the more con-
vinced she became that Annie, uneducated and unwilling
to put herself forward, had accepted defeat too easily in
the matter of her son's burial place. It wasn't likely Annie
had thought of using one of the Richmond newspapers to
get information. Since she could not read, she might not
even know that, every day, the *Dispatch* and other papers
ran column after column of notices from persons seeking
news of their loved ones. "Information wanted," most of
them began, then the name of the person sought, his
company and regiment—and then such details as
"wounded in the fight before Richmond Monday night
last"; "wounded in one of the battles before Richmond":

"understood to be somewhere in the city, sick." Then came a name and address to which information could be sent.

Narcissa guessed that many women must be among the advertisers, preserving their modesty through the use of their initials rather than their Christian names. With that thought, Narcissa hesitated. If she were to put in such a notice on behalf of Annie, what name and address should she leave for the reply? No use in giving Annie's address—even if she knew it—since Annie could not read. Her own name, at the Powerses'? Then she thought, Brit Wallace. It would be easy for anyone having news of James Yates to get a message to the Exchange Hotel. And of course Brit would urge her warmly to involve him, if he were here. Wherever there was a story, Brit's interest quickened. And each of the thousands of advertisements had a story behind it, whether its ending be joyful or tragic.

Paper for the use of the doctors was kept in the drawer of the table at the end of the long room. She selected a piece, dipped the pen in the inkstand, and wrote quickly. In a few minutes it was done: "INFORMATION WANTED—of JAMES YATES, Twenty-fourth Virginia Infantry, mortally wounded at Seven Pines. Anyone knowing the location of his burial will greatly oblige me by sending word to me at the Exchange Hotel. WILLIAM G. WALLACE."

She handed the note to one of the errand boys, along with a handful of Confederate shinplasters in small denominations, with directions to take it to the office of the *Richmond Dispatch*. A moment later she put out her hand to call him back, but he was already out the door. Why this sudden misgiving? The answer came to her with the memory of Annie's face, the feel of her thin shoulder through her sleeve. The woman was so fragile, she might not be able to bear the emotion of a hope raised and then dashed. Not that there was much to hope for in Annie's case—just a space of ground on which her tears could fall. Still, best say nothing to her until—*unless*—there should be that little shred of good news to report.

Louisa Ferncliff met Mirrie at the door and ushered her through the formal rooms into the library, where she poured pale tea into delicate gold-rimmed cups. Mirrie sat very straight on Louisa's low sofa, slipcovered for summer in spotless white. The carpets had been taken up, replaced by rush matting. Net curtains hung at the tall windows, allowing the air to circulate while keeping out mosquitoes and flies. The tea was delicious. Louisa had lemons. But rarely had Mirrie felt less comfortable. She knew Louisa to be a woman who judged quickly, and harshly, and expressed her judgments unsparingly. A year ago Louisa had spoken her mind to Mirrie concerning her engagement to Nat Cohen: it was pure hypocrisy, Louisa said, for a proclaimed abolitionist to betroth herself to a Confederate diplomat. Mirrie feared Louisa would raise the subject again. She found it difficult to defend herself against such a charge, especially since she suspected Louisa might be right.

Louisa leaned forward and set her cup in its saucer. "I was reading in *Harper's Weekly*—the issue for June seventh—"

Only two weeks ago. Mirrie was impressed—as she knew Louisa meant her to be. How had Louisa been able to get a northern newspaper so quickly? It must be true that money could buy anything.

Louisa had paused, perhaps to enjoy the effect of her words on Mirrie. Now she went on. "There was great attention given to the commandeering of a steamer, the

Planter, at Charleston. You heard about that? No? The pilot was a slave. He flew the Secesh flag until he was out of range of the guns, then struck it and raised a white one. I enjoyed that so much." A smile curved the corners of Louisa's mouth.

Mirrie smiled back in appreciation of the irony. "A slave taking possession of a planter, rather than the other way around." Mirrie felt the scintillation of fellow feeling between herself and her hostess.

Louisa took another sip of tea and went on. "There is also a story concerning Jefferson Davis's coachman, William Jackson. He went over to the Union camp at Fredericksburg, some weeks ago now."

Mirrie nodded. Everyone in Richmond knew William Jackson had run for the North. "It's thrilling. How can the myth of the docile, happy slave be maintained when someone like William Jackson gives up his supposedly *honored* position and risks his life for the sake of freedom?"

Louisa set her cup down and walked over to one of the inset shelves that lined the room. She folded the newspaper to the correct page, handed it to Mirrie, then resumed her seat.

Mirrie scanned the article about William Jackson. Words of praise about the coachman's manner and conversation prefaced a summary of his statement made to Union general McDowell. According to Jackson, both Jefferson Davis and his wife, Varina, were despondent about the future of the Confederacy and expecting its imminent demise.

" 'There is much outspoken Union feeling in Richmond,' " she read aloud to Louisa. "Well, here, at least, that's true. But I wonder about this: 'Many of the Richmond people wish the Union troops to come, as they are half starved out.' I don't think that's true, though food is expensive, and supplies often run short—"

Louisa's mouth twisted in a half-smile, half grimace. "There may be some who are turning Unionist because they cannot get a new bonnet or the latest issue of *Godey's*. Those people, I despise." Louisa spoke with such emphasis that Mirrie wondered if she had someone specific in mind.

Mirrie read on, to herself this time. "Jackson has a wife and three children, all slaves, in Richmond. It is a misdemeanor at law in Virginia to teach William Jackson's children to read." There it was again: the horror and the guilt, and herself sharing in it, although she had taught black children in defiance of the law.

Louisa spoke again. "There's an illustration on the page before—an engraving of Jackson's head and shoulders. They made him look very dignified. *Harper's* has been converted. A year ago, southern slaves were a subject for cheap, offensive humor—all blubbery lips and woolly hair."

As Louisa was speaking these words, her black maid-servant appeared in the door behind her. Mirrie glanced away, embarrassed. Had Selah heard what Louisa had said, and did she think—? But Louisa showed no sign of having been caught in a faux pas. *I'm uneasy because I am one of them—a southerner,* Mirrie thought. *I take their guilt on myself, even though Father and I own no slaves.*

"Please excuse me." Louisa got up and followed Selah out into the hall.

Mirrie closed the paper. But her gaze fell on the back page, and she could not look away. On it were line drawings, grotesque and repellent. A skull, its top sawed off, was captioned, "Goblet made from a Yankee's skull." "Necklace of Yankee teeth," said another. Mirrie felt the blood rise in her cheeks. *How dare they say this about us?*

With the blood still pounding in her ears, she thought, Which is *us,* and which *them?* What am I?

In Ward 27, breakfast and morning report were finished. Narcissa had been looking for Annie Yates but had not seen her come in. Now she saw Dr. Wright standing near the foot of the bed in which Annie's young patient, Private Devlin, lay. The bed was the very last in the row, between Sergeant Smith and the wall. The doctor was jotting down observations with a pencil in a little notebook. Narcissa went over to him and stood at a respectful distance, waiting for him to finish.

At last Wright closed the notebook, put it in his pocket, and turned to her. "Yes, Mrs. Powers, what is it?" Wright's face, even the whites of his eyes, had the pink tinge of broken blood vessels, and he gave off the musty-sweet odor of alcohol consumed, not necessarily recently, but often, and in large quantities.

Narcissa was too used to the exaggerated impatience of doctors to be put off by his brusque manner. "I'm wondering if Mrs. Annie Yates has been here today."

"That woman, *Mrs. Yates*"—Wright drew out the name as if it were some sort of insult—"is not welcome in this hospital."

Narcissa stared at him in surprise. "What? Why?"

Wright glared at her. "She's a thief. We're missing half the morphine that was allotted for our patients."

"Missing? But—what makes you think she is the one who took it?"

Wright's cheeks reddened. "One of the orderlies saw it. Now, if you will excuse me—"

As Wright moved away, Narcissa caught a glimpse of Devlin. Something odd there. . . . She made a mental note to check on the patient, then turned to hurry after Wright. She caught up with him and put her hand on his sleeve. "I'm sure you must be mistaken. Her husband and son were killed at Seven Pines."

Wright pulled his arm away and turned on her so fiercely she thought he might slap her. But he collected himself, settled his angry features into an expression of ironic detachment, and said, "Things are not always what they seem, Mrs. Powers. I know that you are the, uh, *friend* of Cameron Archer. Nevertheless, I am in charge here, Dr. Lester backs me up, and Archer has nothing to say in the matter. Now, if you'll excuse me."

Narcissa watched him hurry away down the long center aisle. *Had* one of the orderlies seen something? None of them was close by and at leisure to be questioned. Dr. Wright seemed especially eager for her not to go to Archer with her questions about Annie Yates. Well, that was a good enough reason for her to do just that.

After a moment Narcissa glanced back at Annie's patient, Devlin. He looked the same as he had the day before—eyes closed, head swathed in bandages, hands crossed on top of the sheet. His bandages, shirt, and bedding were clean: obviously one of the orderlies had tended to him fairly recently. His hair wasn't showing, but the beard was brown. She stepped closer, waved away the fly that had settled on his bandaged head, and bent to read the card tacked to the bedpost. It was filled in sketchily, just the last name—Devlin—and the diagnosis, *sopor caroticus. Sopor* meant sleep. What a profound, dreamless state it seemed to be. But she knew she had seen his eyes open, focused, and fully aware only a moment before.

Narcissa stood over the bed, uncertain of what to do. Should she go after Wright again and call him back to examine this patient? What a shame it was not Dr. Coster who was on duty. He was inexperienced, but she sensed his interest in the patients, his compassion. Wright would not be grateful to her for showing him up. In fact, he would likely take out his embarrassment on Devlin.

"I know you can hear me," she whispered. "You must tell them the truth. Tell them you're cured." She smiled a little. "We're past due for a miracle. But if you haven't told them by tonight, then I must. And it will go the worse for you." Then she turned and walked away down the long aisle to the opposite end of the building. Two convalescent soldiers detailed as orderlies were lounging there, one of them smoking a pipe that he hid behind his back at her approach.

"Do you know where Dr. Archer has gone?" she asked. She felt hot again under their appraising eyes—of course, they would think she was pursuing Archer with more than medicine on her mind—and her stomach and her head were aching. She made a detour to retrieve her umbrella, then set off in the direction they indicated. To locate one surgeon in this maze of identical buildings, lining identical streets, would not be easy. But to be out in the air—even in the rain—away from this place. . . . It was searching for him, more than finding him, that she craved—especially since she was far from sure what she would say when she did find him.

Narcissa stepped out the door into the muddy makeshift street. Chimborazo was modeled on similar pavilion hospitals in the Crimea. Onto the flat, grassy plateau called Chimborazo pine planks had been dragged and nailed together into barracks, a hundred and fifty of them, laid out in straight lines, with Ward 27 at the extreme southwest corner of the grid. Viewed from above— as from one of Professor Lowe's hot-air balloons, with which the Union spied upon Richmond and its protecting troops—the hospital must look like a miniature city complete with tiny lead soldiers. But viewed up close, the buildings were raw wood, and almost all the soldiers were broken, missing an arm or a leg, their uniforms faded and stained with blood.

A fat, warm raindrop landed on Narcissa's forehead, calling her out of her morbid imaginings. The other occupants of the street were hurrying for cover. She raised her umbrella and picked up her speed.

Louisa returned at last from talking with her servant and invited Mirrie to come into the garden. Louisa seemed tense and unhappy, and Mirrie wondered again if Selah had given her bad news. They walked out onto the wide, columned portico. On this side, the house overlooked the slope toward the river: first a gentle incline tamed and planted in flowers and fruit trees, then a steep ravine choked with honeysuckle. Below this house were tobacco warehouses, most of them now hospitals or prisons; then the river.

They passed down the steps and in among the roses. It was hard to believe that a few minutes' walk from here would bring them to the edge of Chimborazo. Mirrie thought of what she had seen there—a huge hospital, a city unto itself, really, filled with the suffering and dying and the irretrievably maimed. Louisa's garden seemed a different world—beautiful, comfortable, *sane*.

Why had almost the whole population of the South taken leave of its senses and joined in this suicidal folly? And since they had, why wasn't it possible for her to walk away and leave them to it? But she'd felt the anger beating in her own head just a few moments before, anger at what the northern press had said about *us*.

"I rather envy you," Mirrie ventured. Louisa raised her eyebrows. "Sometimes," Mirrie went on, "I feel like Gulliver when he was tied down by the Lilliputians."

"What do you mean?" asked Louisa.

"I'm tied to the South, to Virginia—by grandparents and great-grandparents, aunts and uncles, cousins . . . three and four generations of marrying and begetting, bequeathing so much more than property with their slaves."

Louisa smiled—a little coldly. "And you envy me? Don't. I was born and grew up in Richmond. My northern-born father was a merchant who grew rich from other people's trafficking in slaves. And he didn't hesitate to take their example: he bought slaves, worked them, and profited from their sale. It was the money paid for human beings—people I loved!—that paid for my northern education. He sold a whole family to a man who owned the property adjoining our country place west of town. I cried for days. At last my father agreed to keep two little girls that had been my pets. But their mother, father, brothers, a baby sister—" Louisa's sharp black eyes clouded over. "After he died, I tried to buy them back, to free them. I offered much more than my father had been paid, but their owner would not sell them to me. He disapproved, he said, of what I was trying to do." Louisa's forehead wrinkled as if she were about to weep.

"I'm sorry, Louisa. I didn't realize—"

Louisa spoke over Mirrie's apology. "We are all guilty, all of us, whoever we are and wherever we live, unless we join in the war against slavery."

Mirrie smarted under the sting of Louisa's words. "Of course, I agree," Mirrie rejoined. "But is this a war against slavery? It isn't now, and it may never be. President Lincoln has made it very clear that he is fighting to preserve the Union, not to end slavery. If he ever does abolish slavery, this will be a holy war. Now it is only a political struggle that brutalizes those on both sides."

Louisa stood very straight. Her eyes seemed to be focused on her rosebushes, but her expression showed she was not thinking of them. She stood that way for several minutes. At last she turned to Mirrie. "*Brutalizes* . . . yes. I'm afraid that is just what this war is doing, to all of us. Selah brought me some rather upsetting news just now. Perhaps this war would be worth it, if only one could be certain, as you say, that the game is worth the candle."

"Selah . . . was she one of the girls you mentioned?"

Louisa nodded. "Yes. They are as dear to me as my own family. I sent them to school in Philadelphia. I can see now that I was trying to atone for my father's sins. But it's not so simple, is it, Mirrie? As you yourself said."

Mirrie was flattered to hear Louisa quoting her opinions back to her. And yet she felt a little prickle of anxiety. Somehow her words came out of Louisa's mouth with a deeper portent than they had had when she herself had spoken them.

✦━◄

It was Archer who found Narcissa. Told that she had been looking for him, he went out into the street, pulling down his slouch hat to keep the rain out of his face. It was easy to spot her, there were so few women about. He hurried up to her. She was asking for his help, he could see it in her brown eyes. Unsure of what to do, he took her umbrella in his right hand and held it over her. She put her right hand through his left arm and stepped close to him so that the umbrella could shelter them both. The raindrops struck the umbrella with a noisy rattle like a snare drum.

"Is he dead?" Archer ventured. "Er . . . Smith?" Thank God he had remembered the man's name. If he hadn't, she would have taken it amiss.

"Oh—no. No, it's not that." Her straight brows contracted in a frown. "Do you know that a woman named Annie Yates has been turned out of the hospital, accused of stealing?"

Archer shook his head. "I know nothing about it."

"Dr. Wright made the accusation. He says one of the orderlies saw it, and that she'd been suspected before."

"Wright." Archer repeated the name. "Very well. I'll look into it." It wouldn't do for Mrs. Powers to see how deeply he despised Thomas Wright. Doctors solved their differences among themselves—or ignored their differences, if they had to. He had his own suspicions of Wright, but the need for surgeons obliged him to be careful. Narcissa was looking at him as if she would not be satisfied with this answer, and he readied himself for an argument. But when she spoke again, he realized that she had more than the Yates woman on her mind.

"I want to know your feelings on a certain matter. But before I tell you, I want you to give me your word that you will do nothing about it, unless I ask you to."

For a moment the surgeon warred with the man. The man won. "I give you my word."

They walked on.

"One of the patients has been shamming."

Archer stopped dead. Whatever he might have expected, it wasn't this. The hospital rats were resourceful, capable of feigning almost everything from deafness to a limp, but—"One of the men in Ward 27?"

Narcissa hesitated, then nodded.

Not Smith. Edwin Booth himself could not feign tetanus. Who, then? The surgeon Archer elbowed the man aside. "Which one?"

Narcissa looked away. "I can't tell you that."

"Are you certain? How did you make this diagnosis?" The reason for his condescending tone was clear—to him, and, he feared, to her: How could you, a mere nurse, spot a sham when the surgeons failed?

"Of course I am certain. I told him he must let the doctors know."

"What did he say?"

"Nothing. But I'm sure he heard me."

Don't say anything stupid, Archer told himself sternly. At last he said, "What makes you think he will do what you asked?"

Narcissa's frown was directed at him now. "What choice does he have? He can't continue to feign indefinitely, even with an drunkard like Wright in charge of the ward. He can't just walk away—how far would he get, with orderlies all around? And he would be a bit conspicuous, wouldn't he, dressed in nothing but his shirt and drawers! If he's found out, he may be prosecuted as a deserter."

Archer returned her frown with one of his own. "Why are you so solicitous of his welfare? The man is a coward. He deserves to be punished. You have to let me handle this."

A shiver ran through Narcissa—Archer could feel it through her arm linked in his. There was bitterness in her voice when she spoke again. "He's young; little more than a boy. And not everyone is so brave as you."

The way she said it, it sounded like a reproach. He opened his mouth to reply, but she was not finished.

"How can you cast judgment so easily? Who knows what he may have suffered to bring him to this point?" She broke off suddenly, slipped her arm from his, and faced him. "What if a woman loves him, and wants him to live?"

Her desperation kindled his, so that he spoke more harshly than he meant. "What kind of woman wants *one man* to live? Her husband? What about her father, her brothers, her sons? Her uncles? Cousins? Her neighbors— they have women who love them too, doesn't she care about them?"

Narcissa shook her head. "I didn't mean—"

But he went on, the full force of his anger and frustration pushing out the words. "A man drills and marches and fights with men he's known since childhood, men he would never betray, not even to save his own life. If one man says, 'No, I'd rather not risk my life,' the whole fabric falls apart."

Narcissa seemed turned to stone. "Maybe that's what they should do. All of them. Then there would be no more war."

The shock of this idea silenced Archer for a moment. "All right," he said at last, "suppose there is no more war. Our hypothetical case has gone home to enjoy the caresses of his wife." God, how cold I must sound to her, he thought. "But he is still a coward. Suppose some villain comes to break into his house, and his wife needs him to protect her and their children, and he cannot do it?"

"You cannot do it now. You are all gone for soldiers."

He had no answer to that.

They walked for a long time, in step with the drumbeats of the rain. At last they came to the edge of the plateau. Below them, the land dropped precipitously, then flattened out again at the floodplain of the James River. He could see its waters, high and brown, in the spaces between the trees. He hadn't done a very good job with the umbrella; Narcissa's skirts were soaked, and her plaited straw hat looked about to fall to pieces. Under the drumming of the rain, he could hear her breathing, they were that close to each other. Her nearness made his skin tingle as if he were about to receive a shock. He had to break the silence.

"Deserters are eaten up with bitterness, because they know they can never go home. Their families are ashamed of them. Their neighbors look at them and remember how they betrayed their husbands, their sons, their brothers. Turning him in is the best thing you can do for him, and for those who love him. Chances are, his regiment will give him another chance."

There, he thought, that should settle it. Narcissa looked close to tears. But there was a steeliness about her, and when she spoke, he realized he hadn't moved her an inch. "But won't it go better for him if he turns himself in? He can . . . come around. Wake up. A doctor will examine him, pronounce him cured. He can go back to his regiment. Maybe he just needed some time."

"This man is diseased, Mrs. Powers—infected. Cowardice spreads like hospital gangrene, and it rots from within." He saw her flinch and regretted his words. How could he mention gangrene to her? The disease had killed her brother—his student; Archer had failed to save him. He had failed her, even before they met.

Very well. He would offer her this. "I give you my word I will not tell anyone what you have told me."

Some of the tension went out of Narcissa's face. "Thank you."

He said nothing. God forbid any of the other surgeons find out he had agreed to this. It made him feel dirty. He had worded his promise carefully. In a matter of minutes he could cross over to Ward 27 and discover for himself who it was that had fooled that imbecile Wright. Of course she would be angry . . . or worse, disappointed in him.

He felt her shiver again, saw her clench her teeth against it. Her skin was ivory pale, her dark eyes shadowed. Her lips were as red as if they'd been kissed, hard.

"Are you quite well, Mrs. Powers?" he asked, feeling foolish. In his eager response to her beauty, he'd overlooked the symptoms of a fever.

Narcissa shook her head. "I'm . . . very cold."

"Let me find someone to take you home."

Again Narcissa shook her head. "Mirrie's . . . at . . . Louisa Ferncliff's."

Louisa Ferncliff. Well, it wouldn't be his choice, but it was close by, and Narcissa would want Mirrie. "All right," he agreed. "I'll send word." He took much of her weight on his arm as he led her toward the headquarters building.

→>—<←

Brit Wallace found the pink Lieutenant Ownby waiting for him, alone this time, at the door of his room on the hotel's third floor. There seemed to be no choice but to let him in. Ownby spent no time in pleasantries but got to business at once.

"Mr. Wallace. You are a war correspondent, are you not, for one of the London papers?"

"You know who I am," Brit replied testily. "By what right are you questioning me?"

"I am attached to Secretary Randolph's office. Now, sir, answer the question."

It was best to answer, Brit supposed; but he could gain the satisfaction of irritating Ownby a little in the process. "I am a correspondent for the London *Argus,* yes. But not precisely a war correspondent. It isn't my job to give the details of the battles or to dissect policies. The *Times* does enough of that—at least, according to my editor. What I write is more *Odyssey* than *Iliad,* you know; more ordinary folk, not so much gods and generals."

Ownby's lips puckered as if he'd bitten into a lemon. "Yet you go around, talking to officers and men, asking questions. You've become quite a well-known figure in the camps." He obviously meant no compliment, but Brit could not keep from smiling, reflecting as he did that Ownby himself wouldn't last a day in the camps, not in those clothes. The lieutenant was no J. E. B. Stuart.

"Well, yes; the war has come to me, you might say. Still, I—"

"You make yourself quite at home with the men in the camps, and with the officers in eating-houses and hotel saloons. You have a way of turning up wherever there is talk concerning the war."

"Where isn't there talk concerning the war?"

"Yet a year ago," Ownby went on, reminding Brit of a hectoring prefect, "you were captured at Manassas, and brought here to Richmond with thousands of Union prisoners. Were you likewise so comfortable with men of the other side?"

"That was a misunderstanding! Were you there, yourself, at Manassas?"

Brit asked the question to needle Ownby, feeling quite sure of the answer. He let Ownby's silence hang in the air for a moment, then went on. "Let me tell you, if you *had* been there, you would know what a jumble it was. I rode down from Washington City as an observer, had my horse stolen, found myself having to aid a soldier whose legs had been blown off—"

Ownby paused in his writing. "Federal, or Confederate?"

"What difference does it make?" Brit was pacing now, waving his arms. "It made none to me at that point, I can tell you! Then a Confederate colonel decided to take out his displeasure with the events of the day by arresting me. So I returned to Richmond, as I had planned to do all along—though not in the way I had planned."

"If you were so eager to return to Richmond, why did you leave in the first place?"

Brit stopped pacing and folded his arms on his chest. This was the question he had hoped would not be asked. "I was asked to leave, by someone purporting to be from the government. Though I've always suspected the charge was trumped up by someone with a more, er, *personal* reason for wanting to me out of town."

"And that was—?"

"I'd rather not say."

Ownby stroked his thin, white-blond beard. If that's the best you can do, shave the damn thing, Brit thought.

"I was told you were asked to leave on account of your dispatch concerning the expected attack by the *Pawnee*."

Brit shrugged. "The dispatch might have ruffled a few feathers in town."

Just after Virginia cast her lot with the seceding states, the rumor of an imminent attack by the Federal sloop-of-war swept through the town, bringing Richmond's fancy-dress militias out to defend the city. Brit had written the scene for comedy; though, if the rumor had been true, the story would certainly have been a tragedy. In the end, the *Pawnee* did not come, and Richmond's would-be defenders went home, a little wiser, perhaps, concerning what it would take to save their city from a hostile power a mere hundred miles away.

Ownby was silent for a moment, studying the notes he had made. Brit wondered whether he would demand an explanation. What would Ownby's reaction be if Brit hinted there was a lady involved? At last Ownby looked up, his expression serious. "You may be interested to know that another, more recent dispatch of yours has come to the attention of the Confederate government. This regards our army's victory at Yorktown."

Victory? An interesting word to use, Brit mused, for a strategic retreat.

"You showed a particular interest in the tactics used by General Magruder." Ownby said the name with a perfectly straight face, as if he himself had not been gossiping about "Prince John" the day before.

Brit smiled. "As you know, Magruder showed himself a brilliant stage manager. First he arranges the scenery, propping up logs to look like cannon. Then he orders his thin line of troops to march back and forth across the stage, as it were, to an accompaniment of gunfire and bugle calls. Of course he judged well his audience in McClellan, who would never believe his fellow West Pointer would violate every military precept by attempting to hold a line with scarcely a thousand troops to the mile."

Ownby was writing in his book again. Then he closed it with a snap and fixed Brit with a cold look. "How do we know you're not sharing these observations of yours with the enemy? This city is under martial law. I can have you arrested."

Brit stood staring, not believing what he heard. "How do you know one of those men you were gossiping to last night isn't a spy? Are you going to have them all arrested?"

Ownby's frown deepened. "Watch yourself." Then he turned and marched down the hall, head up and shoulders back as if he were leading a parade drill. Brit stared after him until he was out of sight, then slammed the door shut with the heel of his hand and dropped backward onto his bed. *Bloody hell.* He sat up, heart pounding, ready to run after Ownby and settle it with fists, man to man. But another thought kept him down. It wasn't just one man against him. Ownby might be attempting to undo the damage of having gossiped in front of a foreigner—worse, a reporter. Still, the lieutenant likely had his superiors' permission to do what he had done to Brit. Rather than launch a counterattack against Ownby, it was probably best to tread carefully—to give no pretext at all for banishment from Richmond and the South.

After a short wait—though it seemed long to Narcissa—Mirrie arrived in Louisa's carriage. The driver lifted Narcissa into the seat, and she lay shivering under a lavender-scented quilt, her head on Mirrie's lap. The carriage stopped in the street in front of one of the largest, most elegant homes in the city. With Mirrie and the coachman supporting her, Narcissa mounted the steps to Louisa's door. The coachman sounded the big brass knocker. In a moment the door was opened by Louisa Ferncliff herself.

"Selah!" Louisa called. A black woman stepped up beside Louisa, and the two exchanged a few words in a low tone. Then Selah stepped forward to help Narcissa. "Come along, come along," Louisa urged.

They made their way up the curving staircase and into a room dominated by a high four-poster bed. "Best get you out of those wet things, miss." The servant unfastened Narcissa's bodice, skirt, and petticoats and let them fall to the floor, then held a silk dressing gown around Narcissa so that she could remove her chemise and drawers. Narcissa was shivering uncontrollably, her skin burning with cold. She didn't speak as Mirrie gathered up a nightgown of fine lawn and worked it over her head and arms. Selah then picked up the sodden clothes from the floor and left the room. Mirrie pulled back the coverlet, and Narcissa fairly dove into the bed, letting herself sink into a snow-drift of feather mattress. She curled herself into a ball, hugging her knees to her chest, praying to get warm.

Brit Wallace found that his evening passed quickly. In those few hours he had composed the dispatch that would raise him from among the hacks and place upon his head the crown of heir apparent to William Howard Russell—"Bull Run" Russell—the best-known war correspondent in the world. With this dispatch, Brit could bid farewell to the *Argus* and take his place among the great men of the *Times,* to whom heads of state played flattering court. . . . Putting together rumors, observations, and the crucial hints provided by Ownby, he had seen, as clearly as if he had been looking down from one of Thaddeus Lowe's airships, the weakness in the Confederacy's defenses.

He scribbled the length of the page, then took up another sheet. Would this be worth trying to smuggle out of the country, when his editor might simply wad it up and throw it away, or use it to light his cigar? But, as always, the thrill of writing ran through his veins like coffee, or brandy, and he smiled to himself as he reread his composition.

War has come home to Richmond, hanging over the city like the threat of a summer storm. The familiar comforts of prosperity have fled along with most of the Confederate government. The Grande Armée of General George McClellan is encamped in a wide arc east of the city, in what amounts to a city of its own—row on row of comfortable tents where pine forest used to be, its hundred thousand men and thirty thousand beasts fed by a supply line that stretches back to White House Landing on the Pamunkey thirty miles away. In fair weather, the airships of Thaddeus Lowe make their ascent to survey the ranks of the defenders.

These are the Confederates, many of whom battle has stripped of superfluities such as overcoats, haversacks, tents, and shoes. Recent events deprived them of their leader, when General Joseph Johnston fell wounded at Seven Pines on the last day of May. The relatively untried General Robert Edward Lee is greeted with some apprehension. Yet this news need not cheer the Federals overmuch, for these are men hardened into determination.

With war comes ever the rumors of war. In the city and in the camps, hope rides on the breeze of human voices. Rumor becomes fact; fact transmogrifies into legend. The exploits of J. E. B. Stuart, leading a force of more than a thousand cavalrymen completely around the Union Army with the loss of only one man, deserve a Joinville or Ville-

hardouin for their chronicler. Every hour, every moment brings news of General "Stonewall" Jackson: he is here, there, everywhere. Soldiers seen marching northward through the city spark whispering of General P. G. T. Beauregard, come up from Mississippi to match his own Napoleonic reputation against that of McClellan. Meanwhile the Confederates' "Prince John" Magruder is on hand to conceal the weak spot in the city's defenses by his usual theatrics. But the playbill has changed from that presented at Big Bethel, where Magruder's puppet show masked a retreat. General Lee has stated that Richmond will not be given up; and so Magruder's troops masquerade as Miles Gloriosus, threatening annihilation with an empty scabbard. The real work will be elsewhere. With every moment, the soldiers await those words that lift the veil between present and future, those words as prescient as anything the witches told the Thane of Cawdor, those words so heavy with omen and portent—the order to cook up three days' rations.

Brit folded the paper and put it in the drawer of the little table. In a very few days, both sides would have played the hands they had been dealt. By the time a dispatch could be shipped across the Atlantic, printed in the newspaper, and shipped in printed form back across the Atlantic to Richmond—a month, at the least—it would no longer pose any threat. From that standpoint, there was no reason not to send it. But there would be the challenge of finding someone he could trust to take it down to Cape Fear or Charleston and get it onto a blockade runner. For if it fell into the wrong hands—Ownby's hands, for instance—well, that wouldn't do.

"Mrs. Powers." A gruff masculine voice spoke in her ear. At first Narcissa had no idea where she was or what man could be speaking to her. Then, squinting against the painful brightness, she recognized Dr. Archer. She saw Mirrie's face, smiling reassurance—and another woman, whose brilliant black eyes seemed to take in everything but give nothing away . . . Louisa Ferncliff.

"Don't distress yourself," Archer ordered. "You're very ill. You need to sleep. Drink this." He held a cordial glass that held a small amount of liquid. *Isn't that just like a doctor, waking me up to give me something to make me sleep?* She sipped it obediently. Archer nodded his approval, then said in a lower tone, "I will try to come see you tomorrow." He left, followed by Mirrie and Louisa.

In the hall, Mirrie put the question to Archer. "What is it, do you think?"

Archer shrugged, but the look on his face told Mirrie that frustration, not lack of concern, inspired the gesture. "It could be almost anything. The next few days should tell. I've given her a few grains of morphine. I will try to come by tomorrow."

Louisa stepped closer. "Mirrie, you and Narcissa must stay here. It would not do to move her in her current condition. And this is so much more convenient to the doctors."

After Archer took his leave, Mirrie was ready to go to Narcissa. Louisa held her back, putting her hand on Mirrie's sleeve. "I want you both to stay here, for a few days at least. I feel safer with you here."

"Safer?" Mirrie asked. The dim light on the landing cast a shadow on Louisa's face so that Mirrie could not read her expression.

"I've sent Claud—my driver—to my farm west of town to take care of some business for me. I have only Selah with me now, and I have to confess I feel uneasy. There are some that hate me."

"You're very generous, Louisa. Thank you. Beulah can take care of Father for a few days. But—should I send for my dog? She's a good watchdog. If anyone came into the yard, she would give the alarm."

Louisa thought for a moment. "A dog? Why not? Yes, it might be a good idea to have a dog here."

Narcissa heard Mirrie come into the room, and she pushed against the enveloping feather tick, struggling to sit up. "Mirrie, can I have some water?" Mirrie filled a glass and held it to her lips. "I'm so hot—" Narcissa pushed at the covers. Mirrie bent over the bed and folded back the quilts and blankets, one by one, until Narcissa was covered with only a sheet. Mirrie poured a little water from the pitcher onto one of the embroidered linen towels hanging on the spool-turned arms of the washstand. She placed the damp towel on Narcissa's forehead. And once again Narcissa fell into sleep.

Since the doctoress and midwife Judah Daniel moved into his house a year ago, John Chapman had gotten used to being woken up at night by the sounds of raised voices and urgent knocking. Usually he turned over and went back to sleep. This time, though, the noise broke into a nightmare and brought him wide awake. His heart beat painfully as he pulled his trousers on and hurried out into the hall. He was sure he'd find Guardsmen at his door, ready to arrest him for taking a tray of biscuits . . .

In the street, rain slanted down. The quivering gleam of far-off lightning showed a lone woman, a dark shawl around her head and shoulders. So it was someone calling on the doctoress after all. But when she stepped closer, he saw it was Susy herself.

"I need you to help me, John, one last time." Her voice

was low, steady, but her eyes glanced up and down the quiet street. The sight of her, here, affected him like a fist in the belly. He drew her inside and shut the door.

"Don't worry," she reassured him. "No one saw me come here. All I need you to do is give me some of your clothes."

"My clothes?" he repeated.

"Men's clothes," she snapped. "They'll be looking for a woman."

Still he couldn't take it in. "What—"

"I've been betrayed."

John turned then and went toward the back of the house. In the hall he passed Judah Daniel. "Go back to bed," he told her, "it ain't for you." Ignoring the question in her eyes, he waited until she was gone, then went into his room. Some of Tyler's things were folded up underneath the bed. The sight of them had made Elda cry. He brought them out, telling himself it wouldn't mean anything, it wouldn't make any difference for the future: when Tyler came back, he could get new clothes.

It was a little less than pitch-dark in the front of the house. John handed the bundle to Susy and then seated himself with his back to her. The warmth he had felt toward her was cooled considerably now that she'd brought her troubles into his house. She didn't seem to want to talk, but there were things he needed to know.

"You Selah's sister, ain't you? Susannah. You was a little girl with her up at the Ferncliffs'. But you went north to school." After so many years he would not have recognized her. She didn't much look like Selah, and he didn't know Selah well: she'd always held herself a little apart from, if not above, the rest of the free black community.

"That's right," Susy assented, her voice muffled by some garment going over her head. "After old Mr. Ferncliff died, Louisa gave us our freedom. She sent Selah and me to Philadelphia, to a Quaker school. Selah only lasted a few months. She wanted to come back, and finally Louisa gave in. Of course, the law says freed slaves have to leave the state, but laws don't apply to folks as rich as Louisa Ferncliff." Susy was silent for a moment, then spoke again, more clearly this time. "I stayed and got my education. I married. Then a few months ago Louisa wrote me that she wanted me to come back. I was hired out as a slave, first one place and then the other. And finally the Davis house."

She didn't seem inclined to say any more, but John was far from satisfied. "What was it come out of that house with them biscuits?"

He heard her sigh. "It was a letter."

"Tell me," he pressed.

"I can't do that."

"I got a right to know," he urged through clenched jaws. He didn't have a plan for what he would do if she refused. But she gave in.

"It was a letter from one of the generals. I read it. What it said—" She hesitated, then the words came out in a rush. "What it said could bring this city down; maybe even bring an end to this war."

Her words raised goose bumps on the back of his neck. His worst imaginings hadn't prepared him for this. Sooner or later, someone would talk about seeing him with her at Davis's, and with Selah at Ferncliff's. . . . He felt a surge of anger at all of them: Susy, Selah, Louisa Ferncliff. "How come you didn't just take it to the Yankees yourself?"

A short, sharp laugh came from Susy. "You think I planned this? I wanted to stay. I fixed it so they wouldn't even know the letter was missing." She walked to the door and pulled it open. He followed her. She looked like a plump, round-bottomed boy with close-cropped hair—

had she worn it that way all along, under her kerchief?—dressed in hand-me-down clothes he hadn't grown into.

"Who you say betrayed you?"

Susy shook her head. "Don't ask me any more questions. I won't answer them. Forget everything you know, or think you know. You shouldn't be in any danger if you tend to your business and keep your mouth shut."

He walked over to her. Her hands were on her hips, her chin tilted at him. He looked her up and down and said, "You best be careful how you look and talk when the Guard stop you. It'd be a shame, after all o' this, if you was to get sold south." He had the bitter satisfaction of seeing fear come into her eyes.

"John." She'd softened her voice. "There's nothing to make them suspect you. Keep doing what you've been doing, going from the Davises' up to Louisa's. Do it for a few days more at least. Give the biscuits to Mattie, like you used to do before I came. And . . . thank you."

John watched as Susy took off into the rain, holding Tyler's old felt hat down on her head. Then he shut the door and bolted it. A stout wooden door . . . a sturdy house, which he and his father had built, largely with their own hands. Home to more than a dozen people: his family. Was it strong enough to survive what was coming?

John Chapman felt the skin crawl on the back of his neck. He was going to be sick to his stomach if he didn't let this secret out to just one person. And of all possible people to tell, she was the best choice. He went to her door and knocked. She opened it right away. There was a tallow candle burning, as if she'd been waiting for him ever since the knock came on the door. They sat together on the low pallet. John clasped his hands together between his knees and began to speak.

"Judah Daniel . . . you know I always done my best to work hard and keep out of other people's trouble. I never seen white men as my enemies. I ain't talking about riffraff like them plug-uglies, it's white *gentlemen* I mean, like my grandfather was. James Chapman was a Virginian, a hero of the Revolutionary War, and he done right by my father—freed him and give him an inheritance. And his other sons, his white sons, honored it. And their sons speak to me when they see me, at the Capitol or around on the streets. Sometimes I want to tell that Baltimore filth just who they're insulting when they speak to me like they does."

John Chapman passed his hand over his hair, steel-gray now but still thick on his head. He was light-skinned, but—Judah Daniel mused—his face was molded on lines too generous, too expressive, for him ever to be taken for a white man. Not that he would have wanted to. He was content. Or he had been.

She waited. John sighed. "It was last Tuesday."

The day after Elda's baby died, Judah Daniel supplied silently.

"I was driving my rounds. Up at the Davis house, somebody new met me at the door. She took me into the kitchen. She told me her name was Susy Reynolds. She asked me if I could take some biscuits up to Church Hill, to Louisa Ferncliff's house. I just laughed. I said I might do that. But I had a bad feeling about it. She was so quiet, speaking so low right in my ear, like she was afraid somebody would hear what she was saying."

John Chapman looked away. "Well, it didn't seem so much to help her out by taking biscuits up to Ferncliff's. But something about the way she done it, I knowed that sooner or later it was going to be more than biscuits I was taking. I worried about it some, back and forth, all that day. But the next morning, there I was, taking biscuits up to Louisa Ferncliff's. It was a far piece out of my way, too, but once I said I'd do it, I didn't want to go back on my word. Then yesterday, I take the tray in to Susy, and I'll be damned if she doesn't give me a tray back with the biscuits already on it! I knowed without her saying what it was she wanted me to do. I took it to Ferncliff's house and handed it to Selah. I don't know how good those biscuits was, seeing as I didn't make them. But I didn't get no complaints."

Judah Daniel thought about what all this might mean. John Chapman had been carefully recruited for the job by someone who knew the right approach to make. And John had taken something from Susy to Selah. The *thing* John took from one to the other could have been anything. Was it something Jeff Davis would miss? That was a frightening thought. "Which one was it come to the door?"

"Susy. She wanted some men's clothes to keep the Guard from knowing her. She's running off to the Yankees. She said she been betrayed. She didn't say by who. Said they didn't have nothing on me."

"What you know about them two—Selah and Susy?"

John must have been mulling over this same question. "I been trying to recollect. Louisa Ferncliff freed them when they was young girls. They was both clever girls, real superior. Didn't mix much with the free blacks *or* the slaves. Ferncliff sent Susannah up north to a Quaker school to be educated. She come back every year 'round Christmas. She turned out to be a real pretty girl. She married a man up there and ain't been back for these many years. Selah never married, never even had a man courting her that I heard of. 'Course Miss Louisa turned against men quite a few years back, and I reckon she ain't encouraged any courtship of Selah."

Susy Reynolds had not come to Richmond and wound up working at the Confederate president's house by chance. Someone—probably Louisa Ferncliff—had thought all this out very carefully. It was like she'd sent her former servant up north twenty years before just for this purpose, getting her ready to spy on a government that hadn't even existed at the time.

She didn't speak these thoughts out loud; she didn't want to add to the worries that had already put a crack in John Chapman's proud demeanor. The plug-uglies would take one look at him and assume he was guilty of something.

"Well, sound to me like the only thing showing you had a hand in this done been buttered and ate."

John's eyebrows rose. Then he laughed, though it was more of a snort than his usual deep, rolling chuckle.

"Keep going for a while, to Davis's house and Ferncliff's too. Show you ain't scared to show your face. Then after a few days—" She stopped, remembering. After a few days, the Yankees might be riding high in the city, and rewarding those who had helped them. "After a few days, we'll see."

CHAPTER THREE

JUNE 24

The first shoppers at John Chapman's bakeshop—two white women—brought the news.

"Did you hear?" one asked. "Another servant done run off from Jefferson Davis. A woman this time."

The second nodded. "Gone over to the Yankees, I reckon, with a bunch of gossip and lies." She glanced over at John. "You heard?"

"Ain't heard no more than that," John lied.

The women made their purchases and walked out, talking in lower tones now. As soon as John was alone, the stiff smile slipped off his face. Earlier that morning, following Judah Daniel's advice, he'd gone back up to Davis's. Mattie had practically jerked the tray out of his hands and disappeared into the house with a swish of skirts. He tried to tell himself he was imagining things—that she was just hurried, not huffy, and it didn't have anything to do with him. Then he'd driven on to Ferncliff's, where he waited for long minutes before Selah appeared and took the tray without so much as meeting his eyes. Neither of the households most involved had spoken a word about what had happened. It was the rest of the town that was buzzing.

He wished he could take Selah by the shoulders and shake her until she told him what she knew. But he was afraid even to speak to Selah, because of that word Susy had used: *betrayed*. Your enemies could hurt you in any number of ways, but they couldn't betray you. Only the people closest to you could do that. And who was closer to Susy than Selah?

Up at Chimborazo, Cameron Archer reviewed the morning's work before him—patients he had to see, reports he had to write—and the additional tasks that had fallen on him as a result of his acquaintance with Narcissa Powers. She had told him about Wright's accusations against Annie Yates. Archer suspected Wright himself had been taking drugs and liquor meant for the patients and using them to dull his own pain, whatever it was. If it weren't for his near-constant state of intoxication, Wright would surely have realized the ward housed a malingerer. Since Wright hadn't realized it—but Narcissa had—that, too, had become Archer's problem. He had worked out who the malingerer must be. Testing out his theory would be the first order of business, he decided; then he could add Wright's failure to spot the faker to his list of complaints to take to the division head, Matthew Lester.

Archer strode purposefully between the rows of patients to the far end. It had to be the case of *sopor caroticus*. The fake would not be hard to prove. The patient would doubtless "revive" after a few moments of having his nose and mouth held shut.

It was there, wasn't it? Archer leaned over the low bed to see a wasted figure, both legs amputated well above the knee. Thinking he'd mistaken the bed, he glanced around. He walked between the rows again, looking more closely this time. The man he was looking for seemed not to be there. Maybe it all worked out as Narcissa had hoped, and the man had turned himself in.

Archer caught sight of the young Douglas Coster—surgeon-in-charge today instead of Wright—and went over to him. "Where's the *sopor caroticus*?"

"You mean Devlin, sir? He died during the night."

"Ah . . . I see. Well, carry on."

Archer walked back out. It was raining again. He pulled his hat well down over his eyes and set off to find Dr. Lester. He felt his cheeks burning with embarrassment. Thank God he'd not made the accusation to Lester that Wright had failed to spot a malingerer. To make such an accusation, based on the unsubstantiated word of a volunteer nurse, would have been a serious breach of both military and medical conduct. Narcissa had taken some kind of involuntary movement of the muscles for sentience—that was all. What had she told him? That she had spoken to the man; not that he had answered.

Archer felt anger rise in him, then ebb away. It was less Narcissa's fault for making a mistake than it was his for believing her. He had offered his belief up to her as a kind of proof of his regard—it was only in hindsight that he recognized this.

"Archer!"

He turned around to see Wright hurrying toward him. He waited.

"Archer!" Wright hailed him again, even though he was now only a few steps away. "How is she faring—your friend Mrs. Powers?"

There was almost enough emphasis on the word *friend* to be insulting—almost, but not quite. Still, Archer had no wish to be interrogated about Mrs. Powers, especially by so unpleasant a specimen as Thomas Wright. As he debated what sort of response to make, Wright's expression shifted from feigned concern to genuine petulance. "We all heard she was very ill with fever. I know she must have been very ill, for you to take morphine meant for the patients."

Archer froze. So he had been seen—by Wright, of all people. It was just a little morphine, not enough to be missed. But he'd be damned before he'd say that, or anything else, to Wright. So he said nothing, just stared at the man.

Wright's face went a deeper shade of red. "You need not worry, Archer. I haven't said anything to Dr. Lester. It's such a small thing; I'm sure it would be overlooked, given all that's going on."

"Tell him, or not, and be damned to you," Archer growled. Wright took a step back. "I was just going to tell him myself." Archer turned and walked away, crunching the wet gravel beneath his boot heels. Of course, he'd not planned on informing Lester about his—*theft,* he may as well call it, it would be a vain pretense to call it borrowing when he had no hope of replacing the morphine. He'd been intending to complain to Lester about Wright. Could Wright somehow have known that? His timing—the bastard—could not have been better. Now anything Archer might say to Lester about Wright would seem like a cowardly attempt at self-protection.

Matthew Lester greeted Archer warmly, shook his hand, offered him a seat, and then reseated himself behind the big desk. Lester had aged in the decade and a half since Archer had been his student. The wiry muttonchop whiskers were showing a great deal of white. But the man's vivid blue eyes still communicated vigor and intelligence. He waited for Archer to begin.

"I want you to know that Thomas Wright may make a complaint against me."

Lester's eyebrows tilted—more of a "please explain" gesture, Archer thought, than one of surprise or concern.

"He may tell you that I took some morphine from the ward yesterday evening. It's true. I took enough for one dose, and that is all. Mrs. Narcissa Powers was here yesterday, taking care of patients, when she fell ill with fever."

"Mrs. Powers! I'm sorry to hear it. She seems to be a very competent nurse."

Archer nodded. "She is, sir. Anyway, she was taken to Louisa Ferncliff's house, where her sister-in-law was visiting. I took her the morphine last night."

"Louisa Ferncliff's, you say?" Lester queried with a frown.

"Her sister-in-law's friend, not hers, I daresay. Mrs. Powers's loyalty is beyond question. She has been volunteering as a nurse at the Medical College Hospital since war was declared. You remember her brother, Charley Wilson, was a medical student until his death a year ago."

"Oh, yes. I'd forgotten she was Wilson's sister. His death was tragic. Well, I understand your feeling in the situation. It's hard to be powerless to help those we—care about. For myself, I miss my wife, but I am not sorry she refugeed. It would be painful to see her suffering through this siege . . . the deprivation, the constant fear."

From what Archer recalled of Mrs. Lester, she would not bear deprivation well. He had no doubt Lester was speaking the truth when he said it was easier for him without his wife. But Narcissa Powers was a different kind of woman altogether.

"It's much easier, for me, that she is in Canada." Lester spoke these last words almost to himself. "Ironic . . . my father spent years in Canada. He backed the wrong side in the last rebellion that was fought on this soil."

Archer wondered if his superior were asking himself what he would have done if someone he cared for needed medicine that by rights belonged to the army. Or perhaps Lester was searching for a gentle way to administer the re-

quired rebuke. He decided to take the whip out of Lester's
hand and lay it on his own back. "It won't happen again,
sir. I know every bit of morphine is needed for the soldiers. And any for sale in the city was certainly stolen from
the hospital, or diverted from military surgeons' use at the
least. I won't let myself be tempted again."

Lester smiled at that. "Don't be too hard on yourself,
Archer. Is that all?"

"Well . . . no, sir. It's humiliating, under the circumstances. . . ."

Lester leaned forward, alert again. "You may speak
freely to me, Archer."

"I think Wright may bring the accusation against me to
forestall my complaining about him. For a while now,
drugs and liquor have been disappearing from the ward.
The amounts taken have been fairly small, and I have not
been inclined to make an accusation. But it's come to my
attention that Dr. Wright has accused one of the volunteer
nurses of the theft and driven her from the hospital."

"Not Mrs. Powers, surely?"

"No, sir. A woman named Annie Yates"—he tried to remember what Narcissa had said of her—"who lost both
her husband and her son at Seven Pines. I believe Wright
is stealing the drugs himself."

Lester made a steeple of his fingers. Archer recognized
the gesture. Then Lester said, "Putting the blame on a
woman who may be innocent is provoking. The misap-
propriation of supplies is provoking. But the sad truth is
that, at some time during your medical training and practice, you've probably condoned worse behavior. I know I
have," he added with a little smile. "Particularly of late."

Archer put his hands on Lester's desk and leaned forward, urging his case. "I admit that I might overlook even
these provocations, if Wright were a better doctor. He's a
fair diagnostician, but he's sloppy. The steward has caught

mistakes in prescriptions—confusion between quinine sulfate and morphine sulfate, for example. Taking all these things together, I have to ask if we would not be better off to dismiss Wright."

Lester considered for a moment, then spoke. "Wright was assigned to Ward 27 to keep him away from the patients that have a better chance of recovery. And I assigned Jonas Bench as steward—he has better than the usual training—to keep an eye on him. I admit that. But tell me, what do you think Wright is doing with the medicines he steals? Selling them, or using them himself?"

Archer answered without hesitation. "I think he is taking them himself, perhaps because it's now more difficult to obtain spirits."

Lester stood up. "I'll watch Wright. I know you will be watching him as well. But this is not a good time to lose a surgeon—even a mediocre one."

Archer nodded. There was nothing he could do but accept Lester's decision, though it left him with a feeling of powerlessness that he hated. All this had done nothing but put him behind in his work for the day—too far behind, for the time being anyway, for him to call at Louisa Ferncliff's and see how Narcissa was faring. He had better send word to Mirrie Powers to call in some physician who was not busy with soldiers . . . if there were any available, which he had to admit was unlikely.

Then another thought struck him. Suppose Wright was not the only one who knew about his theft of the morphine. Had someone else seen him? Were they all gossiping about it even now? Wright had been there in the ward. So had Coster, but that young man held him in too much awe to question anything he did. Jonas Bench, the hospital steward, was a possibility. Bench was a taciturn man whose face gave nothing away. Perhaps he took personally Archer's failure to go through him to obtain the drug (though of course Bench would have refused). There were plenty of other people around, but he doubted whether the convalescent orderlies would know enough about the surgeons' routine to notice he had deviated from it.

Archer reflected on the oddity of human nature—at least his own nature. If Jonas Bench saw, and told, it would be a pettifogging, red-tape-mongering thing to do. If Coster did so, he'd take it as the sincere, though naive, act of a young idealist. But the idea of Wright broadcasting his mistake made him want to call the man out.

Judah Daniel went over again what John Chapman had told her. Susy had come by the Chapman house in the middle of the night. She'd told John what it was he had taken from her hands and put into the hands of Louisa Ferncliff's servant Selah—a letter that could bring down the city, maybe even the Confederacy. She'd asked for men's clothes in which to make her escape from the city into the Union camp. She'd talked about being betrayed, though she'd assured John he was in no danger.

Judah Daniel had encouraged John to trust Susy on that score. What else could she do? He would never run away, not without his old father and his sisters and their husbands and children and his daughter-in-law Elda and most of all, of course, Young John, his grandson. The only thing he could do would be to tell the authorities what had happened, how he'd been a go-between for Susy and Louisa Ferncliff. He could tell them he hadn't suspected anything wrong until Susy had turned up missing; but that now, civic duty forced him to come clean. Well, they might believe it and decide to go after Louisa. She was despised, called a nigger lover and a Yankee lover; still, she was a wealthy white woman. It would be her word—*and* her money—against that of a man who would not even be allowed to testify in a court of law because of the color of his skin. Judah Daniel had little doubt who would come out on top in that fight. But if John was suspected, it might be worth a try.

She had to find out, if she could, who had betrayed Susy, and whether that person might be likely to do the same thing to John. Her greatest fear was that it was someone in Jefferson Davis's household—someone who had seen John Chapman come and go.

Mattie Peat, the Davises' cook, would be the best one to approach. Judah Daniel had met Mattie a few times at the farmers' market and at church. Mattie knew she and John were close friends. If Mattie suspected John, or knew others suspected him, it would come out somehow, in her words or in her face.

Mattie greeted Judah Daniel at the door of the kitchen, invited her in, and gave her a cup of real coffee. It was a hot day already, but the treat was too good to turn down. Judah Daniel sat at the table, holding the cup with both hands, and watched as Mattie kneaded bread dough. Mattie stood barely five feet high; she bobbed up and down on her toes as she kneaded, putting her whole body into the effort as well as her strong arms and blunt-fingered hands. "I reckon I know what you come about," she announced to Judah Daniel. "It's all over town about that housemaid Susy running off."

Judah Daniel nodded. She told herself not to make too much of Mattie's reaction. Might be others had called on the cook with an eye to getting the latest gossip. "Folks is saying this and that about it. I reckon you know more than most. What do *you* say?"

"I say, good riddance!" Mattie declared, giving a forceful whack to the dough. "Susy Reynolds hadn't got no more sense than a day-old biddie. She didn't know nothing about how a house ought to be run. If Mrs. Davis was here, she'd have straightened her out right quick-like. She don't know how to set a table or get stains out of a tablecloth. And you ought to seen the biscuits she made." Mattie gave a sideways glance in Judah Daniel's direction. "Reckon I know what she was up to with that. Reckon that's why you here."

Judah Daniel struggled to keep her mask of bland interest in place. *Jesus God,* she prayed silently, *don't let this be going where I think it's going.* She set her cup down for fear it would shake in her hands.

"She done set her cap for John Chapman." Mattie nodded several times, slapping the dough harder than ever. Judah Daniel breathed again. Mattie went on. "Thought she could sweeten him up with her baking, I reckon. Hah! That was the sorriest-looking batch of biscuits I ever seen. I reckon John took 'em from her just to be nice and throwed 'em in a ditch somewhere. After that, I don't know, might be he said something to her. She come to me all in a huff and asked if I'd meet him at the door from then on. I said I would. I been doing it before she ever come here; she asked special to do it. Setting her cap at him, I reckon. Now I wish I'd told her not to go nosing around men who got better sense than to be interested in the likes of her."

"It surprise you, her running off like that?"

Mattie shrugged. "She was flighty. I ain't altogether sure she run off to the Yankees anyhow. Might be some man give her the eye and she run off with him."

Judah Daniel thought about that. Did Susy have another man helping her smuggle out secrets? "You see anyone else hanging around her?"

"No," Mattie admitted, "but I didn't have no time to watch her comings and goings."

Judah Daniel nudged the talk in a different direction.

"Might be it was somebody from where she used to work. Where was that—you remember?"

Mattie shrugged again. "Mrs. Davis hired her, back before she left town. There was lots more folks in the house then, white folks and servants both. I didn't take much notice of her. Some lady who was refugeeing, closing up the house, and needed to find a place for Susy."

"Did she live around here?"

Mattie thought a moment, then nodded. "Seem like she live up on Church Hill. I don't think Susy was one of her own slaves. She hired her out. Who owns her, I don't rightly know. Might be somebody out in the country. Susy had a man back there, maybe; didn't look like she was above trying to replace him, though. You know," she added, her tone suddenly warmer, "John didn't do nothing to lead her on. Don't you go thinking he did. He got better sense than that."

Judah Daniel saw what Mattie was leading up to and steered her away. "Does the president and them seem very upset by it?"

"Hmph!" Mattie snorted, amused. "They got more important things to do than worry about some uppity housemaid running off. They's a big storm brewing, Judah Daniel, and won't be long before it breaks."

→>—<←

Archer's first sight of Douglas Coster reassured him that the young man had not heard any accusation that Archer had taken drugs from the hospital. Coster was standing at the end of the long ward building with a stack of patients' cards in his hand, making notes with a pencil. When he caught sight of Archer, his face relaxed into a welcoming smile. Archer went over to him.

"It's the damnedest thing," Coster said. "That *sopor caroticus* up and died."

"Well," Archer replied cautiously, "you can never tell with closed head injuries."

Coster held the pencil between his teeth and riffled through the papers. Then he took the pencil out and said, "There's no death certificate that I've been able to find." He paused, then added, "Wright was on duty."

"So he didn't do the paperwork," Archer hazarded. "It wouldn't be the first time."

"The *sopor* case had only been here a couple of days. I'm not sure he ever had a thorough examination. I wonder if he might have been malingering."

"In which case—what?" Archer prompted.

"I wonder if Wright gave him a pass, so to speak."

Archer thought about this. To be sure, Wright wasn't a scrupulous physician, but he didn't seem a man to do a favor without some reward for himself. What could a malingerer who had nothing but the clothes on his back, and few enough of them, use to bribe a doctor?

"I'm not proud of saying that about another doctor," Coster added. "If it were anyone but Wright—"

Archer felt the thrill of a rather evil excitement. If Wright had aided a deserter, there were grounds for a court-martial. But how in the world could it be proved? He asked Coster, "Would you recognize the *sopor* case if you saw him?"

Coster thought for a moment, then shook his head. "Not a chance. And there was no information about him—not his regiment or state, not even his real name. They called him Devlin or something like that. If he did escape, by now he's blended in with all the other skulkers in the city, or hightailed it for the Yankee camp. No—we'll never see *him* again." Coster looked crestfallen.

"Well." Archer decided to take the angle of the older, more experienced physician. "You know, really, Coster, it's more than likely that the man is dead. It's hard to feign

complete unconsciousness for days at a time. Someone
would have noticed." *Someone other than a young woman
with no experience in such matters,* he added to himself. "I
know you feel as I do about Wright. But the truth will
come out. One of these days he'll make a slip that can't be
overlooked."

Coster nodded his acceptance of Archer's counsel.
Archer felt a twinge of guilt at the young man's easy ac-
ceptance of his words. Still, he couldn't tell Coster that he
planned to look through the death certificates to find if
Wright had verified the demise of the man known as
Devlin.

✦➤✦◄✦

Judah Daniel was back walking the streets of Church Hill,
eyeing the fine homes to try to find the one most likely to
have employed Susy Reynolds before the Davises. A few of
the houses' owners had left them more than a year before,
when the war broke out, leaving them to be rented by
high-ranking officers and their families. Other owners
stayed on, riding out the siege like the rest of the city.
When she saw a maid sweeping steps or polishing a door-
knob, she stopped to talk. She learned nothing of interest
until she came upon an old man deadheading the roses in
the side yard of a house on East Marshall Street. He was
dressed in the clothes of a house servant, tailored to fit
him; but he had taken off the white gloves and settled an
old felt hat on his head to shade his eyes in the out-of-
doors. He handled the knife like he wasn't accustomed to
it; probably he'd been drafted into service as a gardener
only lately. She remembered his name: Ash Chalmers.

"What you doing there, Ash? You got to let the hips
form on them roses. If you leave them on until the first
frost, they make right good jelly."

Ash made a droll face and lifted the beat-up old hat in

greeting. "Don't you think I told Mrs. Riley that? She won't hear of it. Say, keep her roses looking pretty; it takes her mind off the Yankees. If *they* come riding in, though, I got orders to chop these bushes down. Right after I hide the silver and missus' jewelry." He gave a sigh and applied the knife to another overblown blossom. "Yes, I reckon I be right busy if the Yankees ride in."

Judah Daniel stepped closer. "There's some that ain't waiting for the Yankees to come get 'em. You hear about that maidservant run away from the Davises? Come to think of it, didn't I hear she worked around here? For some folks that refugeed sometime in the past few months."

Ash shook his head. But it turned out he didn't mean *no*; he went on to say, "I didn't expect nothing good out of that woman."

"Oh—you knew her?"

"Met her. Name of Susy Reynolds. Worked for Dr. Lester's family. I asked her to come to a worship service." Ash was a deacon at the First African Baptist Church. "She swished her head and told me she was a *different religion*. Well, what would that be? I asked her, but she didn't say. Reckon she weren't no religion at all. Not more than a week after that, she went to work over to the Davises. I could have told them she didn't have no good character. 'Course nobody asked me."

"Where do the Lesters live?"

"Down Grace Street." Ash pointed. "On the corner of Twenty-third."

Grace and Twenty-third—catty-corner across the street from Louisa Ferncliff. Judah Daniel frowned. "You said the family refugeed. But he still here, ain't he—the doctor?"

Ash chuckled. "Oh, yes, ma'am. He still here, though he don't come to the house from one week to the next. He

pretty much living at the hospital. It was that wife of his.
I heard she went to Canada. Sent the servants out to the
country somewheres—reckon she couldn't take them
with her, seeing as, in Canada, they got laws against keeping slaves. Susy Reynolds, she got hired at the Davises.
Susy was strutting about it like she was somebody important. Guess she found out work is work, no matter how
fancy the folks is. So she run off."

"The servants who got sent to the country, where'd
they go?"

Ash's forehead creased. "I don't know. I don't think
they was expecting it to be long. But don't none of us
know what to expect, and that's the truth of it. I can ask
around if you want me to."

"If it ain't too much trouble," Judah Daniel replied. She
didn't hold out much hope of learning more about the
missing slaves. Still, she had the information she'd
wanted. Dr. Lester's wife had taken Susy Reynolds into the
White House, and then gotten about as far away from
Richmond as she could go without crossing an ocean.
Canada. The best-known routes to freedom led there—
the place where the Fugitive Slave Laws lost their power.
Maybe Dr. Lester's wife had her eyes on more than society
luster when she placed Susy in the president's house. But
she owned several slaves—not what you'd expect from an
abolitionist. Judah Daniel talked a little while more with
Ash, then took her leave.

Dr. Lester's house was smaller and plainer than Louisa
Ferncliff's, and situated on a much smaller lot; but it was
still a fine house, made of brick and rising three stories
over an English basement. Judah Daniel looked first into
the kitchen behind the house. Finding no one there, she
walked in. The kitchen had not seen use in quite some
time; no fire burned in the big fireplace, which had not
even been swept out after its last use. Mice had gnawed

into a flour sack that drooped against the wall and speckled the bag with their droppings. The doctor's cook would have a fit when she came back from wherever the family servants had been sent to wait out the siege.

Judah Daniel went back outside and looked up at the house. The shutters were closed, and the house looked empty. There was nothing interesting about it except its closeness to Louisa Ferncliff's. She decided she'd best move on. It wouldn't do for her to be seen here. Empty houses were sometimes broken into; if it happened here, she didn't want to get the blame.

Narcissa awakened to the gray light of another rainy day. For a long time she felt as if it were more than she could do to get out of the bed. She lay there, hot and miserable, trapped in the oversoft mattress like a fly in molasses. At last she sat up and swung her legs over the side of the bed. She sat there for a minute, gathering her strength, then slid gingerly to her feet. Her legs could hardly support her. The touch of the air as she moved through it was enough to make her skin hurt. Carefully, holding on to the furniture, she made her way to the night stool. On her way back to the bed, something on the floor caught her attention, something dark on the light summer matting. She leaned over to see what it was—a big spider, smashed flat. The sight brought back a memory. Once she had found a spider in her bedroom and hit it with her shoe. The bursting body released thousands of tiny babies that ran like water into the space between the floorboards.

Back in bed, in a state that was neither sleep nor waking, she felt spiders crawling on her skin. She twitched away from the feeling, relaxed for a moment . . . then they came again, their thin, dry legs scratching her. Now they'd gotten inside her skin, breaking out from the painful place in her abdomen and swarming in her blood.

"Narcissa?" It was Mirrie. The sight of her face had never seemed so welcome. Mirrie slipped her arm under Narcissa's shoulders and helped her to sit up, then held to her lips a glass of cool water. Narcissa sipped it gratefully. The water seemed to sizzle away as it touched her mouth—to evaporate as if it had fallen on a hot griddle.

"That spider," she told Mirrie, pointing. She saw Mirrie look, frown, look back at her as if considering.

"I'll get something to clean it up," Mirrie told her soothingly, rising from her perch on the high bed.

"No." Narcissa clutched her arm. It would be worse to be here alone with them—

"There's no one I can call," Mirrie explained. "I've no idea where Selah is. Louisa is lying down with a headache. I wish Beulah would bring Friday. She could keep you company."

Narcissa smiled her thanks. Yes, the little dog would be a welcome companion. It was horrible to be alone with the thing that had taken over her body and her mind—dull and deadening at best, and at worst almost maddening.

→>—<+

Mirrie stayed with Narcissa all morning, giving her drinks of water and cool compresses when she woke, and when she slept, returning to her volume of Spenser. In the early afternoon Louisa knocked on the door and asked if she would come down to dinner. Narcissa seemed to be sleeping soundly; Mirrie agreed. On the dining table were a Virginia ham, a big dish of butterbeans, biscuits, strawberry preserves, watermelon pickles, and a pitcher of cold tea. Mirrie felt a pang of guilt, wondering if Louisa had assembled it all herself, since Selah was nowhere in evidence.

Even as she had the thought, Louisa answered the

question. "I must apologize for this poor dinner. Selah was out this morning. When she came in she told me another servant has run away from Davis's household. A maid this time."

"Well!" Mirrie replied lightly. "I suppose in a few weeks' time we will be reading about her in the northern papers."

Louisa smiled her thin, unhappy smile. "They say her name was Susy Reynolds. I hope she is carrying more than gossip—unlike poor William Jackson. If only these intelligent Negroes could be more patient . . . wait a little longer . . ."

"Wait?" Mirrie asked. "Why, what would they be waiting for?"

Louisa's smile was drawn tighter even than usual, as if she were holding her temper with an effort. "Isn't it obvious? Placed as they are, in positions of trust, in the very heart of the Confederate government, all they would have to do is keep their eyes and ears open. They could be very successful spies, once the real war commences—the war to end slavery."

Louisa's tone made Mirrie blush with irritation, but she held back an angry reply. "I suppose it is hard for them to wait, when the opportunity for freedom presents itself, and they have been suffering for so long."

Louisa got up. "I apologize for my bad temper. I am too used to living alone. Now I really think I must lie down again. My head is splitting."

—>—<—

Narcissa woke to see Mirrie standing over her, arms full of red roses still wet with rain. "Mr. Wallace brought these," Mirrie said, smiling. "And Dr. Archer is here to see you."

Cameron Archer stepped into the room. Mirrie carried the roses over to the mantel and began arranging them in a tall Chinese vase.

Archer seated himself in the chair next to the bed. "How are you, Mrs. Powers?"

"Better. Thank you—"

Archer shifted, stretching his legs out in front of him and then drawing them back as if worried that he shouldn't appear too comfortable. Narcissa wondered if he were here as a doctor or a friend, and thought he might be wondering as well.

"That *sopor caroticus*," he began, then stopped. "That man you thought was malingering. There can be no doubt that he's dead. I found the surgeon's certificate. Dr. Lester signed it himself."

"Oh," Narcissa answered. She must have imagined what she saw. With all that she'd imagined since then, it seemed possible. "Well . . . thank you for finding out for me."

Archer stayed a few more minutes. Then Mirrie accompanied him out of the room. When the door closed, leaving her alone again, Narcissa almost wept. Time had slowed to an agonizing crawl. Only those too-brief visits gave evidence that, beyond the walls of her sickroom, the world went on as before, and that she was still a part of it. Maybe I'm feeling what the men in the hospital feel, she thought. Maybe that is why they always seem so glad to see us.

➤><◄

Mirrie went out into the hall. The door to Louisa's room was open. She walked up to it and called out, "Are you feeling better?"

"Oh, Mirrie. Come in."

This was the first look Mirrie had had at Louisa's private rooms. The furnishings were delicate, feminine. The walls were papered in soft moss green. The rose-patterned carpet had been left down despite the summer heat—

possibly because it was enormous, running almost to the walls of the big room. Real roses from the garden had been gathered into vases on the mantel. Louisa was working hard at maintaining the niceties of a gracious life, though surely it was Selah who was doing most of the actual work.

Louisa sounded quite strong, and looked it as well. She was dressed and was sitting very straight-backed on a low bench with curved arms. She was holding something in her lap. "Come sit by me. You asked about the young women who were my wards."

Mirrie recalled the two slave girls whom Louisa had been able to free and to keep with her—only the two, with the rest of the family sold away by Louisa's father. "It's a sad story."

"This is their likeness." Louisa's hands held a little leather case lying open to reveal paired daguerreotypes. Mirrie took the case and tilted it so that she could see the images. The young women shared a family resemblance. The younger and prettier looked to be between twenty and twenty-five; the elder, whom Mirrie recognized as Selah, was several years older. They were dressed, coiffed, and posed not as servants but as young ladies. Their hair was uncovered, smoothed back. Their print dresses had broad white collars trimmed in lace. "That's Selah, isn't it?"

"The photograph was taken in Philadelphia," Louisa said. "Selah and I visited Susannah there a few years ago, before the South lost its mind. Susannah was educated there."

"Not Selah?" Mirrie asked.

Louisa frowned. "I sent her as well, but she did not take to it; she complained that the letters and numbers scrambled themselves in her head." Louisa's tight smile showed that the young Selah's complaint had not met with sympathy. "Susannah wrote to me about her, the school wrote to me; she was miserable, crying, not eating. Of course one cannot do schoolwork when one makes up one's mind not to. In the end, I gave in and brought her home."

"I'm sure she's been a comfort to you," Mirrie ventured.

"Susannah did very well. She won awards. She taught at the school for a time, then had some success as a speaker at abolitionist meetings. I was disappointed when she married; I feared it would deflect her from the important work she had to do. Of course the young man was a dedicated abolitionist as well."

"And did it—deflect her, I mean?" Mirrie prompted. She was becoming very interested in the story of Louisa's two wards.

Again, Louisa did not answer the question, responding instead to some voice inside her own head. "They were like my own children."

Louisa held out her hand for the case, and Mirrie gave it to her. Louisa took it and set it on the little table among some other *objets*, the most prominent being an elaborate hair wreath under a glass dome set on a wooden base.

Louisa followed her gaze. "My mother's hair, my father's, and my two brothers'. They died very young. See how light their baby hair is, how blond. You southerners view such mementos as holy relics. I do not. Nor do I grieve over the ones who are gone—even the little boys. If they had grown up to be like my father, God was merciful to take them."

Mirrie looked away from the wreath, from the innocent white-gold hair of the young boys. She had adored her brother, Rives, but . . . suppose her father had sold a family of slaves, dividing them, despite her begging him not to do it. Then suppose—but no, it wasn't possible; she couldn't imagine growing up in such a family.

"Where is Susannah now?" she asked, mostly to change the subject.

Louisa turned to look at her. "We've lost touch."

"Oh, but—that's a shame." More sorrow, thought Mirrie. "Perhaps, when this dreadful war is ended, you will find each other again."

"Perhaps." On the word, Louisa's lips shut as tight as the little leather case that held the two daguerreotypes.

Brit Wallace wandered back to his room at the Exchange Hotel, feeling at sixes and sevens. Narcissa had a serious fever. A fear he wouldn't name prickled at the back of his neck.

The door to his room was ajar. Some servant had been careless, he supposed, and pushed it open. The tiny space looked as if a tornado had blown through. Books and papers from the shelves and table, pictures from the walls, his bedclothes and his clothing—even the clothes hidden away under the bed—all were dumped in the middle of the room, and looked to have been thoroughly shredded. Ink from the inkstand had been poured on the papers. He felt under the mattress to see if his little cache of money was still there. It was gone. But he knew that this was no robbery. He thought of Ownby's piggy face, and he thought of the dispatch he had written. Thank goodness it had been in his pocket, not here in the room for Ownby to find and use as evidence of indiscretion. Well . . . best gather up what was left of his possessions and look for another place to stay—preferably one where Ownby would not be likely to find him.

By nightfall, Narcissa's fever had broken. Mirrie was with Louisa, so Narcissa took Friday out into the front garden.

Friday chased fireflies among the big boxwoods. Though
the little dog was quick, Narcissa was relieved to see that
the pretty insects she'd loved as a child were quicker. The
roses were drooping, heavy with the rain that had fallen
earlier in the day. Dark clouds still clustered overhead, but
in the distance a shaft of sunlight broke through. With the
waning of the fever, life's concerns returned. Dr. Archer
had come with medicine, Brit Wallace with roses. The two
men were as different from one another as the gifts they
had brought, but both were important to her.

Then there were the other things that had been on her
mind twenty-four hours before: Robert Smith, the
tetanus victim; Annie Yates, accused of theft; and the patient with the diagnosis of *sopor caroticus* who had looked
so wide-awake. In her weakened condition, she'd accepted
Archer's word without a murmur, but now she wasn't so
sure. A mistake could have been made—by Lester, or by
Archer, or by someone else in the long chain of official-
dom. She had lost a day; but tomorrow she would go back
up to Chimborazo. She'd set things right.

CHAPTER FOUR

JUNE 25

In the early hours of the morning Narcissa woke with a start. The sound that had woken her still vibrated in her ears—the crack of a shot. It sounded so close that it brought her to her feet. She peered out the window but saw nothing. Then she went to the door, turned the knob . . . it was locked. She felt for the key but didn't find it.

"Mirrie." Her voice came out in a croak. But the fever was gone—really gone. She felt almost as usual, just a little tired, though her throat was still dry. She raised her fist to pound on the door, but she hesitated. No alarm was being raised. Perhaps those who lived this close to the lines were used to such noises. She'd been locked in, doubtless, for her own protection, lest the fever return. With these halfhearted assurances, she returned to bed.

Sometime later, she heard the key turn in the lock. She sat up and called, "Who's there?" The door opened. She saw Mirrie's red-blond curls haloed against the light.

"It's all right," Mirrie responded soothingly.

"That shot . . . it sounded so close—"

Mirrie poured water from the pitcher into a glass, then gathered her nightgown around her and perched on the edge of the featherbed, handing the glass to Narcissa. "I wondered, too. But it was nothing. See, it's quiet now."

Narcissa drank a little water from the glass, then handed it back. "Mirrie, why was my door locked from the outside?"

Mirrie didn't answer for a moment. "Louisa is afraid you will have nightmares," she said at last, "and walk in your sleep."

Narcissa frowned, but said nothing. If a complaint had to be made, she should make it to Louisa, not Mirrie. But she noticed, when Mirrie left the room, that she did not hear the key turn to relock the door. She settled herself back down, determined to sleep. She would need all her strength for the day ahead.

➤►◄◄

John Chapman was not given to questioning his beliefs or his actions. He had never stepped that far outside his own skin. To him, his beliefs were the truth, and his actions were steps toward that truth, taken with the trust of a child toddling toward its mother. If he had thought about it at all, he would have considered himself blessed.

Then, night before last, Susy had come to his house. *Betrayed* was the word she'd used. She'd told him not to worry, but he couldn't help it.

Now it seemed to him that there were two John Chapmans. He was doing the same things he had done before—baking biscuits, then going about the city delivering them, passing the time with friends, with acquaintances, and with those like the Home Guard who were his natural enemies, as much as the dogs are to the fox. But now he did these things as two people: John Chapman, actor, and John Chapman, spectator at the performance. He might as well black his face with burned cork and take up the banjo, he thought, and smiled at the notion, but it was a wry smile. He felt the pangs of loss for his old, simpler self.

At President Davis's house, he met the gaze of Mattie, the cook, with eyes as guarded as hers. Up on Church Hill, he stopped on the street in front of the Ferncliff house and found he could hardly get down from the wagon for worry over how he should appear when walking up the path to the house. A jaunty step? No, best not call attention. Eyes down, shuffling? No, too different from his usual way of walking. Come to think of it, how had he walked, before?

As usual, Selah had little to say to him. Did she know her sister had left town, headed for the Yankee camp? Was she the one who had betrayed Susy?

Chapman turned the wagon to drive along the brick wall enclosing St. John's churchyard. The church was talked about as a meeting place for Unionists. And it had a history of rebellion going back much further than that.

This simple wooden church and its graveyard—old as anything in the city of Richmond—had always filled him with troubling awe. Maybe it was the spirit of Patrick Henry. Here he had spoken the words "Give me liberty or give me death"—words that inspired not only the white warriors of rebellion but Prosser's Gabriel, the slave who'd led an uprising with the cry "Death or liberty." Henry had found liberty. Gabriel had found death. Both of them were long dead now, but their words lived on, provoking restless souls like his son, Tyler, to give up everything for a dream.

Raven's plodding steps slowed, then stopped. The reins hung slack in John's hands. *Walk in the churchyard.* He could hear the words as if someone sitting beside him had whispered them. He could feel the little hairs in his ear tingling, it was so real. Without hesitating, he climbed down from the wagon. He tugged at his homespun waistcoat and settled his felt hat more firmly on his head. Then

he walked up to the iron gate that led into the churchyard.
By this point he'd begun to question the wisdom of following an order given by an invisible speaker. But he
wasn't taking any chances. Most likely the churchyard was
empty. Even in this time of so many deaths, it was a rare
thing nowadays for anyone to be buried here—so rare
that the sexton had been called out to work on the defenses.

He walked about among the gravestones, eyeing them
curiously. The oldest seemed to be the simple white ones
with curlicued tops. Newer-looking were simple brick
vaults, just big enough to hold a coffin, topped with granite slabs. He read the inscription on one and learned that
it covered a young woman and her two-month-old baby.
He swallowed a lump in his throat, thinking of the baby
Elda had lost. Pray God she didn't follow it in death. He
glanced around, looking for something—he hoped he'd
know what it was when he saw it—then strode up the hill
through shaggy, overgrown grass toward the table-shaped
tombs at the back of the church. What were *they* for? A
picnic on the Day of Judgment? Were these folks so sure
of their salvation?

There came a sound, a little ways off—someone gulp-
ing in air . . . then a low wail that made the hairs on his
neck prickle. No one and nothing moved around him.
Then his eyes probed lower, down amid the thick-
growing ivy. *There,* near that gravestone, something was
moving, down low to the ground. He made out a bundle
of rags. His mind questioned the truth of what he was
seeing even as he stumbled forward, stopped, stared,
reached out careful hands . . . a baby, tiny, dark-skinned,
crying so softly he could hardly hear even as he lifted it
up, baby and bundle, into his arms.

John Chapman hurried back to the wagon, cradling
the baby in its filthy rags. He looked all around. Far down

the hill, through gaps in the trees, he could see the river. The docks were quieter than usual, almost deserted. Around him, the big houses kept their blank eyes trained on the river. But the mansions' lives were lived behind their faces, in between the servants' quarters, the kitchens, and the less formal rooms of the houses themselves. It seemed no one saw him, though he could not be sure.

The baby seemed healthy enough, with a strong, square face and bright eyes. John fumbled with the rags to see—yes, it was a boy.

"Moses," whispered John Chapman to the baby. "These ain't no bulrushes, but they'll do."

→>—<—

Judah Daniel met John Chapman at the door. She saw the baby in his arms. For a moment she had the wild notion that John, crazed by the loss of his grandson, had stolen a child to replace him. But John wasted no time turning the baby over to her. "Found him in the graveyard up at St. John's Church, when I was making my deliveries," was all he said.

John Chapman's sister Phyllis came up then. "A baby?" She peered at the bundle in Judah Daniel's arms. "Well, he a little prince, ain't he? Whose is he?"

John answered. "Somebody left him like this, up on the bluff on Church Hill. I call him Moses." With that brief answer, John walked out of the room. Judah Daniel wondered a bit why, this time, John hadn't named the place where he'd found the boy. She supposed he had his reasons.

The news spread through the house, and one by one the other members of the family gathered. Phyllis made a sugar tit, tying a little carefully hoarded sugar in a clean rag and dipping it in water, and gave it to the baby to suck while they got the filthy wrappings off of him. Darcy, Judah Daniel's ten-year-old ward and apprentice, held one of the cloths up by a corner to show her. "This here's a piece of a quilt." Judah Daniel glanced at the cloth. It was about three feet square, ragged-edged on two sides as if cut from a bigger quilt, wet through, and so filthy it was hard to see the pattern or the colors. Darcy dropped the piece into the bucket with the rest of the filthy cloths.

Rose fetched a basin of warm water, and they washed the baby, who seemed to take it in good spirit, watching them with bright dark eyes. Young Chapman cousins came with pots of salve, stacks of clean cloths, and a long dress for the baby.

Darcy smiled as she gently rubbed the baby clean. "What we going to call him?"

Phyllis answered. "John said he call him Moses."

Darcy's soft face bunched into lines of worry as she took in the significance of the name. "He a slave, you reckon?"

Judah Daniel shook her head, not answering the question No, but denying the question itself. It might be that someone would claim this baby as his property. But no amount of claiming would ever make it true.

"Elda can have *this* baby now." The speaker was six-year-old Becca. She grabbed Young John under his arms and held him up so he could see the baby. "Maybe she won't cry so much once she got a new baby."

Judah Daniel smiled at Becca. "But this baby got a momma someplace. Suppose she missing him and crying for him?"

Becca frowned, thinking it over. Judah Daniel didn't say the other thing that was in her mind: that maybe the baby's mother had left him to be found . . . or not.

"You all run on now," Judah Daniel shooed the children. John followed the children out. Judah Daniel gathered up Moses, dry and sweet-smelling now. As she did so, the baby—who'd been quiet all this time—started to cry, just a little at first, then heartily, his eyes squeezed shut and his mouth wide open, showing toothless gums. Judah Daniel bounced him in her arms, but it was no use—he was hungry. Moses hushed for a minute, getting his breath back, and in the quiet Judah Daniel heard a soft step behind her. She looked around to see Elda staring at her and at the baby in her arms. Elda's cotton nightgown had two wet patches in front where her milk had come in, her body's response to the baby's crying. Elda held her arms out for the baby, took him without a word, and went to sit in the split-cane rocker. Judah Daniel walked away without looking back, closed the door behind her, and waited. In a few moments the crying stopped. Well, that was a blessing anyhow.

John Chapman came out into the hall where Judah Daniel was standing. "Poor little thing," he muttered. "You reckon his momma left him out there?"

Judah Daniel raised her thin eyebrows, questioning. "Might be somebody done it for her."

John frowned down at the floor. "Might be his momma ran off to the Yankees."

Judah Daniel said nothing.

At last John let out his breath in a sigh. "Might be I made a mistake bringing him here. God forgive me if I been the cause of Elda's heart getting broke one more time."

Judah Daniel put a comforting hand on his shoulder. "You bringing him here saved that baby's life. Don't you feel the least bit sorry about what you done. How come you to go up in that graveyard in the first place, but by God's will?"

>-><-<

Narcissa found her dress, brushed and tidied, lying over a chair. Her undergarments had been washed and pressed. She wondered if there were other servants in the house in addition to the sulky-looking Selah. If there weren't, it was no wonder Selah was unhappy.

Narcissa dressed quickly, passed down the grand staircase without meeting anyone, and followed the scent of food into the dining room. There on the sideboard were fluffy biscuits, butter, peach preserves, eggs, Virginia ham with the salty rind curling at its edges. It was months since Narcissa had seen a breakfast like this prepared to be eaten by civilians. The very abundance made her throat close against it. This food should go to the soldiers.

But she could not resist the smell of coffee. Real coffee. Hardly anyone had it these days; instead they roasted and brewed whatever was to hand, chicory root, sweet potatoes . . . Investigating the contents of a big silver coffeepot, she poured a dark stream of the rich-smelling liquid into a delicate cup. Well, if she did not drink it, it would be thrown away. She drained every drop from the cup and refilled it without bothering to carry it to the table. Then she noticed Selah had come into the room. Narcissa smiled at her, embarrassed to have a witness to her lack of restraint.

Selah's manner was no warmer than it had been the night before. "Miss Ferncliff will be with you in a minute, ma'am. Miss Powers still in bed."

Narcissa nodded, but Selah had already left the room. The coffee was having its effect, clearing her head and rekindling her spirit.

When Louisa Ferncliff came into the room, a man was with her. With a shock of surprise, Narcissa recognized Dr. Matthew Lester, one of the division chiefs at Chimborazo. The doctor stepped up to Narcissa and held out his hand. She reached out to shake it, but he took her hand in his, turned it over, and put his fingers on the inside of her wrist. For the moment, she was his patient.

"Cameron Archer told me you'd fallen ill. I'm glad to see you've made a good recovery, Mrs. Powers. How did you sleep?"

"Very well," Narcissa answered. "Except for the shot."

With raised eyebrows, Lester queried Louisa Ferncliff, who answered him with a dismissive shrug. "I'm sorry you were disturbed," she said to Narcissa. "We are not so very far from the Confederate picket lines."

Lester smiled. "Perhaps one of them had his slumbers disturbed by a possum or a raccoon—or even a Yankee. I can only hope he got the varmint." Lester glanced aside as if to show Narcissa the remark was directed at Louisa, who was standing behind him; but Louisa gave no sign of having heard. "I'll send my carriage to take you home."

"That won't be necessary." Though Louisa Ferncliff had been born in Richmond, her voice had nothing of the southern lady's drawling softness. Rather she had formed her accent after her northern-bred parents and teachers. It might be that, no matter what Louisa's mood or message, her voice would always sound harsh and hurried to Narcissa's ears. Now it certainly did. Ferncliff went on, "Mrs. Powers and her sister-in-law Miss Mirrie Powers are staying with me indefinitely." Louisa directed a tight-lipped smile at Lester, who was now standing facing her.

Lester turned to look at Narcissa. "Is this your wish, Mrs. Powers?"

"It's very gracious of Miss Ferncliff," she answered. "If Mirrie . . . if that's what she wants. . . ." Her mind was outpacing her words. It was convenient to be here, close to Chimborazo. And Mirrie, eager-souled abolitionist, no doubt found a kindred spirit in Louisa Ferncliff, though whether that was a good thing. . . . After all, why worry? *Indefinite* meant just that. And she had the distinct impression that Louisa had chosen her words for their effect on Dr. Lester.

Louisa nodded as if she read acquiescence in Narcissa's face, then looked over again at Lester. Narcissa had seen his frown reduce medical students, nurses, even fully fledged surgeons to red-faced stammering, but it had no visible effect on Louisa Ferncliff. If anything, her smile grew broader. "That will be all, then, Doctor?" she said calmly, as if here, in her house, Lester's uniform and surgeon's status meant nothing. Rather to Narcissa's surprise, the surgeon accepted his dismissal.

With a rustle of stiff silk, Louisa came over to Narcissa, who stood looking down on her hostess. Louisa's hair was dressed in ringlets—more work on the part of Selah, who likely had tied up the strands of hair the night before and brushed them out this morning.

Narcissa smothered her doubts about Louisa's intentions and spoke warmly. "I'm very much obliged to you for the invitation."

Louisa inclined her head to acknowledge the remark. "I assume you plan to stay here and rest today. I don't have a servant to accompany you around town. I freed all our servants after my father's death. Most of them continued to work for me. Now my gardener, my butler, and the boy I employed to run errands have all been impressed by the Confederate government. Ironic, is it not? Only my driver is left to me. I've sent him out of town, to my country place, lest I lose him as well. And Selah, of course."

Anger radiated from Louisa Ferncliff. Narcissa took a step back, as if from a too-hot fire, and saw Louisa smile as if she had won the point. They talked for a few more minutes, playing the roles of hostess and guest. Then Narcissa excused herself.

"Where are you going?" Louisa demanded, her voice rather shrill.

"To Chimborazo," Narcissa answered. "Don't worry. I have no need of a servant to accompany me."

Louisa frowned. "I am sure Dr. Lester would advise against your returning to Chimborazo, so soon after your illness."

"He has more important matters to concern him," Narcissa replied, her irritation imperfectly concealed.

"No doubt," Louisa agreed dryly, "he would be the first to say so."

Judah Daniel slipped away from the Chapmans' house. She didn't want, just now, to have to tell them all that she was going looking for the mother of the baby that had raised their spirits. Only Elda seemed not to care much for Moses, accepting him at her breast just as she'd accepted the mullein-leaf poultice. Judah Daniel didn't know whether to be glad or sorry for Elda's coolness. Everything about this baby—aside from Moses himself, who seemed a God-touched child—troubled her. Who would tend to a baby so carefully, then leave him in a churchyard? No woman would, not of her own will anyway. But where did will end, and force begin? It wasn't always easy to tell, especially with slaves. And it was likely, just because there were so many more of them than of free blacks, that a slave had given birth to Moses.

The fact that Moses had been found in the churchyard at St. John's might mean that his mother served in one of the houses near there. It seemed right to start there. Like most of Richmond, Church Hill was home to a wide range of people, rich and poor and all the stages in between. Many of them—the poorer ones at least—she had served in the capacity of midwife and doctoress. To her knowledge, no women here had delivered babies in the past few weeks. But people came and went in times like these, and old ties got stretched and broken.

And in times like these, it seemed like nothing was simple. What could be more natural than to try to bring together a baby and his mother? But human sin had reached down even to that most basic tie and twisted it, so that it was possible a baby could be better off without his mother. If the fact of his birth shamed or threatened her. If his needs ran counter to her own. Or if someone else— the woman's husband, the baby's father?—didn't want the child around. So Judah Daniel knew she had to be careful how she talked about the baby, and to whom.

In a little frame house on Twenty-ninth Street, Kezia Holt, a free black woman whose last two children Judah Daniel had delivered, listened carefully to what she had to say. Could she think of anyone who'd had a baby in the last few weeks? Kezia shook her head and pulled her own baby to her breast as if the fear of losing her had walked into the room with Judah Daniel. Kezia's next-door neighbor and cousin, Rebekah, was scornful—*some o' them worthless Negroes just hike they skirts and take off after the Yankees, don't care nothing about they babies*—but there was a haunted look in her eyes as well.

Leaving Kezia's, Judah Daniel saw Esther Mann walking ahead of her on the street with a basket over her arm. Esther was a slave belonging to the Butlers, one of the well-to-do merchant families of Church Hill, and she was always one to know the goings-on of the people who lived there, black and white. Judah Daniel picked up her pace and caught up with Esther. A soft, persistent rain was falling. No one else was in sight along the length of the street.

"How do, Judah Daniel? What you doing here? Ain't no babies coming into the world at this time of day!" Esther laughed with her whole body, planting her feet wide apart and throwing her head back. No wonder people loved to tell her their news, and other people's too.

"No, I come up here looking for somebody might know something. And you, Esther, know pretty much everything."

The laughter bubbled up again. Judah Daniel felt her own spirits rising, not for any reason but naturally, as wood floats up on water.

"Well, I don't reckon I lived all these years without knowing *something*. What you want to find out?"

"Was anybody round here expecting a baby in, say, the last month?"

Esther thought. "Black or white?"

Judah Daniel hesitated a moment. "Either."

"Well, I know two was expecting—one of each. Suppose you tell me why you want to know?"

Judah Daniel sighed. "Somebody left a baby up in the churchyard, last night or this morning." She tilted her head in the direction of St. John's. "John Chapman found it—healthy baby, a boy, dark-complected, about two weeks old."

"Sweet Jesus," Esther murmured. "Elda's boy died, and some woman with no more morals than a cat done give hers up."

"Give him up, or got him took from her," Judah Daniel corrected.

"Well, the ones I knowed of was Janie, who's the daughter of some cousins of the Butlers. She married to a soldier. She come up here to be with him, but when her time got close, she wanted to go to her momma down in North Carolina. She be gone about a month. And the other one was a slave of the same family. Cordella Otis was her name. She was one of a bunch got sold off south, couple weeks after Christmas. She was just beginning to show, and I reckon that been six months ago."

"But you ain't seen her, or heard she was back?"

Esther shook her head. "No, I ain't. And I'd know if she was. Oh, Lord—there's Sam, looking for me!" Esther shifted the basket on her arm and hitched her skirts, then turned back. "That child meant to be Elda's. Don't question God's plan."

Judah Daniel watched Esther hurry away toward the black-suited servant who stood, arms folded, waiting for her. Remembering Esther's parting words, Judah Daniel let her eyes close and her mind drift into prayerfulness. *Show me your will. . . .*

Should she turn left or right on Franklin Street? Looking down to the left, where Franklin Street made a dead end at Bloody Run, she saw a house lot she'd never noticed before. The house itself was barely visible through the tangle of trees and bushes that had taken over the neglected yard. It looked like the kind of place where someone might choose to hide.

She walked down the slope to the yard. Seen up close, it was no more welcoming. There were pokeweeds taller than her head in there. She put her hand on the gate to open it, then froze. Something—it could have been the cracking of a twig—raised the hairs on her arms and brought her head up sharp. She turned to find herself staring into the muzzle of an old horse pistol, held by a thin-faced white woman whose steady hands and narrowed eyes showed she knew what she was doing. Judah Daniel hadn't heard her coming; it seemed like she'd been standing nearby, hidden in the heavy dark green shadows of the overgrown yard, for some time.

"Get away from here," the woman whispered. "I ain't got nothing for you to steal."

"Beg pardon, ma'am, but I ain't no thief." Judah Daniel spoke softly, watching the woman's face and her hands.

"Well, get along, then."

There wasn't any use arguing or explaining. Judah Daniel nodded, then set off down Grace Street toward the house she had saved for last. She didn't have to turn around to know the woman still had the pistol trained on her back.

➤➤◄◄

Narcissa entered Ward 27 by one of the main doorways— not that there was any difference between the paired openings at both ends of the long building, except that two gave out onto the rough slope bordering the plateau, while two led onto one of the streets that ran arrow-straight through the Chimborazo encampment. It was at the latter that the orderlies lingered and the doctors gossiped, and so she had always thought of it as the main doorway. She walked the length of the building to the next-to-last bed, occupied by Sergeant Smith. He looked the same—no improvement, but she could only feel relieved that his condition did not seem to have worsened. He lay in that unnatural back-bending arch, the tendons standing out like ropes in his neck and arms. His eyes were closed, his breathing labored.

She took a deep breath, steadied herself, and looked over to the next bed where the patient with the diagnosis of *sopor caroticus* had lain. It was a different man. She looked at the nearby beds, then retraced her steps to the doorway.

"Where is the man who was there two days ago? The one with his head bandaged?"

One of the orderlies, a recovering private named Reid, frowned. "Dead."

She'd expected the answer, but she didn't intend to accept it without question. "Are you sure?"

"Well, ma'am, I reckon so," Reid replied slowly, seeming puzzled by her disbelief. "They carried his body out night before last. He been hurt real bad. He was here three, four days; never even come to. That's why we give him the name of Devlin, since we didn't know his real one. 'Poor devil.' Beg pardon, ma'am."

Narcissa stared. "You mean Devlin wasn't his real name?"

Reid shook his head. "Didn't know his real name, his rank, his regiment, nothing. He come in his shirt and pants, and with a great big bloody bandage around his head, limp as a rag doll. 'Course, we thought somebody'd come by and claim him, but they never did."

Another orderly, Coudreau, joined in. "Couldn't talk, nothing on him but trousers and a shirt. You'd of had to been looking for him particular, to find him."

Everything about Devlin was false—even his name. "Who carried him away?"

"Just a couple boys from the dead house, I reckon. One black, one white. They was pretty pitiful specimens, but I reckon you'd have to be, to work there."

Was it possible to consign a man to the dead house when he was still alive? If so, could he still be there—unburied? She told herself it wasn't possible, but still the thought galvanized her. She had to see with her own eyes that it wasn't true.

The little buildings called dead houses stood near the headquarters of the hospital. Narcissa had never had cause to go in them, nor did she much wish to now. She thought of all the wives and mothers, fathers and brothers, who had come here searching for their loved ones, and the sights they had to bear.

At the door of the dead house allotted to the Sixth Division, an elderly man dressed in civilian clothes inquired what her business was. "A man died the night before last in Ward 27," she told him. "I wanted to know if he is here."

"Have you come a long way, ma'am?" His long, white-whiskered face was solemn.

How many sad stories has he heard? Narcissa wondered. She shook her head. "I am helping with the wounded men here in the hospital. I'm Mrs. Narcissa Powers," she added.

The old man took her offered hand and shook it. His skin felt cool and tough, like leather. "Albert Johnson. Pleased to make your acquaintance, ma'am."

Narcissa went on. "The man I'm looking for was called Devlin. He was in Ward 27. He was brought here night before last."

Johnson looked thoughtful. "I don't recollect seeing that name." He pulled out a notebook and looked through it, running his index finger down the pages. "No. Ain't had nobody here by the name of Devlin anytime lately."

"He had a head injury," Narcissa offered. "He had a brown beard—straight, not wiry. Really, that's all I know about him."

Johnson made no reply.

"Do you . . . may I look?" It had occurred to her that someone might have discovered Devlin's real name, after all, and recorded his death under that name. Johnson handed her the notebook without comment, and she looked through the list. There were twenty-seven deaths recorded within the approximate time period—from measles sequelae, from gangrene, from various forms of fever—but nothing from head injury. She handed the notebook back to him. "Maybe I've got the name wrong. Could I look for him—in there?" She nodded toward the dead house.

Johnson cleared his throat. "Somebody died day before yesterday, he ought to be buried by now. But we been having trouble getting enough coffins. I reckon you can take a look." He stood aside to let her pass through the door. In the pale light that came through the windows she counted sixteen bodies lying on low pallets. The cause of death for most was readily apparent: missing limbs, wasted flesh. It struck her how blessed a thing death could be. Whatever agony had racked their bodies, their souls were now at peace. *God, thank you for these brave men. Keep them with you in eternity.* She walked around the small space, peering into the faces of the dead. She had seen so little of Devlin, and what she had seen—a growth of brown beard—was so common among the soldiers. . . . But she didn't think he was one of these men.

She walked out again, the fresh air striking her damp clothes with a sudden chill. Thunder boomed in the distance. "There are only sixteen men in there. Where are the rest?"

"Claimed by their loved ones."

At last she gave up and started away, thinking. Maybe someone had claimed Devlin at last, given him his right name, and taken his body. But if he'd been brought to the dead house, why would there be no record of it? And how would she ever know what had happened to him, since she could not even give a description of him?

There must be someone in Ward 27 who had gotten a closer look at Devlin. The best thing to do was to go back there. At the very least she could get a better description of the man—his age, the color of his hair, an estimation of his height. Maybe she could also get some sense of how close he had been to death. Then she thought, Annie Yates nursed him; maybe she would know.

It no longer seemed to Narcissa that Devlin had been feigning unconsciousness. No one would let himself be carried off to the dead house. It would be reassuring to think of Devlin as dead . . . at peace . . . rather than contemplate the possibility that he'd been buried alive.

Another distant rumble interrupted her thoughts. She knew this time that it wasn't thunder, but cannon fire. She could see its effect now in the streets. Surgeons were going for their horses, drivers for their wagons. Close behind them came the men on crutches, or with arms in slings—eager to get a view of the action that had seemed so long in coming. She stopped, all other concerns forgotten in an instant of fear for the city and the soldiers guarding it. Then she gathered herself and hurried on. Soon there would be work to do, and she would be needed. But first she would make one last attempt to find out what had become of Devlin.

She caught sight of three young boys running barefoot down the street, headed east toward the sound of the cannon. She waved to them, and they changed course to intercept her.

"They's fighting over to Seven Pines again," the tallest boy called. "Hurrah!" and "We'll drive 'em!" the others shouted. Despite their bold words, their eyes were round and worried. No doubt they had seen the thousands of wounded brought into the city from Seven Pines just over three weeks before. Everyone in the city had seen them.

"Come on, Tom!" One of the smaller boys tugged at the tallest boy's sleeve. Before they could run off again, Narcissa asked, "Do you want to make some money?"

The tallest boy frowned. "How much?"

Narcissa knew she would have to make her offer good enough to compete with the sound and smoke of battle. "Mrs. Annie Yates has a house near here. If you can tell me where, I'll give you each a dollar."

This got their attention. "Confederate?" their spokesman asked.

"Yes," Narcissa admitted.

The boys' smiles faded, but they nodded. "All right."

"I'm Mrs. Powers."

"I'm Tom," offered the tallest boy, "and this here is Jack and Will."

"Bring me word at Ward 27," Narcissa called after them. How the boys of the town got their information, she wasn't sure, but she had never known them to fail.

At last Judah Daniel came to the Ferncliff house. Thinking of what John Chapman had told her, she knew she had to be careful. Both Louisa Ferncliff and her servant Selah were likely to be jumpy—though the sight of a lone black woman at the door, rather than a contingent of Guardsmen, ought to reassure them, she thought as she climbed the steps and rapped the knocker against the door. She would ask for Selah. She hoped Louisa wasn't the kind of mistress who hung around to hear what servants said to each other, although she suspected that was just the kind Louisa was.

But it was Selah who came to the door. Selah was neglecting her appearance today—wisps of dark hair stuck out from her headscarf, and rings of sweat stained her dress under the arms. She didn't look like the sight of Judah Daniel was raising her spirits any, either. She looked blank, lids half-down over her eyes. Judah Daniel knew what the look meant; she used it herself sometimes. When a woman had this look on her face, you might as well try talking to a stone wall.

"Selah, I sure am sorry for bothering you like this"— Selah nodded impatiently—"but I wonder if you know anything about a baby been found up in the churchyard." Judah Daniel gestured in the direction of St. John's Church, catty-corner across the street from Miss Ferncliff's.

Selah stiffened up a little bit, and her eyes widened, but she said, "I don't know anything about it."

"Well, this baby—little boy, just a couple weeks old—was found this morning, early." Judah Daniel was leaving John Chapman's name out of the story for the time being—why, she wasn't sure.

Selah's eyes were wide open now, the pupils big and dark. "A baby? Nobody with him?"

"That's right. A little Negro boy, wrapped up in a raggedy piece of quilt." Judah Daniel answered patiently, holding back a hotter rejoinder—*What did you think I said, an elephant?* "You know if any woman around here had a baby recently?"

Selah was holding herself very still. "No. I—"

Selah broke off and turned to look behind her, then put out her arm the way a mother or a nursemaid would to keep a child from running into the street. But it was Louisa Ferncliff. Louisa stepped into the open doorway so that Selah had to move or be knocked out of the way. "What's all this about?" the white woman demanded, looking first at Selah, then at Judah Daniel.

Selah said nothing, so Judah Daniel spoke up. "Beg pardon, ma'am, but a baby was found up in St. John's churchyard early this morning. A Negro baby, just a few weeks old—"

"Alive?" Ferncliff broke in.

"Yes, ma'am, he's fine—"

"Who found him?"

Judah Daniel hesitated, then said, "John Chapman."

She saw the two women exchange glances. Then Louisa Ferncliff commanded, in tones that would allow no argument, "Bring the baby to me. I will see he's taken care of."

What, Judah Daniel wondered, did Ferncliff expect? For her to nod, mumble "Thank-ee, ma'am," and shuffle off to get the baby?

"He's fine," Judah Daniel said again, more firmly this time.

Selah touched her mistress's sleeve. "Judah Daniel is a midwife and a doctoress. She'd know what's best for—"

Ferncliff glanced at Selah, then fixed her eyes again on Judah Daniel. "I want to see him. Bring him to me."

"The woman nursing him ain't well enough to travel," Judah Daniel answered.

There were spots of color now on Ferncliff's bony face—where the cheeks would have been on a younger, plumper woman. "When she is well enough, then." Ferncliff put her hand on the door, making Selah take another step out of the way, and was raring back to slam it shut when another figure appeared behind the mistress and servant.

"Judah Daniel!" It was Mirrie Powers. "I know her," she explained to Ferncliff and Selah as she pushed past them out the door.

Mirrie stopped short, and Judah Daniel watched as she collected herself—smoothed her hair, veiled the eager expression in her blue-green eyes. Mirrie put her hand on Judah Daniel's arm and led her down the steps, away from the sharp-eyed attention of Ferncliff and Selah.

"What brings you here, Judah Daniel?"

"You remember John Chapman. He was driving the bakeshop wagon up here this morning and found a baby, over there"—she pointed—"in the churchyard. A colored baby, only a few weeks old. No sign of the mother. I been going around trying to find out if anybody seen anything."

Mirrie looked over her gold-rimmed spectacles, her eyes intent on Judah Daniel's face. "Is the baby all right?"

Judah Daniel nodded. "John Chapman's daughter Elda nursing him."

Mirrie nodded. Then her gaze shifted away, and Judah Daniel could see her thoughts had shifted as well. Mirrie said, "I suppose you are surprised to find me here. Miss

Ferncliff is a friend of mine. Narcissa is staying here as well, for a few days at least. She was ill yesterday with a fever. But she is better today. If she falls ill again, may I call on you? It's just that the surgeons are so busy. And after today"—Judah Daniel knew she meant the battle that was raging just beyond the city, which by nightfall would be filling the city yet again with wounded soldiers—"it will only be worse."

"Yes, ma'am, you can send for me up to John Chapman's." As Judah Daniel said these words, she glanced up at the porch of the Ferncliff mansion. The door was open, a wide crack of a foot or ten inches, letting in the flies. . . . A dark face peered out: Selah was watching them, slyly, or fearfully—as if she were plotting mischief, or thought they were.

Mirrie turned, following Judah Daniel's gaze. The door was hastily closed. Mirrie turned back to Judah Daniel. "About the baby: you think Selah may know something, don't you?"

"Yes, ma'am, I think so," Judah Daniel answered carefully.

"I shall keep that in mind." Mirrie gave her a long look, then turned and mounted the steps to the house.

By the time Narcissa returned to Ward 27, the rumors were confirmed: the enemy had been engaged at several points east of town between the Chickahominy and the White Oak swamps. But as the cannon fire died away and the surgeons returned one by one to their wards, it became clear that today's engagement had been far less costly than the last major battle, at Seven Pines almost a month before. It seemed clear, too, that Richmond would not surrender—not today, at any rate.

Twilight was falling when Tom—alone this time—

came into the ward. Narcissa caught sight of him at the door, waving his cap to get her attention, and went over to him. "Mrs. Yates been staying at a house at the end of Franklin Street, past Twenty-ninth," he told her, then held his hand out for the money.

She pressed three dollar bills into his hand. "Don't forget to give Jack and Will their share."

Tom grinned and took off again.

She'd been at the hospital about ten hours, she guessed. Luckily Annie Yates's place was close by, only a few steps out of her way on the route she would be taking to Louisa's. It was time to go, anyway, Narcissa told herself. If she spent any time at all speaking with Annie Yates, it would be dark before she got to Louisa Ferncliff's. She was very tired. But it was hardly surprising if yesterday's fever had left her in need of rest.

Narcissa walked outside and looked up at the dome of heaven that covered the treeless plateau of Chimborazo like an upturned bowl. The storm clouds were retreating eastward, gray and lowering, touched here and there with fantastic shades of pink and gold. Angel armies, they seemed. Did they engage themselves in the struggles of men? And if so, which side did they fight for?

The Young Men's Christian Association had become a subject of laughter in the town when some enterprising soul opened a disorderly house directly across the street from it—with scantily dressed females cavorting in full view of its windows. Now, with the city under siege and its enemies camped just a few miles away, the bawdy house had drawn its shades. Brit wondered idly if the women inside were sewing Union decorations for their dresses and hair, readying for a change in clientele.

Brit had come there hoping to find a place where

Ownby wouldn't locate him quickly. And indeed the
YMCA was a sad contrast to the Exchange Hotel. There
were no beds available, but fortune had smiled, albeit
weakly: he'd secured a chair in the reading room with
table space enough to lay his head. He knew he could
sleep when sleep became irresistible: soldiers fell asleep
on the march, though the collision with hard ground usually woke them. He turned his mind resolutely from the
notion of Zetelle's chophouse: he couldn't afford it. There
was also the question of whether he could afford to be
seen there. After a dreary day spent in the confines of the
YMCA, he was beginning to think he had taken fright too
easily. After all, Ownby didn't have a valid complaint
against him. Still, in these days of martial law, a valid
complaint might not be needed.

At last he grew tired of worrying over the same questions. He drew out a deck of cards from the same pocket
and dealt himself a hand of solitaire.

At the house said to be occupied by Annie Yates, the
wrought-iron gate first resisted, then gave way to open
with a creak. Narcissa stepped through it onto the path.
Broad leaves, weighed down by the rain, released fresh
showers as she brushed past. They weren't even trees, but
weeds that towered over her head, their pulpy trunks as
thick as her wrists. Anything could be hiding in here—
snakes, rats—she suppressed a shiver. The flagstones had
sunk deep enough in places to hold an inch of rainwater.
Her first glimpse of the house surprised Narcissa. It was a
big, old-fashioned clapboard house she would have said
belonged to someone much more prosperous than Annie
Yates. Then she took in the gray-green patches of mildew
spreading on the white clapboards, the drifts of last winter's leaves decaying in the corners of the porch. Maybe

the house's owners had left Annie as caretaker; but it was more likely they'd left town in a panic, and had never heard of Annie Yates.

She was standing in the path, wondering how to proceed, when a black-clad figure came around the corner of the house. "Annie!" she called, relieved she would not have to mount those stairs and knock on that door.

Annie approached slowly, giving no sign of recognition and certainly no sign of welcome. Well, the woman had reason to be cautious, Narcissa mused. She'd been accused of theft at the hospital, and she might be wondering if she was about to be accused of trespassing on this property. Her hands were in the pockets of her apron. The apron and the dress beneath it were filthy with mud. Is she just come from her husband's grave? Narcissa wondered. Now Annie had nothing else to do but mourn.

"It's Narcissa Powers," she called out. "I came to see how you are doing."

Annie stopped a few yards away. "I heard the guns, earlier."

"A minor engagement, they say; a matter of a few yards gained or lost." Narcissa avoided the comparison with Seven Pines, fearing the reference would distress Annie, who was holding her shoulders back and her head tilted a little as if bracing herself for a blow. "Only a few dozen men of our men were wounded. Listen, Annie—did you know the patient you were caring for, Devlin, has died? Only a short time after you last saw him."

Narcissa watched the blood drain from Annie's face. "No," Annie said at last. "I didn't know that."

"Did it seem to you he was so very ill?"

Annie's eyes seemed to search her face. "The doctors said he was."

"I wondered . . ." Narcissa was having a hard time putting into words the doubt that had made her come here and disturb Annie Yates with questions. "They had no record of him at the dead house."

Annie shook her head. She took a step toward Narcissa. "The ones somebody going to come asking about, them's the ones they put in coffins. The ones like . . . like Devlin, they throw in a ditch."

Narcissa shuddered again, chilly beneath her wet clothes. She was watching Annie, noting the tension in her face, the anger behind her words. Annie saw Devlin's fate in the light of what had happened to her son—saw it as a pattern being repeated. Narcissa understood only too well. She did the same thing herself whenever she heard about the death of a child: her mind brought up the loss of her own baby after a few hours of life, so that, if she were told that the child in question was three years old, or five, she was always surprised. Still, there must be something she could learn from Annie. "What did he look like? Could you describe him? Would you recognize him if you saw him again?"

Annie thought for a moment. "He had a brown beard. Tan skin. He were twenty-five year old, a bit more or a bit less. I reckon he was middling tall. Would I know him again? Maybe—if he was to lay down and shut his eyes. But walking around—" She shrugged. "I ain't sure."

Narcissa had been watching Annie; now she noticed Annie was watching her as well.

"You feeling all right, Mrs. Powers?"

Narcissa hadn't time to reply. Cold broke over her in a wave, and she bent double, folding her arms over her stomach. Her teeth chattered so she could not speak.

Annie stepped closer. "You best get on home. You're burning up."

Narcissa nodded. She wanted more than anything to get away. She couldn't bear to be taken—though it would be a kindness on Annie's part—into that decaying, awful house.

Annie took her arm. "I'll take you back to the hospital."

Narcissa shook her head. "Take me to Louisa Ferncliff's."

Annie's hand tightened on her arm. "Ferncliff? What you got to do with her?"

Just then, Louisa's political views mattered much less than her clean sheets, and above all Mirrie. "Mirrie's there . . . my friend . . . *please.*"

"All right. Lean on me." Annie put her arm around Narcissa's waist. Despite Annie's starved look, she was strong, and Narcissa leaned gratefully on her supporting strength.

Mirrie thought the room Louisa Ferncliff had given to Narcissa must have belonged to old Mr. Ferncliff. The massive furniture and wine-red wallpaper made the room as dark as a cave. The bedposts rose almost to the ceiling, and the mattress was a good three feet off the ground. In that mattress, a heap of bedclothes topped by a crocheted counterpane covered a mounded shape. As Mirrie looked, the pile of covers shook as if whatever was under them was fighting to get free. She thought for an instant that the little dog, Friday, had gotten in and hidden among the bedclothes—but there was Narcissa's black hair, spread out in a tangle on the pillow. She was lying on her side, hugging her knees to her body.

Mirrie perched on the bed. She watched as the shuddering spasm racked Narcissa's body. After a few moments it subsided, and Narcissa sank into exhausted quiet. Then the shuddering came again. It was uncanny that someone could be freezing cold, when even now, after sundown, the heat and damp clung like a sodden garment. But Dr. Lester, who had examined Narcissa earlier in the evening, had identified her illness as tertian fever. It was not often fatal, thank God, but always exhausting and debilitating. The bouts of shivering, chills, and fever recurred on a regular schedule, every forty-eight hours, then—eventually—vanished as mysteriously as they had come. The cause was thought to be bad air from the swamps; hence the name, *mal-aria*, and the nickname given by the soldiers camped near the swamps around Richmond: Chickahominy fever.

Shiver and burn. Sooner or later, depending on when this attack had come on, the burning would set in. Narcissa would throw off all the covers, tear open the buttons at her throat, soak the bedclothes with perspiration. The burning could be relieved with cooling drinks and compresses. Now, though, it seemed most merciful to let her sleep.

Mirrie went down the stairs to the dining room. "She's asleep," she told Louisa, who was sitting at the big table. "A day of fever, a day well, another day of fever. Of course it's malaria, there can be little doubt now."

Louisa beckoned to Mirrie to sit beside her at the table. The yellowing light of the gasolier gave Louisa's pale face a jaundiced pallor and deepened the hollows under her eyes and cheekbones. She looked worried; was it for Narcissa's sake, or for the trouble Narcissa's illness might bring to Louisa herself? Mirrie pushed the thought aside. Long years of feeling superior to everyone and everything around her had made Louisa difficult to like. But it was impossible—for Mirrie, at least—not to respect her for the depth of her commitment to ideals, if not to people.

Mirrie went on. "Quinine could relieve the symptoms, but it has to be smuggled through the blockade, and so many are sick—they say there's none to be had." Selah was nowhere in sight, Mirrie noted as she helped herself to cold chicken, corn, and a biscuit. "But there are other remedies, using native plants. Judah Daniel will know of them—the doctoress who was here earlier today."

Louisa stiffened at the mention of Judah Daniel's name. "That woman who came to the door, asking questions? I don't want her here. Selah was very distressed by her questions."

Mirrie waited, hiding her interest, then commented, "Judah Daniel was trying to find the mother of a baby found up in the churchyard. Why would Selah be distressed by that?"

Louisa shot her a sideways glance. "I suppose the idea that any mother could abandon her child is upsetting."

"Do you think the mother went over to the Union camp?"

"It's possible," Louisa answered. There was a note of defiance in her voice—as if she were arguing for a point of view she found difficult to defend. "Very likely," she asserted, more firmly this time. "And the church steps have always been the place where babies are left. It derives from the ancient idea of sanctuary, I suppose."

Mirrie took a bite of her biscuit, then a sip of tea. She patted her lips with the linen napkin and remarked, all mildness, "It seemed to me that Selah was trying to protect *you* from distress. She looked as if she wanted to keep you from hearing what Judah Daniel was saying."

"*Me?*" Ferncliff fixed her with an angry gaze. "What could she possibly want to keep from me?"

Mirrie shrugged. "Perhaps there is some unpleasant, sordid story, some neighborhood gossip that she'd rather you not know. It would not be a bad thing if she were protective of you."

Louisa dropped her napkin onto the table, pushed back her chair, and turned to face Mirrie. "It would be a very bad thing if Selah were keeping things from me. I do not believe it. That woman, Judah Daniel, was merely being officious. She should have brought the baby to me, as I asked, instead of bustling all over town asking questions and upsetting people. You may consult her about Mrs. Powers, if you feel you must; but when her work is done, she must leave."

Mirrie's anger flashed. "She need not come here at all. We will leave as soon as Narcissa is well enough to travel. If she is indeed suffering from tertian fever, this episode will be over in twenty-four hours. We can leave the day after tomorrow—Friday."

Mirrie saw Louisa shrink slightly away from her. *So that's it. Return fire, and she backs down.*

"No! No, I didn't mean that," said Louisa. "I said I wanted you here, and I do—now more than ever." She reached out a thin, blue-veined hand and touched Mirrie's sleeve. "Please, say that you'll stay until . . . until all this is over."

What did Louisa mean by "all this?" The siege? The war? "Louisa, I'm sorry," Mirrie said at last. "It was ungracious of me. We will certainly stay a few more days at least."

Louisa reseated herself on the edge of her chair. Her thin lips curved in their usual slight smile, which spoke more of iron control than of good humor. "What would you say if I told you I had the means to stop this war—to bring about a Union victory?"

Mirrie stared. "To stop the war? It's not possible."

Louisa shrugged. "If Richmond were to fall . . . if Lee's army could be taken, and Davis captured. . . . And would it be so difficult, after all? The Union has more men, more guns, better equipment. General McClellan would have taken Richmond by now if Lincoln had given him his full support."

"Lincoln is afraid Jackson will attack Washington City. He's determined to protect it at all costs."

"Then Lincoln is a fool," Louisa snapped. "Lee and most of the other generals are Virginians, first and last. They will protect Richmond at all costs. 'Stonewall' is on his way here—I'm sure of it. And so, in a few days' time, the chance for an easy Union victory will be lost. It's in my hands, don't you see? But it's as you said; the war must go on until Lincoln ends slavery. If it were to end now, it would be so easy for things to go on as before."

She means it, Mirrie thought. Is she insane?

Louisa's smile broadened. "You think I'm raving. I assure you, I am not. You see, I placed a servant in Davis's house. It took a year of planning, and months of preparation—of course, she could not go there directly from me. I hired her out to friends, acquaintances, until the trail back to me was obscured. Her last employer, before the Davises, refugeed just before the siege. Varina Davis took her on, then left town—perfect! But my plan succeeded too well, too quickly."

Mirrie realized what she was getting at, but still she could not believe it. "You mean, Susy Reynolds is your Susannah?"

Louisa nodded. Her face was serious, but there was a suppressed excitement about her. Louisa had been longing to tell someone, Mirrie realized. That was why Louisa had invited her here, kept her here—because Louisa so badly wanted someone she could talk to about what she had done. Or someone she could convince of a lie?

Louisa went on. "Susy got hold of a letter and smuggled it out to me. It detailed the weakness in the Confederate defenses around Richmond. She expected me to get it out to the Union camp so that they could take the city. But talking to you confirmed my sense that it was too early to end the war. I let her know I would not send it out. After that, it seems she lost her nerve. I don't know why. She should not have been in any danger at Davis's, if she was careful. After all my work getting her in, I expected she would make it worth my while. It was a fiasco, really."

Talking to me? So that was what had been on Louisa's mind that day . . . the day before yesterday now. That was why Louisa's repetition of her words had carried a weight of meaning that Mirrie herself had not understood. Their exchange of words had been a contest, a battle for possession of the moral high ground. How could Louisa have confused it with reality? To bring down the city, to end the war—was it possible that Louisa Ferncliff had the power to do this? How many lives would be saved if the war ended now, instead of a year from now? How many would be lost if Richmond fell to its enemies? But the equation was not that simple, because some of those lives belonged to men she knew and loved—and despite her abolitionism, more of those men fought on the Confederate side. "If the letter helped the Union Army enter Richmond, wouldn't many of the defenders be killed—or executed?"

Louisa shrugged. "I don't think that's likely. Remember how closely related we are, North and South. And the higher one's class, or rank as an officer, the more likely one is to have relations on the other side. Lincoln's own wife has brothers in the Confederate army. If he had them hanged, he would have to answer to her. No—I don't think mass reprisals would be the order of the day."

How can she be so calm, so matter-of-fact? Can it really be true? Mirrie wondered. "Do you still have it—the letter?"

"The letter is in a safe place."

"But, Louisa," protested Mirrie, "it's dangerous to keep such a thing. Now that Susannah's run away, all her activities are sure to come under suspicion. Someone may figure out that she stole the letter and brought it here. You'd better dispose of it right away."

Louisa's lips curled derisively. "What? And put a notice in the paper announcing I've destroyed the letter that was stolen from Davis's, so there is no need for anyone to come looking for it? Don't be foolish. Even if someone should suspect that the letter is here, no one could find it. Besides, there is still time for Lincoln to repent his cowardly compromise and decree slavery illegal. If he does, I will dispatch the letter and Richmond will fall. If he does not . . . well, the letter may be of more use *after* the chance to use it is lost. A paradox? But it's true. The power of this letter does not end when this siege is lifted. Imagine if I were to refugee north some months from now and carry this letter with me. Imagine if I were to release it to the northern papers with an explanation of how the letter *could have* ended the war—if only Lincoln's timidity had not forced me to hold it back. Why, the president would be humiliated. Think of the outrage as people realized how many lives could have been saved, how much suffering averted, if only Lincoln had had the backbone to free the slaves. The clamor would rise to the heavens. Lincoln would have to act, or be swept out of office!"

Louisa's eyes were glittering with a fanatical light. Again Mirrie thought it could not be true. Something might have been taken from Davis's, some correspondence. . . . But Louisa was no general, how could she judge whether a letter could bring down the city, much less end the war? In her unbridled egoism, Louisa was making herself the equal—no, the superior—of Abraham Lincoln. To think that governments, presidents, the lives of thousands of men, and, through them, the lives of a million other men, women, and children, depended on the whim of one woman. . . . No; it could not be true.

Mirrie stood. "I have to go see how Narcissa is doing."

"I know you won't speak of this to Mrs. Powers." Louisa made the remark with a quiet confidence. Mirrie wondered how she could be so sure. But in another instant, she knew Louisa was right. She caught one last glimpse of Louisa's mocking smile as she fled.

Sitting by Narcissa's bed, Mirrie thought about what Louisa had told her. Susannah—Susy—McRae, educated to be the equal of a white lady, yet brought up somehow free from the shackles of convention that ruled the lives of most of them—of *us*. Susy had been bold enough to come down into enemy territory and live among people who would gladly have hanged her without a trial had they known who she was and what she planned. And then, when things went wrong, this woman had lost her nerve? That's what Louisa had said. . . . But Louisa could say that, because Louisa—even if she were exaggerating the importance of the letter—was risking everything. Louisa had planned all this and brought it about while living in the midst of the enemy.

Was that why it seemed to Louisa that Susy had failed, just as William Jackson had failed—and just as Selah had failed her years ago by refusing to stay in school? Was that why Louisa wanted that baby: as a sort of replacement for Susy and Selah? But it was too strange to think of Louisa wanting to bring a baby here, and now, of all times. . . . What had frightened Susy off? It would have to be more than a vague threat.

Louisa's home offered no safe haven from the war. It was a battlefield with linen napkins, that was all.

Brit slept, but fitfully. For a moment, it seemed, he would be able to forget he was in an awkward position, in more ways than one. Then some particular discomfort—the crick in his neck or the ache in his arms—would rouse him. Nevertheless, the touch on his shoulder surprised him; he'd slept through the approach of whoever it was. He looked up through bleary eyes to see the earnest face of his friend Yancey.

"Good God, Wallace, you're the soundest sleeper here," Yancey whispered in his ear. "You wouldn't believe what these other fellows have been saying. Pretty rough for a Christian Association."

Brit laced his fingers together and cracked his knuckles. How could the simple act of falling asleep in a chair make one hurt all over? "What are you doing here, Yancey?"

"Come to warn you." Yancey shot him a serious look. "The authorities are looking for you. Came to the telegraph office, asking all sorts of questions."

"Was it Ownby? Young lieutenant, looks like a piglet?"

Yancey grinned. "That's him, all right. He was most put out to find you'd left your lodgings."

Brit sat up straight, rubbing his face. The stubble was growing into a beard. "That's ironic, considering he left it in a shambles. Thanks for coming to find me, Yancey. I'll be all right."

"Good luck." Yancey made as if to go, then turned back. "You'd best get out of here on the double-quick. If they went to the trouble to find me—"

Yes, it was serious, Brit thought. He didn't dare go to any of his friends for shelter. It would put them in an uncomfortable, if not dangerous, position. He thought of Narcissa . . . staying at Louisa Ferncliff's, she didn't need any more damage to her reputation. And yet she was loyal!—as was he, come to that. He gripped the table's edge, hard. He could have turned it over, thrown the chair through the window; that would suit his feelings, but it wouldn't help. He needed the protection of someone who was not a friend, someone whose reputation he couldn't hurt. . . . Then he thought of Cameron Archer. They were sometimes enemies, sometimes uneasy allies, always rivals. But Archer's own loyalty was beyond question. And Archer knew what Brit had done after Seven Pines, how he had gone out to bring in the wounded and risked his own life a time or two, though more from overenthusiasm than heroism. Archer was dividing his time between the medical college hospital and Chimborazo. Well, he would go on up to Chimborazo. If Narcissa was still at Ferncliff's, he would be closer to her, even if he dared not visit, or even write to her, for fear of doing her harm.

Narcissa stared into the darkness. She told herself that Mirrie slept in the chair beside her bed, that the candle had gone out. But she was afraid to reach out—afraid she would touch the hand of a dead man. They were all around her, broken, no life left . . . but they whispered together, a sound like rain falling. She could not make out the words, but she thought they were calling to her to help them. She turned over and put the pillow over her head, leaving just enough room to breathe. They seemed to press on her; her neck and back and anyplace where one part of her body touched another was wet with their blood. Then she was looking down into a grave, a pit, looking down at dead men, and she was falling, she fell among them, they were soft and damp and yielding beneath her weight—

Her own screaming woke her. A moment later Mirrie was there. "It's all right, Narcissa, you were dreaming."

"The dead men," she whispered. "So many of them."

"I know," Mirrie answered. "I know."

The softness she felt beneath her was Louisa's mattress . . . and she was wet with the heavy perspiration of the breaking fever. But the war was not a dream. It seemed to follow the pattern of the fever, building, cresting, dying down, then breaking out again. Not that malaria actually killed so many—maybe one in a dozen or fifteen—but it was easy to imagine how it killed the spirit and the will. And the fever of malaria ran in the blood of many of those fighting, as well as of their leaders. Jefferson Davis himself was sometimes afflicted, as was Abraham Lincoln, and doubtless scores of others among the highest officers on both sides. Maybe that was why this siege dragged on so, because the leaders were too weakened from bouts of chill and fever to force a victory. And as they delayed, the fever claimed more men every day.

CHAPTER FIVE

JUNE 26

In the morning, responding to Mirrie's summons, Judah Daniel went out to gather three kinds of bark—dogwood, poplar, and willow—for the fixings to treat Narcissa's fever. She had some of the mixture on hand, but she'd best make more now, since the ground-up bark had to soak in the whiskey for two weeks. Mirrie had sent some whiskey along with her request—a good thing, for it was hard to come by. Judah Daniel used the mixture for many kinds of fever, but not often for malaria, which seemed to choose white people as its victims. What made them think this land belonged to them, when the very air they breathed here made them sick?

Dogwood and poplar were easy, but to gather willow she had to go down along the river, avoiding the Guards. At last she decided she had plenty and headed back up to Main Street. John Chapman was closing up the bakeshop, ready to go home. She waited until he was done, got up on the wagon beside him for the short ride back to Navy Hill. John didn't seem like himself. He looked costive, Judah Daniel thought, and wondered if she'd soon have another patient on her hands. He spoke hesitantly, like he was afraid to rile her. "I got—I want to talk to you."

Judah Daniel knew better than to seem too curious and risk driving him into silence. She waited.

John glanced sideways at her, his face grave. "You been over to Ferncliff's. How's Selah look to you?"

"How d'you mean?"

"She look excited? Like she waiting for something?"

Judah Daniel recalled Selah's blank, unfriendly face. "Well, she don't look like she expecting anything good to happen, if that's what you mean."

John sighed, exasperated. "You telling me, Selah don't look like she expecting the Yankees to ride in and bow down to her and Louisa Ferncliff."

"No, she don't look like that."

"Can't you go see Mattie again? See if anybody at Davis's is asking questions, or—?"

Judah Daniel shook her head. "Best leave well enough alone."

John brought his fist down on his knee. He let loose a string of curses in a rumbling voice that was almost a sob. "Susy told me that letter could bring down the city. Three days done passed. . . ." He took a deep breath and let it out, then went on. "Not that it make that much difference to me if the Yankees take Richmond. If they was to ride in and give you and me the key to the city, what of it? Stand to reason they got to ride out someday. And then what do you reckon would happen to us? Way I figure it, if you was to take this whole city and turn it upside down, the same people would come out on top as is on top now. Might take some time, but it'd happen. Whereas the poor people and the black people would wind up as bad off as they is now—maybe worse. But I can stand that if I have to. What I can't stand is not knowing what become of that letter. If it was to get back to Davis I had a hand in taking it, how can I keep my family safe? If I run away, they might punish them instead of me. If I stay, they might punish them just to break me down."

Judah Daniel gathered her thoughts. John had a bad case

of nerves, and it wouldn't help a thing if she caught it. At last she said, "Selah don't look like she fixing to greet McClellan. Then again, don't look like they packing to make a run for it. They just waiting; and that's all you can do. Don't you go running off. That'd just make you look guilty."

"Yeah, I reckon I can see that," John said. "Still, I feel like a damn fool, just sitting around waiting for them to put the shackles on me."

"What I can't figure out," Judah Daniel went on, "is why Ferncliff say to bring Moses to her. What she be wanting with a baby?"

John looked over at her, then away. "Might be you best give him to her."

"You that much afraid of Louisa Ferncliff?" Judah Daniel asked, arching her thin brows and staring him down.

"No! No. It's just that . . . well, some of them treat that baby like he was part of the family. Like he took the place of Elda's real baby, my grandbaby. Except for Elda, and me—we the ones still hurting from the loss. Seem like the longer Moses stay with us, the more *we* feel it. Might come a time when we can't stand it no more. And then what we going to do?"

Judah Daniel got down at the front door of the Chapmans' house. John took Raven to his stall out back. Judah Daniel's feet had hardly touched the steps leading up to the porch when Darcy was there, a worried look on her face. Darcy put her hand on Judah Daniel's arm and whispered, "Elda done give the baby away."

She can't mean that, Judah Daniel told herself, but her heart turned cold and stone-heavy. "What you mean, *give away?*" Then, seeing Darcy's face, she realized the girl was blaming herself for what had happened. She laid a comforting arm on Darcy's shoulder and drew the girl to her.

"I was in the kitchen, giving Young John his dinner. When I come in to see if Elda wanted something to eat, the baby weren't nowhere around. She told me a woman come for the baby."

"You didn't see the woman?"

Darcy shook her head. They were walking toward the house now, Judah Daniel listening and comforting but eager to get to Elda.

"Was it his mother?"

Darcy shook her head again. "Elda didn't say so. Elda—she like a rag doll. It's like her heart and her head ain't connected. How come she just give him away?"

Judah Daniel squeezed Darcy's thin shoulder. "I'll talk to her," she assured the girl. "You keep Young John out of mischief."

Elda had allowed the baby, Moses, to suckle. Beyond that, it was like John had said—she just hadn't warmed up to him. If, in time, the raising of a stranger's baby would bring Elda back to herself—or whether her older son might do it—these were the questions Judah Daniel had asked herself. But never had she wondered if Elda would harm the child. She walked into Elda's room almost holding her breath. Elda was lying half on her side, covers pushed down, her brown skin glistening with sweat.

"Elda, where's the baby?"

Elda looked up, dull-eyed. "A woman took him."

"His mother?" But Judah Daniel knew—without knowing how she knew—that Moses's mother had not come for him.

Elda hesitated, then shook her head no. "She told me her mistress wanted the baby and she had money and a fine house." Elda fiddled with the loose tie of her nightdress. "She told me the baby be better off with her mistress than with me. Then she took him away."

Selah. It had to be. Acting on behalf of Louisa Ferncliff, who had ordered—tried to order—Judah Daniel herself to bring the baby to her. But it still didn't make any sense.

"You going to get him back?" Elda was watching her, looking for signs of—what? Anger? Chiding? But Judah Daniel didn't feel angry, at least not at Elda. What anger she felt was directed at Selah, and Louisa Ferncliff. And at herself, for asking too much of Elda. There was no point in going to get Moses, if Elda would not take him. "Elda, do you *want* him back?"

Elda turned her head a little on the pillow to look Judah Daniel full in the face. "That woman told me he be better off with her mistress. She send him up north to be educated."

Judah Daniel released an exasperated breath that flared her nostrils. "Elda, he not but a couple weeks old. What do *you* think? This little while, you been the closest thing to a momma that baby got. You think some other woman nurse him better 'cause a rich white lady paid her to?"

Elda stared at her for a long time. At last she whispered, "No."

"Well, do you want me to get him back or not?"

The answer came on a let-out breath: "Yes."

Judah Daniel heard John Chapman's heavy step in the hall, then his voice calling her, sounding excited or upset. He's heard about Moses, she thought, and came out to meet him. He could drive her up to Church Hill, it would save time— But John stood in the doorway with a bundle in his arms, looking just as he had when he brought Moses to the house for the first time. It *was* Moses, there in his arms, fast asleep.

"I'll take him to Elda," John said softly. "It was Selah took him. I don't trust that woman a lick. If this baby go to another home, it ain't going to be with her."

Judah Daniel followed John into the room where Elda

was lying. She saw Elda reach out to take the baby. John sat on the side of the bed and settled Moses into Elda's arms. Judah Daniel eased out of the room.

After a minute, John followed her out. "It'll be all right," he assured her.

"How'd you come to get him back?"

John looked as perplexed as Judah Daniel felt. "Selah come out of nowhere and give him to me, out there in the yard. Said she made a mistake, he belong here with us. She held him out like she was going to drop him, so I took him, and she lit out on the double-quick. First Susy, now Selah—and Louisa Ferncliff sitting back pulling the strings, I reckon—it's like they's all been dining on run-mad mush."

Judah Daniel breathed out a sigh. John was getting his spirit back, at least, praise God. "It seem like Selah talked Elda into giving the baby to her, told her Miss Ferncliff wanted him, planned to send him to school and such. But Selah weren't gone away from here long enough to get to Church Hill and back. Selah either made it all up or she changed her mind on her own."

Darcy came up to Judah Daniel. "I think that woman took that piece of quilt. You know—the one Moses wrapped in when he come here."

"The quilt?" Judah Daniel repeated, wondering. "She took it to wrap him up in?"

Darcy shrugged. "I washed it out yesterday and hung it up in Elda's room. What with all this rain, it weren't even dry yet. I reckon she seen it when she come into the room."

"John—did Selah give you the quilt as well?"

"The quilt?" John repeated, as puzzled as if he'd never heard the word. "No—I didn't see no quilt. Maybe she throwed it away."

Judah Daniel ran out on the porch. There was no sign of Selah, no sign of the quilt. She searched around the yard, then went back onto the porch. Darcy and John were standing there, looking as if they thought she, too, had dined on run-mad mush.

Judah Daniel put off answering their questions. She hadn't worked it out enough in her own mind. It just seemed to her that even Selah would have sense enough not to wrap a baby in a damp quilt. But if she hadn't just taken it for that reason, and hadn't given it back to John with the baby, then the quilt had a meaning for Selah.

Well, quilts did carry meanings aplenty—messages about the kind of place, maybe the kind of mother, Moses had come from. Slaves rarely had the leisure to quilt with tiny stitches; more often they tied their quilts with pieces of string. How this quilt had been made, she hadn't noticed. Whether the quilter had access to fine fabrics made a difference too. Judah Daniel thought back on the pattern she had glimpsed in the filthy quilt, the material, the colors—madder-dyed reds and browns, mostly, but green and blue as well. The maker of the quilt might have been a house servant rewarded with scraps of her mistress's dresses. And quilts that looked the same to outsiders carried other messages as well to those who knew how to read them—messages as to who made them, what family she belonged to. . . .

"See if you can recollect the pattern," she told Darcy. "Sketch it for me, good as you can recall."

This drew a smile from Darcy. The baby's ordeal scared her, that was only natural. Darcy herself hadn't had an easy childhood. The broad scar on her cheek . . . Judah Daniel hoped Darcy had forgotten the pain and fear of the wounding that might not have been an accident. After the burn, Darcy had stopped talking, and her owners, judging her not only scarred but stupid, had sold her cheap to Judah Daniel.

Why had Selah kept the quilt, and not the baby? Could it have been the quilt Selah wanted all along? She wanted to run after Selah and shake the truth out of her, but that wouldn't work—not with a woman like Selah. There was another way, though. Armed with a flask full of bark medicine that made do for quinine, she could walk right in to Louisa Ferncliff's house and make herself at home. Once there, she could poke about for the thread that ran between two things that couldn't, on the face of them, be more different—the letter stolen from Jefferson Davis, and the quilt that had wrapped a given-up child.

→>←

At Louisa Ferncliff's, Selah opened the door to Judah Daniel and led her upstairs without saying much of anything. Mirrie met Judah Daniel on the landing and thanked Selah in words that told her—but politely—to take herself off. Then Mirrie drew Judah Daniel into a room she assumed was Narcissa's until she saw there was no one in the bed.

"I see you've brought the medicine. Good." Mirrie was strung very tight. Judah Daniel could see it in her tensed shoulders and flushed cheeks. "Narcissa is sleeping now. I think it's best to let her sleep, don't you, until she wakes of her own accord."

Judah Daniel nodded, waiting.

"Please—sit down," Mirrie told her, pointing to a slipper chair. Mirrie seated herself on a little low bench at the end of the bed. Judah Daniel sat on the chair. "The baby you told me about. Have you found his family?"

"No, ma'am," Judah Daniel answered. She didn't add

anything. Mirrie had something on her mind, and it was best to wait and see what that was.

"Did you hear about the servant who ran away from the Davises? The woman, I mean—Susannah Reynolds?"

Judah Daniel's heart quickened. "Yes'm, I heard about it."

Mirrie played with the tasseled trim of her pagoda sleeve. "I know not much goes on that you don't know about. So you may know that Susy Reynolds is Selah's sister, and that she once lived in this house."

Judah Daniel nodded, taking care not to say anything that would turn Mirrie away from her purpose.

"Louisa is my friend." Mirrie stood up and began pacing. "She is a Unionist and abolitionist. She's what Richmonders call a Black Republican, and worse names. They think she's disloyal. I now know their suspicions are justified. Louisa placed Susy in the Davises' household as a spy. Susy stole a letter." Mirrie turned to face Judah Daniel, who knew that it was time to speak.

"I know about that. My friend John Chapman brung it here. Susy come to him for men's clothes so's she could run away to the Yankee camp."

Judah Daniel's words seemed to knock the wind out of Mirrie, who sat back down on the bench, gripping it with her hands as if it needed keeping still.

Judah Daniel went on. "She told him the letter could bring down the city. She told him she had to run away—she been betrayed."

"Betrayed." Mirrie echoed the word, her eyes wide behind her spectacles. "By whom?"

"She didn't say."

Mirrie got up and started pacing again. At last she said, "The letter is here, I think. Louisa has it. She won't let it out, because Lincoln hasn't freed the slaves. It could be that was the betrayal Susy complained of. I kept telling myself it couldn't be true. But it is true, isn't it?"

Judah Daniel nodded again.

Mirrie stopped and looked down at her. "Something happened, the night before John Chapman found the baby. A shot was fired, very close to here; maybe up in the churchyard. Someone—it must have been Louisa, or Selah—had locked Narcissa in her room. They must have known about—whatever it was, before it happened. And then Louisa wanted the baby. . . ."

It was strange to be sitting herself when the white woman was standing. Judah Daniel got up. "There was something else that Louisa wanted. A quilt the baby was wrapped in."

Mirrie stared at her. "A baby, a quilt. What could they have to do with the stolen letter? Well, I suppose you will explain it, when you know. Meanwhile, I'm frightened for Narcissa. Or frightened *of* her," she added in a dry voice. "She's never been a fire-eating secessionist, but I can't fool myself that she would accept the state of affairs. She would go after Louisa herself first, I imagine; but when that failed, she might go to the authorities. Louisa, Selah, John Chapman, you, me—I don't know if we would be enough to keep her quiet, if she believed the soldiers' safety depended on her not keeping quiet. She mustn't find out. We must find the letter ourselves, and destroy it."

"From what you said," Judah Daniel rejoined, "Louisa ain't going to let that happen."

"We have to try. You watch Selah, I will watch Louisa. Sooner or later one of them will make a slip."

Late in the afternoon, the guns began to sound in earnest. After the ominous silence, the sound was almost a relief.

With Judah Daniel caring for Narcissa, Mirrie had decided to keep Louisa company. They'd been sitting in the back parlor, reading newspapers—though it required some effort to pretend that the news from last week, or even from two days ago, meant anything today.

Mirrie was surprised to hear a firm rap on Louisa's front door—Louisa didn't seem to have many visitors. It was Mrs. Stedman, the wife of an older physician who was a good friend of Professor Powers. Mirrie wondered a bit that Mrs. Stedman, obviously a loyal Confederate, would call on Louisa Ferncliff; but then Rosalie Stedman would have known that she and Narcissa were there. She had a way of knowing things like that.

Mirrie embraced Mrs. Stedman while Louisa looked on with a tight little smile. "I've come to take you up to the Hebrew cemetery," Mrs. Stedman announced briskly. "We can see the battle from there—at least, the smoke of it. Won't you come?"

While Mirrie was hesitating, Louisa spoke up. "Yes, let's go. The doctoress"—meaning Judah Daniel—"can look after Mrs. Powers."

"All right," Mirrie agreed.

Mrs. Stedman nodded approval. "There is quite a crowd gathered already. We must be quick, before my carriage is taken out from under us. It's been used as an ambulance before—but I think the bloodstains have all dried."

The Stedmans' carriage was pulled by two well-cared-for horses that, so far at least, the army had let alone. The driver handed the women in, then mounted to his seat and flicked the reins. The horses started forward with a lurch.

To fill the silence, Mirrie asked after Mrs. Stedman's grown daughters.

"Lord, those silly girls!" Mrs. Stedman smiled proudly. "They are just like geese. And the baby is a fuzzy-headed little gosling, isn't he? It's a wonder he knows which one is his mother, they all fuss over him so."

As Mrs. Stedman chatted on, Mirrie wondered at her courage. To hear her talk, there was nothing the matter in the world; but in fact the baby's father was an officer who even now might be risking his life. She sneaked a glance at Louisa and saw on her face the same composed smile she almost always wore. What in the world would Rosalie Stedman think if she knew what Louisa had done—and what she still might do?

They crept down the precipitous slope of Church Hill to Shockoe Valley. Mrs. Stedman laughed. "If Rosinante and Bayard miss their footing," she quipped, "we'll have the cart before the horse indeed."

The sun was almost directly overhead, but the air was cooler and less humid than it had been for the past few days, so that lines of light and shadow seemed redrawn with a firmer hand. Birds chirped and warbled in the full-leaved trees, and now and then a breeze brought the sweetness of honeysuckle or magnolia. But with the fresh air and breeze came the sound of guns firing, not very far away. When the ground leveled off in the valley, Mrs. Stedman consulted a little gold watch at her waistband. As they began the climb up Shockoe Hill, she looked at it again and said, "Five minutes, ninety-seven guns. I believe the expectations of a battle are not exaggerated."

Mirrie looked over at Louisa. Their eyes met for an instant, but Louisa turned away before Mirrie had time to decipher her expression.

When Broad Street began its steep ascent up Shockoe Hill, the driver got out to lead the horses.

"What is the news?" Mirrie asked Mrs. Stedman.

Mrs. Stedman shrugged. "Rumors, reports. The wilder

they are, the more currency they find. The fact is, General Lee has imposed a code of silence. I hear that officers returning from furlough cannot ascertain where their regiments are, and must obtain passports to Lee's headquarters. *But*," she added with a wink, "I heard the boys were up early this morning, frying bacon. So I think that we have taken the offensive."

Mirrie tried to push away the thought that it would likely be the last meal some of those boys would eat.

Broad Street began to level out again just past Monumental Church. It seemed the traffic, foot, horseback, and carriage, was all tending the same way. And sure enough, a crowd had gathered up on the hill overlooking the Mechanicsville Turnpike. In the distance dark smoke hung over the ground. The booming of the cannon was louder now. It was beyond Mirrie to interpret anything from the noise and haze, but some said that guns had been heard to the left, in the direction of the Pamunkey River.

"That is Jackson!" one man exclaimed. "And he is in their rear, behind their right wing."

"Naw, not Stonewall! He ain't within a hundred miles of here," another man answered back. He slurred his words a little, as if he'd been drinking. The crowd hushed to hear what he had to say—seeming ready to jump up and give him a good whipping if he had any criticism to allege against their hero. "He's about to take Washington City!" Laughter erupted, and the speaker was warmly congratulated by his companions. Just to hear the name of Stonewall Jackson seemed to spread comfort among the group.

They were acting as if they'd gathered to watch a horse race, with nothing more than a little money riding on the outcome. Mirrie began to wish she hadn't come. What was happening down there was something out of Dante or Milton, a scene from hell erupting in the fields of Virginia. With each thunderous boom of cannon fire, men were falling dead or wounded. Before long they would be coming into the city—another long procession of broken bodies, headed for the hospitals and the graves.

Louisa looked so composed. Was it really possible, as she had claimed, that she had the power to end this carnage? Rosalie Stedman, too—she volunteered in the hospitals, she knew firsthand what was happening out there, yet she looked as calm as if she'd been sitting in her own parlor.

The pounding grew closer, the reports coming only seconds apart. At last the rattle of small arms fire could be heard, and then two guns on the right, followed by others. Louisa and Mrs. Stedman had found something to talk about. The sun sank low behind their backs, and yet the firing continued, growing—Mirrie thought—even stronger. The eastern sky turned gray-blue, dimmed by the smoke from the battlefield. The first star appeared. The flashes of the guns could be seen now, and the explosions of shells. Still the battle rumbled on, echoing like thunder.

→>-<←

Up at Chimborazo, the noise of distant guns injected all but the sickest patients with a kind of wary energy. The young medical students seemed the most affected. With pressing needs attended to, Cameron Archer rallied his medical troops to move closer to the scene of battle. Brit Wallace—who, it turned out, had chosen a good day to offer his services—drove a grocery wagon that could serve as an ambulance to bring the wounded back into town. They rode out the Mechanicsville Turnpike toward the Chickahominy Swamp, following the path taken by the soldiers a few hours before. Along the way Archer dispersed the students to help the surgeons already at work until only Brit Wallace was left.

"The fellows who make it back here on their own are the least wounded," Archer grumbled. "The artillery's gone out now, behind the infantry. The firing's too hot for men to help each other to the rear. Let's take that grocer's wagon of yours and go and get the ones who're really in need."

The sky was clear; over the last few days the rain had tapered off, leaving the roads at that ideal state in between sticking mud and choking dust. Brit and Archer were led by the sound of firing in the direction of the Meadow Bridge. They followed the road along the tracks of the Virginia Central to the Chickahominy—a narrow brown stream with a stretch of low marshy land on either side. A causeway carried the railroad tracks across the Chickahominy. They stepped onto the causeway, Brit noting the detritus of the Federal pickets who had fled this post at the advance of the Confederates—blankets, knapsacks, a coffeepot lying on its side near the remains of the fire.

"Let's gather up a few of these canteens," Archer said. "We'll have need of water."

They rummaged among the abandoned articles and salvaged two or three canteens each. Brit opened one and tipped it toward his open mouth, then turned it upside down and watched a few drops of water speckle the worn leather of his brogans. They gathered up the canteens and resumed walking. Brit gestured at the sidearm Archer wore. "You should have found me a pistol. We'll need more than one if we get in a fix."

Archer laughed, his teeth white against his tanned skin. "More than two, if we're up against artillery. But it's not the enemy that surgeons are armed against. *This*"—he patted the pistol in its holster—"is to protect the medical supplies. There are plenty of men on our own side who would put a ball in your head for a draught of laudanum or morphine. Here—what's this?"

Brit followed Archer's gaze to a pile of—something—on the side of the road as it resumed on the other side of the swamp. More supplies abandoned by the Federals? Another glance, and he could make out the shapes of a half-dozen men stretched out under blankets. Asleep, with the tramp of passage along this road? Of course not; they were dead. Archer uncovered the first: half his face was shot away. And the next: arm and shoulder almost off. Archer seemed obliged, now, to try them all. By the sixth and last, Brit found that shock had given way to a sort of desperate numbness.

Archer flicked the blankets back up over the bodies and dusted off his hands. His face was expressionless. "Let's get that water."

"All right." Brit turned away, relieved, and started down the bank where the log underpinnings of the causeway gave support to his feet. He had uncorked the first canteen and was stooping to fill it when he saw just upstream, half hidden in the shadow of the causeway, another dead man. The gentle motion of the water laved the blue uniform and the red wound. Brit took a step back, then turned and scrambled back up the bank, motioning Archer to move to a spot farther upstream. They filled the canteens and returned to the wagon without another word exchanged.

Ascending a low hill, they at last came upon a soldier they could help—an infantryman, slender and light-haired, pale from loss of blood. With his arrival, Archer became businesslike. "I'll set up here. See what it's like ahead."

Brit went on alone. The roar of guns, the crackle of muskets, the shrieking and bursting of shot and shell, grew louder at his approach. He came into a grove of oaks from which he could look down on the buildings of Mechanicsville—just a few wooden structures, now knocked almost to pieces by the battle that had since moved on ahead, leaving its pall of bitter smoke, blasted landscape, and broken bodies. The Union forces were falling back. It would be safe to bring the wagon forward to this point, he noted, and there were men who could use the help—but the thunder of battle drew him on. He pressed forward toward a small hill. There were the caissons, under protection of the hill. Above them were the guns, manned by grim-faced cannoneers. As he watched, an officer came toward him, limping, holding his boot in his hand. Brit gestured to the man and, when he came closer, called out, "Just a little ways back." Should he turn now and help the captain? There was a man going to his aid, offering whatever rough rescue could be performed under such conditions. So Brit, even as he wondered, kept moving closer, watching the precision-drill performance of the cannoneers. One man went for a shell, placed it in the muzzle of the gun, and withdrew his hand just in time for the other man to put in the rammer and throw his weight on it to force the cartridge home. All this was done amid the pounding of shot and bursting of shells from the enemy, together with the roar of their comrades' guns on the left and right. The earth under his feet, the sky above, every vein in his body, shook with the force of it. There, at the corner of his eye—he turned his head to a break in the rhythm of loading and firing. A man had fallen across the gun axle. The ball that had hit him, as big as an orange, rolled down the incline, covered in gore. The second man at the gun dropped the rammer and thrust his hand through the spokes of the wheel, knocking his fallen comrade out of the way. Another was coming to take his place as Brit ran forward, keeping low to the ground. He came up under the gun and took hold of the fallen man, drag-

ging him out of the way—a corpse, he saw now, for the
ball had passed right through his chest. An instant later
Brit felt the ground buck under him. He had a brief sen-
sation of flying before everything went black.

When Brit came to, there was a uniformed man bending
over him. Cameron Archer. His lips were moving, but Brit
couldn't hear the words over the roaring in his ears. What
did he want so godawful much? Then his head cleared,
and he realized—to save his life.

Narcissa was lying propped up in bed, with Judah Daniel
seated nearby. It was nine o'clock. The guns—so close at
times that their firing had rattled the windows—were
silent at last. They hadn't heard any news or even seen
anyone for hours—not since Selah had brought Judah
Daniel up to the room. Mirrie and Louisa had gone out
with Mrs. Stedman; surely they should be back by now.

At last a knock came at the door. Narcissa sat up
straight, expecting Mirrie with news of the battle. But it
was someone who seemed so out of place at Louisa's that
Narcissa didn't recognize her at first.

"Mrs. Powers, I brung you some soup." It was Annie
Yates. The smell of chicken soup reached Narcissa; bless-
edly, it provoked hunger rather than nausea.

"Oh, Annie, how kind of you. Do come in. What news
of the battle?" Narcissa asked eagerly.

"They's lots more wounded men coming into the city.
Hundreds, thousands maybe. Prisoners too. They saying
we drove 'em, but I reckon they drove us right hard as
well." Annie was as calm as if she were discussing the
weather. Narcissa understood for the first time that Annie
didn't care much about the distinctions of Union or Confederate. It was her husband and son who had mattered to

her, not the cause for which they had died or the fate of the city—not even her own fate, maybe. And yet she'd reacted so strongly the day before when Narcissa had said the name Louisa Ferncliff. It was surprising she was here, come to that—but perhaps Annie knew, as she herself had learned, how loneliness works upon the mind of someone who's sick.

Annie stepped closer. "I heard you got the tertian fever." Then Annie looked across the room to where Judah Daniel was sitting, and froze. She looked so appalled Narcissa feared she would drop the bowl of soup.

"Put it down here," Narcissa said quickly, indicating the nightstand beside the bed. Annie set the bowl down and pulled off the cloth it was wrapped in.

"I didn't bring no spoon," Annie grumbled. She sounded angry, almost, as if someone had accused her of an oversight.

Selah had already left the room. "I'll go get one," Judah Daniel offered. Narcissa smiled her thanks.

Annie's eyes followed Judah Daniel until she was out of the room. "Do you know that colored woman?" Annie asked.

"Yes—quite well. That's Judah Daniel. She's made up the medicine to help break the fever. She's quite a well-known doctoress in town. She helped my brother's wife in her confinement—among other things."

"A midwife too," Annie remarked. "Well—I reckon I made a mistake. I thought I seen her someplace. Well, I got to be going."

"Annie—thank you!" Narcissa called after her.

A few moments later, Judah Daniel reappeared, carrying a silver spoon. Narcissa started in on the soup with a good appetite. "Why is Annie Yates so frightened of you?" she asked Judah Daniel.

"She must have took me for somebody else," Judah Daniel answered. "Or maybe she just ain't used to black people. She from the mountains, ain't she?"

"Well, yes, but by now you would think. . . . Anyway, it was kind of her to bring this. Where do you suppose she got a chicken? I wouldn't offend her by offering to pay for it, but I wish there was something I could do for her." Saying the words, Narcissa remembered for the first time in days the notice she'd arranged to run in the newspaper. What better could she do for Annie than find out the location of her son's grave? But the notice had directed replies to Brit Wallace at the Exchange Hotel, and she hadn't thought to tell him that she had placed the notice. He'd called here, brought her flowers, but she'd been ill with fever. If he received a reply to the notice without knowing what it was, he probably wouldn't think to ask her what it meant. He might even throw it away.

"I believe I'll get dressed and go downstairs," she told Judah Daniel. "There's a letter I need to write."

Back now at Chimborazo, with no lingering ill effects save a stiff neck and aching head, Brit was detailed to nurses' duty. He was cleaning and bandaging the wounds of one of the Marylanders, David Schlitz. "Is it your arm?" Brit asked—the man's right sleeve was soaked in blood up to the elbow. Schlitz looked at his sleeve and hand, likewise dyed red, and shook his head. He pulled his arms out of the sleeves and laid the jacket aside. "That ain't my blood," he explained. "Mine's in the leg. Shrapnel, most likely. I'm a gunner, I was out of range of the musket fire."

Then Brit could see the blood that had run down his inside trousers leg. "Take them off, too. Do you need me to help you?"

Together they worked the trousers down so that Brit

could see the wound on the inside of his right thigh. "Doctor—over here, please."

Archer looked and probed with his finger. Brit could see Schlitz biting his lip against a scream of pain. "It's a flesh wound," Archer said. "Clean it up so I can get a better look at it."

Brit had been given a sponge and a basin. He thought he'd like to change the water, which was dyed red with the blood of several men, but time seemed to be of the essence. He wrung out the sponge and dabbed the wound. It appeared to be a shallow trough several inches long.

Schlitz winced, took a deep breath, and began to talk. "It was a beautiful day for a fight. Does that sound strange? But it was. We all knew something important was about to happen. You should have seen us, the way we went about our business. We were graceful as dancing masters, not a foot wrong. We were ready.

"But they made us wait, and wait. I don't know why. The weather was perfect. There was no mud to mire our guns. The infantry went ahead of us toward the Chickahominy. The sun came up right over our heads and then passed over and threw our shadows the other way. It was hard to see *it* moving, when *we* weren't.

"Then at last, about two or three o'clock in the afternoon, our two rifle guns were ordered ahead. We all saluted each other. We had a thing we said to each other— 'We part "Richmond besieged," we meet "Richmond relieved." ' We'd shake hands, and say that, and 'Take care of yourself.'

"The rest of our battery was still waiting. At last we heard the musket fire start up beyond the swamp. A volley, and then another volley. And then the cannons' roar."

Schlitz was propped up on his elbows now, and Brit suspended his cleaning of the wound to listen.

"At last it was our turn. 'Drivers mount! Cannoneers to your guns! Forward!' Our battery drew out into the road and made our way to the swamp. We were advancing in the direction of the Meadow Bridge.

"Well, you know," Schlitz went on, "it was a good thing for us the creek was high. We filled our sponge buckets there—every time we fire the gun, we have to quench the sparks before we ram the next load in."

Brit nodded his understanding.

"We went on across and up a hill. We saw some men dead, and others coming back wounded. We met those sights with a cold eye. When the time comes, it's like—it's not that you're not afraid, but you don't *feel* it, any more than you feel a blister on your foot at that time. We had a job to do, and the devil himself couldn't stop us from doing it.

"The firing was getting louder now, artillery and musketry, and then we could see the smoke, and then the men moving in it. We knew the enemy had strong fortifications at Beaver Dam Creek. We got to Mechanicsville and halted. It was hot now. Cannonballs were flying through the air, hitting the buildings or the dirt, or passing through the line of our guns. Well, we'd been in artillery duels before, so we didn't flinch, but we always hated the sound of shells—that whistle and catch"—Schlitz pursed his lips and blew a faint approximation of the sound—"so you can't tell where it is or where it's going.

"We got orders to move again, and went past the buildings to the slope of a little hill. Stevens and I agreed to take turns handling the rammer—that's the hardest job. We went into position there and opened fire." Schlitz smiled, remembering. "There's nothing like it. The noise goes all the way through your body, the air shakes, it . . . quivers, like the worst storm you've ever been in, but it doesn't stop. We were firing like *we* were machines, not just our guns.

"We saw men coming back across the field, limping. And then it was my turn. It hit me from the back, as I was stepping in to ram the cartridge in—a piece of a shell, I reckon. It pulled the fabric of my trousers into the meat of my leg. When I stood up, my trousers pulled tight, and it came out. I reckoned when I felt it come out, it might mean I could keep my leg. I'd just about made up my mind to die rather than have one of those surgeons sawing on me.

"My leg was numb," Schlitz said, "but I kept going. We all kept going, until it was too dark to see. When I tried to walk, I fell down. They carried me to the rear. Most of us gunners were struck in the legs. One man and three horses were killed."

As Schlitz fell silent, Brit moistened the sponge and resumed his careful dabbing.

Schlitz winced, then spoke through gritted teeth, "Tell me, we were talking about this earlier, maybe you know— who is this General Lee?"

Brit glanced around the ward. Everyone knew Stonewall, everyone knew Longstreet, but Robert Lee by contrast did not bear a glorious name. But he did not want to let Schlitz and his comrades think that their sacrifice would be wasted.

"He is as brave a soldier as you yourself. He is a man of honor."

Schlitz seemed to mull over Brit's statement. "They'll patch me up, then, and send me back. Better that, than Richmond should fall. God willing, we'll see victory."

"You will," Brit answered. "I'm sure of it." He realized he had almost said, We will.

Narcissa had gone into the back parlor to write to Brit Wallace concerning the newspaper notice. Judah Daniel was off doing something in the kitchen. All at once Selah burst into the parlor, quick-step. "You've got to do something about that dog. It's like to bark its head off."

Narcissa jumped to her feet. "Oh, no! No one's given Friday her dinner. Selah, please gather up some table scraps." She could have done it herself, but she could not resist meting out a small punishment for Selah, who had so completely taken on the domineering manner of her mistress. "I'll take it out to her."

Carrying the bowl of scraps, Narcissa hurried out into the yard. The air was scented with magnolia and honeysuckle. The stars would be out soon; already the lightning bugs were twinkling among the trees. She picked her way through the wet grass, holding up her skirts. Friday was howling now, a mournful and desperate sound. Selah would be out here with a muzzle, Narcissa knew, if she didn't hurry and quiet the dog.

Friday had gotten the rope wound around the stake until she had only a few feet of play. Yet Friday was making it worse on herself by straining the length of the rope toward something, a sound or a smell, that was beckoning her. A coon or a possum, most likely. Narcissa put the bowl down and went to her. "Friday! Hush!" The dog put her head down and switched her tail low to the ground, apologizing. Narcissa bent to take her head in her hands and scratch behind her ears. Friday licked her hands and wagged harder. "You were lonely, weren't you, girl? Here, let me get you untangled—" Narcissa fumbled with the knot at Friday's collar. The rope was slippery and swollen with rain. Narcissa tugged at the loops, but they didn't budge. "Damn," she swore quietly, then smiled to herself. *If those soldiers who are always apologizing to me for their cussing could hear me now!* Friday squirmed and licked her cheek. Narcissa pulled: it seemed hopeless. Pulled again: maybe . . . yes! The knot gave. One more tug, and the rope came free from the collar. But Friday, her desire for human attention overcome by a more ancient impulse, shook herself, and was gone.

"Damn!" She said it aloud this time, looking on helplessly as Friday pursued a zigzag course across the lawn, nose down, tail waving like a defiant battle flag. *"Friday!"*

Well. Dogs are dogs, Narcissa told herself, and that's why we love them. There was nothing to be served by standing here screaming the dog's name and adding to Selah's list of complaints. The longer she waited, the more likely it became that Friday would give her the slip entirely. Narcissa gathered up the length of rope, hiked up her skirts again, and strode to the gate. She reached the street just in time to see Friday's madly wagging tail charging up the hilly ascent to St. John's Church. *"Friday!"* she called once again, but the dog gave no sign of having heard. At the edge of the street, Narcissa hesitated. Friday had slipped between the iron bars of the gate and disappeared into the tree-shaded gloom of the cemetery.

Narcissa could see it in her mind's eye: some animal had made its rounds of the Ferncliff house, found a tidbit or two perhaps, then, scared off by Friday's barking, had taken off into the churchyard. Even now it was escaping down a hole or up a tree. Friday would stand guard for a while, but eventually she would tire of the game—and return to Ferncliff's with a loud clamor, probably in the middle of the night. This would anger Ferncliff and Selah, but it would distress Mirrie, and Narcissa knew that she herself would worry until Friday was brought back safe. As she stood debating, there came out of the dark silence of the cemetery an unearthly howl that brushed up the hairs on the back of her neck.

She started across the street at a run that carried her up the incline to the fence. There she stopped and walked along its iron bars, came to the gate, lifted the latch. The gate swung silent on oiled hinges. She stepped into the churchyard. The moss-covered stones were slick beneath the thin soles of her shoes.

"Friday!" She was calling softly now, more for the comfort of hearing her own voice than from any hope that the dog would come. She had to calm herself; another howl like the last one would send her out of her skin.

She stopped to listen. Cicadas were singing their ragged song. And a scratching, and whimpering—she followed the sounds to the far end of the cemetery. She caught sight of Friday's tail again, where the dog was busily digging. Maybe the animal, whatever it was, had gone to earth there; if it felt threatened, it might turn and fight, and Friday might be hurt.

Narcissa started to run. Then something—the root of a tree, or a half-buried gravestone—caught her foot and sent her sprawling. She lay on the wet ground, spitting dirt out of her mouth. Friday was only a few feet from her now. She pushed herself up to a crouch, felt around for the rope, gathered it up, and made ready to jump, to catch the dog by surprise so that she wouldn't take off again. Friday had stopped digging now, but— Had she caught the thing? She had something in her mouth and was worrying it as if to drag it from the hole . . . something limp and brown and . . . Oh, God! Bile filled Narcissa's mouth, and she spat again. Friday had dug into a grave. It wasn't an animal she had in her mouth, but a human hand.

"Friday! No! Leave it!" Narcissa's voice came out in a hoarse whisper. She pushed forward, still on her knees, lunged, and got hold of Friday's collar. She was relieved to see that Friday's teeth gripped the fabric of a sleeve, not the flesh. The dog let go of her grisly prize and stood quietly enough while Narcissa gathered her up and threaded the rope through the ring on her collar.

Narcissa sat back on her heels. Her heart was pounding, but she forced herself to look again. The hand and forearm, clad in a sleeve of what looked like homespun fabric, protruded from a mounded pile of earth. She had heard of shallow graves dug on the field of battle, graves that yielded up their dead to the carrion eaters. But in St. John's churchyard? No, there was definitely something wrong here.

Friday gave a low warning growl, then a bark.

Narcissa tightened her grip on Friday's collar. The pale shapes of the tombstones seemed to shift in the shadows. Something was moving. Some*one*. The figure was very close to her, towering over her where she crouched holding Friday. One long stride, and whoever it was would be upon her.

The figure stopped. It was a man, by the clothes—that was all she could tell. Then he spoke, his voice little more than a hoarse whisper. "Don't you know who I am? You was looking for me, asking questions."

She strained to see his face—the bottom part covered with a brown beard, the upper part with a bloodstained bandage. He was wearing what looked to be a uniform. "You're Devlin, aren't you? I knew you hadn't died."

He came a step closer. Friday growled low in her throat. "You scared of me?" he asked Narcissa.

"Did you kill this man?"

"Those women down there." He gestured toward Louisa's. "They killed him. If you trust them, you're a fool."

"What women?"

"Those women got no hearts. You best get away from them, before they turn on you." He took another step toward her.

"Don't come any closer. I'll set the dog on you." Her voice was shaking.

"Ha! That little bitch don't scare me none," Devlin

jeered. But he took a step back, then another, and then was gone.

Narcissa got to her feet. She looped Friday's leash around her hand, then began to move slowly backward, never moving her gaze from the spot where Devlin had stood. She passed slowly through the cemetery, eyes probing the shadows, feeling her way with her feet because she dared not look down, and she dared not risk a fall. Friday was tugging on the leash, wondering why she was going so slowly. At last she came to the gate. She lifted the latch and passed through, then went down the hill at a run.

When she reached Louisa's yard, she slowed, then stopped, keeping in shadow. She was still trembling from the shock of finding the dead man, and from her encounter with Devlin. While she'd been looking for Devlin, wondering what had happened to him, he'd been watching her. He knew where she was staying, he knew she'd been looking for him. . . . He even knew Friday was a female, something he couldn't have seen in the darkness or guessed from her name.

He had told her not to be afraid of him. It was the women, the women in this house, who'd killed that man. Maybe he'd been watching them, too, and seen them do it. But whom did he mean? Louisa, Selah? Surely not Mirrie, or Judah Daniel. But Mirrie might be on Louisa's side, and so might Judah Daniel. *If you trust them, you're a fool. . . .*

For good or evil, she had allowed Devlin to escape detection as a malingerer. Then he'd gotten away, carried out of the hospital by men who must have known he wasn't dead. Dr. Lester had signed his death certificate; he, too, must have known Devlin was alive. She had saved Devlin, and now he was trying to return the favor by warning her against Louisa.

Or—it could be that Devlin had been watching

Louisa's house, watching *her*, looking for an opportunity to turn her against Louisa. But why? He hadn't asked her for anything, just told her to save herself. What selfish motive could he have in that? It made more sense to think he meant to help her. And so she should be careful.

Well . . . she'd tell them about the body, but keep Devlin's appearance a secret—for now, at least.

Narcissa found Judah Daniel in the kitchen and led her to the place where she had found the body. They dug around the body until they uncovered a dark-skinned black man dressed in rough clothing—a shirt, vest, and trousers held up with a rope. The stiffness of rigor mortis had passed away, and the body had begun to soften and swell.

"Do you recognize him?" she asked Judah Daniel.

Judah Daniel shook her head. She pulled the shirt away to reveal a massive wound on the left side of the man's chest. "He was shot."

Narcissa thought of the shot she had heard two nights before. She had a feeling this man had been its target. But who had held the gun? Louisa? Selah? Or had Devlin lied?

"The shovel was to hand, I reckon." Judah Daniel pointed, and Narcissa saw it, propped against the iron fence railing. "Somebody scooped up a little trench, dropped the body in it, and covered it up. Sweet Jesus—look at his hands. You think the dog . . . ?"

Narcissa looked. The finger ends were torn up so that the bones showed through. She shook her head. "No. Friday had one of the sleeves in her teeth. She didn't touch the—the fingers."

Judah Daniel was still examining the wounds. "Maybe it was rats," she said at last. "But I wonder: where's the woman?"

Those women—Devlin's hoarse whisper echoed in Narcissa's mind. "What do you mean? I didn't see any woman."

"I reckon you don't know. John Chapman found a baby here yesterday morning. This man's been dead for a while, a couple days at least. Might be this here's the baby's father."

"Oh, God, a baby? Was it all right?" Devlin hadn't said anything about a baby. Had he known? Was that what he meant by "hard hearts"?

"Yes. He weren't parted very long from his mama—or a wet nurse, at the least."

"Could his mother be here as well? Let's look and see if there's another grave."

They walked slowly through the cemetery, holding the lantern down low. There was no sign that any other body had been buried recently, and in a hurry.

"Look, Judah Daniel—there's the Stedmans' carriage. Mirrie and Louisa are back. I'll ask Mrs. Stedman to go for the police."

When they reached the door, they found Mirrie had complained of a headache and gone straight up to her room. Narcissa managed to exchange a few words with Rosalie Stedman, who was heading up to Chimborazo and promised to send down someone to take charge of the body. Louisa saw them talking together and came up. "What are you two talking about?"

Narcissa turned to answer her. "I was up in the churchyard, trying to catch Friday. I found the body of a man— a black man; he'd been shot, a day or two ago I would guess by his appearance. I've asked Mrs. Stedman to tell someone up at Chimborazo."

Louisa looked shaken. "A black man, you say? Take me up there, show me—"

Rosalie Stedman intervened. "Louisa, I'm sure it would do you no good to see such a thing. If the man has been dead for more than a day, in this heat—I assure you, it would be most unpleasant."

Louisa's eyes flashed, and she drew herself up as if to argue, but Rosalie was a match for her. "Go along inside, Louisa. We don't have time to argue the point." Louisa gave up then and walked away toward the house.

Narcissa and Judah Daniel went into the house. There was no sign of Louisa or Selah, and Louisa's door was shut. They went on to Mirrie's room, where they found Mirrie sitting in the chair next to her bed. Narcissa noted her red-rimmed eyes and knew she had been crying.

"We won, they say," Mirrie told them.

Narcissa sat on the bed near Mirrie. But there was a distance between them, and not all on her own side, Narcissa felt. It would take more than the words of a deserting soldier to separate her from Mirrie—but Mirrie herself seemed withdrawn.

"I'm afraid I have more bad news," Narcissa told her, as gently as she could. She went on to describe how she'd found the body. As the story unfolded, Mirrie sat up straighter, and the color came back into her cheeks. When Narcissa got to the part about John Chapman finding the baby, Mirrie surprised her by saying, "I knew about that. Judah Daniel came here on Wednesday—it was while you were sick—and asked Selah if she knew whose baby it could be. Louisa Ferncliff came out and asked for the baby to be brought here! Judah Daniel refused—politely, but she held her ground."

"You knew? Why didn't you tell me?"

Mirrie looked down. "I should have, I suppose, but you were sick. I didn't want to worry you."

"What would Louisa want with a baby?" Narcissa asked wonderingly.

"I've been asking myself that same question. All I can think is, she's a lonely woman; she wants someone to care for."

Narcissa frowned. "I can't put such a pleasant face on it, Mirrie. After everything she's done, to bring a baby into this house—"

"It's worse than you think. You don't know about the letter."

"What letter?" asked Narcissa.

Mirrie looked at Judah Daniel. "We have to tell her."

Judah Daniel nodded. Narcissa looked from one to the other, her frustration growing into anger.

Mirrie spoke again. Her voice sounded cold, distant still, as if she were reading words someone else had written. "Louisa should not have let you come and stay here, knowing the position it would put you in. So I will tell you. Judah Daniel, please add anything you know, or correct anything I get wrong.

"There was a letter stolen from Jefferson Davis's home. Louisa had placed a servant in the house—Susy Reynolds, Selah's sister. The letter wound up here, in Louisa's possession, the day I came here for a visit."

Narcissa felt chilled. Devlin had told the truth about the women of this house. Louisa and her servants were spies. Mirrie had known.

Mirrie was still speaking in a cool, flat voice Narcissa hardly recognized. "I don't think Louisa expected anything to be brought out of Davis's so soon, or she might not have invited me; but once we were here, she was eager for us to stay. She told me it made her feel safer to have us here. I suppose she thought we—or you at least—might deflect suspicion from her. The letter supposedly detailed information about troop placements that would help the Union army take Richmond."

Our soldiers, Narcissa thought. They would die in battle, or be executed. Hard-hearted—yes. "And Louisa couldn't wait to pass it on."

"No! Louisa doesn't want to do anything that would help the Union win."

"I don't believe you." Narcissa's own voice sounded strange to her—cold, hateful.

"She doesn't!" Mirrie was almost sobbing now. "Not until the laws are passed to free the slaves. Don't you see? She believes that, if the Union won now, things might go back to the way they were: slave states, free states, laws that send escaped slaves back to their masters. That was the reason she wanted me here, from the first, I think—to listen to her reasons and support her—though she didn't tell me all the truth, not right away. She didn't tell me that she had placed Susy in Jefferson Davis's household, or about the letter. She kept circling around it, wanting me to understand why it was she hated slavery so much. Louisa, Susy, and Selah have been all in all to each other. When Louisa was young, her father sold the rest of the family, save for Selah and Susy, to the owner of the farm next to theirs. Years later, when Louisa inherited her father's wealth, she tried to buy them back. The owner refused. Can't you understand, knowing that, why Louisa feels as she does about slavery?"

Narcissa shook her head, rejecting what Mirrie seemed to think was a defense of Louisa. Mirrie was naive—that was the kindest interpretation she could make of her condoning treachery. And so Mirrie sympathized with the traitor, and believed what she said. Or agreed to lie to Narcissa. "Where is it now—this letter?"

Mirrie sighed, almost a sob. "She says she has it in a safe place—a place where she can get it, should Lincoln decide to free the slaves. Judah Daniel, what do you know?"

Judah Daniel too.

"I reckon Louisa'd been planning this for quite some time—maybe since the war broke out. She brung Susy down here from up north. Susy got work in Dr. Lester's house first, then with the Davises, like you said."

Dr. Lester. Jefferson Davis. How could two brilliant men be taken in this way? But perhaps they were the easiest to fool, these men who bore the burdens of the new government and the war. They would take for granted what they had always taken for granted—the running of their households, their servants. And perhaps they were not prepared to contemplate the idea that someone they saw every day could be harboring disloyal thoughts behind a mask of deference.

"Three days ago," Judah Daniel continued, "Susy give John Chapman something from there to take to Selah. I don't reckon he knowed what he was doing. He lost his son and his grandson just a few weeks back. Later Susy told John about the letter. She talked about it to him the same as Miss Ferncliff did to you—like it could end the war, but didn't say how. She told him somebody betrayed her. That's why she run away."

"Judah Daniel." Mirrie's voice was low, hesitant. "If this letter came into your hands somehow, what would you do with it?"

"Put it in the fire." Judah Daniel spoke with finality. "If it got into the hands of the Guard, and they found out the one who stole it from Davis's got away, it'd fall that much harder on anybody they thought helped. It'd be like turning loose a pack of wild dogs. Who knows who they'd fasten on?"

"What about the soldiers?" Narcissa heard the edge in her voice again, but this time she owned it hers. "Have you forgotten what that letter could do to *them* if it got out to the Union camp? I think Louisa is behind that man's death. He must have seen something. . . . Don't believe what she says to you, Mirrie. Even if she had feelings of love and loyalty once, they've turned to stone."

"If the dead man seen something," Judah Daniel offered, "might be the woman—the baby's mother—seen it too. If she ain't dead, I got an idea where she might be."

"If you're going to look for this letter," Narcissa told them, "I will help you. And I will see it destroyed. I don't trust you—either of you." She went around to the other side of the bed so that she could not see them. In a few moments they slipped away, leaving her alone. She felt as ill as if the fever were upon her again. She wished she were ill again—anything to escape the awful reality that two people who'd been close to her heart were traitors.

It wasn't long after Rosalie Stedman left the house that two detectives came to the door. The entire household was awakened and asked to gather in the front parlor. One of the detectives, a man named Parsons, asked Narcissa how she had found the body. She told him, and tried to watch the reactions of Louisa and Selah. She thought both looked tense and unhappy, but that proved nothing—under the circumstances, who would look otherwise?

Then Parsons turned on Louisa, who, despite the late hour, was fully dressed and bright-eyed as ever.

"There've been stories about you, ma'am, to the effect that you smuggle runaway slaves through your house. Was this man coming here?"

Louisa tilted up her chin and faced him. "No such charge has ever been proven against me, officer. But I can say this: if he had come to me for help, I would have given it to him to the best of my power."

Louisa was as much as admitting she'd smuggled slaves to freedom, and daring this Parsons to prove it. Narcissa felt her suspicions tilt away from Louisa, toward Devlin. If

Judah Daniel was right, that one percussive burst had blasted away a man's life and blown his family apart. Could Louisa, committed as she was to abolitionism, have done that? Or had the first explanation offered been the correct one: an accident, a nervous young man taking target practice at something that spooked him in the cemetery? Or could Devlin himself be after the letter? She wondered for a second if she should tell these men about the letter. If she could have pinned the blame on Louisa alone, she thought she would have told. But Mirrie, Judah Daniel . . . she had to keep them safe, whatever they might have done.

Narcissa had retired to her room and was preparing for bed when she heard Friday barking again, even more frantically than before. She went to the window. In a moment she saw what was exciting the dog. At the far end of the yard, a fire was burning in one of the wooden outbuildings. Friday, who was tied near the kitchen, was sounding the alarm. "It's a fire," Narcissa yelled to Judah Daniel. Selah was there already, knocking on Louisa's door and calling. Mirrie was pulling her wrapper around her. "Come on," Narcissa called, and led the way down the stairs.

In a few minutes the entire household—Louisa and Selah, Narcissa, Mirrie, and Judah Daniel—had run into the yard with pots, pitchers, and basins. They formed a line at the pump to fill the containers and pass them down to be hurled onto the fire. Judah Daniel—the strongest, by virtue of her work in the hospital laundry—stationed herself closest to the flames. Selah worked the pump. Louisa Ferncliff, wearing a lacy cap and a light silk wrapper, took her place in the line between Mirrie and Narcissa. As each load of water found its target, the flames hissed and spat with a kind of elemental anger. But the fire was small, the ground damp from days of rain. In ten minutes, more or less, it was over.

They stood for a moment. Louisa, red-faced and breathing hard, leaned on Selah. Judah Daniel used a stick to poke around in the sodden pile of ashes and charred wood, searching for any remaining spark.

"They hate me, you know." Louisa Ferncliff addressed the remark to Mirrie. "My neighbors, the soldiers, the city police. Any one of them could have done this, just to harass me, just to show me they could get to me any time."

Narcissa said nothing, but she wondered: Could it have been Devlin? Was he out there now, standing in the shadows, watching them? If he was, he would know she hadn't taken his advice to get away from Louisa Ferncliff's house. Why did he hate Louisa so? She was an abolitionist, a Unionist, disloyal in spirit if not in act; but he was a deserter—what cause would he have to fault someone else's loyalty?

Mirrie was standing holding on to Friday's leash. "If Friday hadn't barked, we might not have known until the fire had spread."

Louisa looked down at Friday, who gave her a crooked smile, one side of her mouth caught on a tooth. Louisa didn't smile back, but she said, "Very well. You may bring the dog into the house."

It was grudging, but Mirrie said simply, "Thank you."

Narcissa saw Selah turn toward Louisa, open her mouth as if to speak, then shut it and look down at the ground. Selah disagreed with Louisa's decision to admit Friday into the house—vehemently, if the expression on her face was any indication. Yet she did not speak. For all Louisa's rhetoric on the subject of freeing the slaves, Selah was still her servant, and Selah knew her place. Unless . . .

perhaps Selah was trying to save her mistress the embarrassment of public questioning. Maybe Selah intended to put her case in private. Would Louisa come back later and announce that she had changed her mind about having the dog in the house? If so, Narcissa would suspect Selah of having persuaded her. But it was hard to believe anyone could persuade Louisa Ferncliff of anything. At least Friday would be brought into the house, where she would be safer, and could raise the alarm if needed.

"Let's go in," Louisa ordered her servant. They moved slowly back toward the house, Narcissa last of all, imagining she felt Devlin's gaze.

Judah Daniel woke in the night, unsure of what had disturbed her. She got up and went over to the bed. Narcissa's forehead was cool, her breathing regular.

But before she could settle back into her chair beside the bed, Judah Daniel heard a little noise out in the hall—footfalls, and a whispered voice—had it said, "Selah"? She padded silently to the door and peered out from behind the doorframe into the dimly lit hall. Hurrying down the stairs, hunched over like she was crying, was Selah.

In a moment, Judah Daniel was after her. She walked softly, keeping near the wall so that the floorboards wouldn't squeak. From the top of the stairs, she glimpsed Selah going in the direction of the door that led to the side yard. But by the time Judah Daniel got to the door, Selah was nowhere to be seen.

Maybe she's gone to the privy? No sign that Selah or anyone else had been there in the last little while. *The kitchen?* No one there. *Hmm.* Over the kitchen were the servants' quarters. Strange, Selah living there alone, while Louisa stayed alone in the big house. Judah Daniel shrugged and went up the outside stairs to the door. After a few min-

utes, Selah answered her knock. She did look like she had
had an upset: her headcloth was askew, her skirt pulled
sideways. Likely she'd been getting undressed when Judah
Daniel knocked. Selah stood holding the candle while
they looked at each other.

Judah Daniel spoke first. "You and your mistress been
showing a lot of interest in that baby John Chapman
found near here."

Selah shrugged, an awkward movement of her shoulders that made the candle's flame bob. "Miss Ferncliff said
she wanted to help," Selah muttered.

"You done what she told you," Judah Daniel agreed.
"But then you changed your mind. Why?"

Selah looked away. "It seemed Elda was taking good
care of the child. It might not be so easy to get a wet nurse,
with things the way they are."

"How did Miss Ferncliff take it, you going against her
like that?"

Selah looked at her then. "Miss Ferncliff wants her way,
all right. But if it's something she can't have, she doesn't
waste time fretting about it."

"What about the quilt?"

The question caught Selah off her guard. Her eyes, her
hand, the candle, all wavered. "What quilt?"

"You took a quilt from the Chapmans' house."

"I—I used it to wrap the baby in." Selah's fingers fret-
ted with a button on her bodice.

Judah Daniel shook her head, not accepting the answer. "You brung back the baby but not the quilt."

Selah shrugged. "It was just a rag."

"I reckon it was you set the fire, to burn that quilt—not
somebody aiming to scare Miss Ferncliff. There was some
of them northern papers in it, like Miss Ferncliff got. And
you was the first to sound the alarm. Reckon you didn't
want any real harm done."

But Selah was on her guard now. The charge of having set the fire—which Judah Daniel had been counting on to shock her—drew only a little tightening of the mouth.

Judah Daniel pressed harder. "It was the quilt you wanted in the first place. Little babies look right much alike, don't they? But somebody see that quilt—somebody who knowed about fabrics and patterns and stitching—they'd know who the baby was and where he come from, as good or better than if they seen his face. And if they knowed where the baby come from, reckon they'd figure out where that black man buried in St. John's churchyard come from too."

Selah got very still. The candle lit her face from below, turning it into a mask. "You're poking around in what doesn't concern you, Judah Daniel. It doesn't concern John Chapman either. It'd be best for everybody if you don't ask any more questions."

Judah Daniel thought about what she'd seen just a few minutes before—Selah running away from her mistress's room, bent over like she was in pain, or in tears. "You think Louisa Ferncliff know what's best for you, and John Chapman, and your sister, and all of us? You went against Louisa about the baby, and she didn't like it, did she?"

Selah shook her head, not saying no, but saying there would be no more talking about it. The door swung shut; the bolt dropped into place. Selah had taken the candle, leaving Judah Daniel in the dark.

CHAPTER SIX

Brit had fallen asleep propped up against the wall of the hospital building. He remembered having sat there to rest for a few minutes. He had no idea how he'd managed to fall asleep, with all the noise and activity going on around him—the groaning of the wounded, the shouted commands of the surgeons, the horrible grating of saw on bone. It was hot; he reached into his jacket for his handkerchief. As he pulled it out, he realized there was something that should have been there, something he was missing: his dispatch. He felt again. It wasn't there. He felt around him on the floor, then sat up and ripped off the crumpled, sweat-soaked jacket. Nothing. He looked on the floor. Nothing. He thrust his hand into each shoe. Nothing.

His frantic activity caught the attention of a passing orderly. "Lose something?"

"Yes," Brit croaked. "My lucky charm."

"Ha!" The fellow laughed heartily. "Rats ate it, more'n likely."

Brit sat, head in hands. Could that be it? Could, would, rats eat a piece of paper? He realized he wouldn't be giving this notion a moment's thought, except that it was preferable to all the other explanations he could come up with.

He heard his name called and looked up. Cameron

Archer was beckoning to him. "All right, Wallace, I trust you're feeling rested." Brit had to smile at the grim joke. "We're going back out."

Brit joined the group of doctors, ambulance men, and orderlies that was moving out into the new day. At least, where he was going, Ownby would have the devil of a time trying to find him.

→>—<←

After breakfast, Narcissa told Mirrie that she felt strong enough to go with Judah Daniel to find the mother who'd left her baby in St. John's churchyard. It was warm already, turning hot. Judah Daniel had on a wide-brimmed straw hat she had plaited to shield her eyes against the sun's glare. Narcissa's small bonnet offered no defense from the sun, but the old black umbrella she carried cast a little circle of shade. It was one thing for a lady to wear a patched dress, quite another to allow sunlight to darken her skin.

And it was quiet. The continual sputtering of small arms fire—snipers, pickets, bored soldiers taking target practice at rabbits—had become as familiar to the ears of Richmonders as the sound of the river. As quiet as it was now, you could come close to forgetting that, a few miles away, deadly enemies faced each other.

"What makes you think Moses's mother might be at the Negro jail?" Narcissa asked Judah Daniel as they walked.

"News like somebody missing—a baby missing—don't take long to get around," replied Judah Daniel.

"Has it been in the papers? I haven't seen anything."

Judah Daniel smiled a little. "Folks passing this kind of news don't need the papers. One family's driver tell another family's cook, or two maid passing at the market, one tell the other. But since nobody heard nothing about this baby, nobody missing him, I figure he's not from around here. The dead man, too—could be he run away from someplace. They put up notices in front of the jail about runaways. Might be there's notices up about the man and the woman. Might be they even got her there."

"Do you think the patrollers could have caught up with them—shot him, and taken her to the jail?"

"Might be," Judah Daniel answered. " 'Course, the patrollers wouldn't kill him if they could help it. He belong to somebody, after all. And if they did kill him, stand to reason they'd not hide the body. They'd bring it back to show his owners and claim they had to do it."

Narcissa wasn't done with questions. "But the woman: her husband had just been shot. How could she have left her baby?"

"Well," Judah Daniel replied, "I figure it's like this. If there's a snake in the grass, or a crow circling, a mother bird leave the nest. Sometime she even act like she got a broken wing. Might be the woman doing the same thing—trying to draw the danger after her, away from her baby."

Narcissa nodded. She looked like she was swallowing something bitter. Despite the kind nature Narcissa had always shown, Judah Daniel wondered if she understood how black folks lived: not by laws—which were forged like chains to hold them in their place—but by mother-wit. It must seem to the people who made the laws that they were engraved in stone by God's own hand, like the Ten Commandments, but it wasn't so. The events of this day—or if not this day, some other day soon—could put the bottom rail on top in Richmond . . . could make Narcissa Powers one of those who had to take orders from Yankees. Narcissa had said nothing about this possibility, but it stood to reason she must think on it. Of course, John Chapman was probably right that the white folks would find a way, sooner or later, to get themselves back to giving the orders. Still, it might be good to let them see how the shoe pinched when it was on their feet.

Judah Daniel and Narcissa passed down Lumpkin Alley to the Negro Jail. They stopped outside to look at the bills offering rewards for the return of escaped slaves, describing their height, physique, skin tone, teeth, scars. There were dozens of the notices posted. With all the ruction of war and siege, there must be many more slaves escaping now than a couple of years ago. Then again, it might be harder to get the word out.

Narcissa scanned all the bills in turn, reading some portions aloud to Judah Daniel, who tried to keep her eyes from following the words. If the jailer suspected she could read, he might decide to question her, or her supposed mistress.

At last Narcissa turned back and whispered to Judah Daniel, "The man I found fits the bill for ten or a dozen escapees. But none of them describes a woman and a baby under a month old." Narcissa led the way to the door, where the jailer grinned, stretched himself, and sauntered over to meet them. "Name's Murphy. Can I help you, ma'am?"

Narcissa smiled back at him. "I would be most obliged to you. I'm Mrs. Bowman. A girl has run off from my brother's place in Hanover County. My brother's in the army, and my sister-in-law never had to manage by herself before. The girl was getting uppity, and my sister gave her a beating. The next morning, she was gone. She took her new baby with her. I expect she's doing a Yankee's laundry by now, but I promised my sister-in-law I would look for her."

The jailer seemed interested; whether he knew anything or enjoyed the attention of Narcissa Powers—*Mrs. Bowman!*—Judah Daniel could not tell, but he asked, "What's she look like?"

Narcissa hesitated just a moment. "They've had her less than a year. I've never seen her. She's a middling-brown color, and she's young and strong, but shiftless. My sister-in-law thinks she will give up the baby if it becomes too burdensome, and that's one reason she's anxious to get her back. After all, that baby is my brother's property."

The jailer nodded. "Yes'm, well, maybe I got the gal you looking for. They brung her in a couple days ago. She been sick ever since. I had my wife look at her. She said she had a problem with her females, like she done had a baby. But the girl told her the baby died."

"Oh, can I talk to her?" Narcissa asked eagerly. The jailer turned to lead the way, and Narcissa followed a few steps, then called back over her shoulder, her voice rougher than the honeyed tones she'd used with the jailer. "Come *on*, Judith."

Judah Daniel hurried to catch up. *Judith*—her name in slavery. She had told that name to Narcissa, but this was the first time the white woman had called her by it. Narcissa Powers fell easily into the role of mistress. But Judah Daniel could not resent it. Even now she might be about to find the woman who was Moses's mother.

The jailer Murphy opened a door into a small, stinking cell. It was as hot as a washhouse, and so dark that Judah Daniel could just make out the figure on the pallet.

"What's the name of your sister's gal?" the jailer asked Narcissa.

"Tabitha," Narcissa answered. "It's in the Bible. Peter raised Tabitha from the dead."

"Well, best of luck to you in doing the same. Now if you'll excuse me—" The jailer stepped aside. Judah Daniel turned her head just a fraction to watch as he disappeared out the door and into what was, by contrast, the cool, fresh air of morning. Then she went in and crouched down next to the figure on the pallet. As her eyes grew accustomed to the dark, she could see that it was a young woman. She put her hand on her shoulder. The woman's skin was hot and dry. Judah Daniel increased the pressure a little, and spoke to her in a gentle voice. The woman turned her head away from the sound.

Just behind Judah Daniel, Narcissa murmured, "The poor thing. Is there anything you can do for her?"

"I got to get a better look at her."

"I'll get a candle." Narcissa hurried out. Judah Daniel found a glazed clay cup with water in it and held it to the woman's lips. A little might have trickled into her mouth, but the rest ran unheeded down her cheek and onto the sheet.

After a few moments, Narcissa returned with a tallow candle. By its light Judah Daniel could see a woman of about twenty, wearing a skirt and a man's shirt worn soft by many washings—the gift of Murphy's wife, maybe, who must have a little more feeling in her than her husband. Judah Daniel pulled the shirt up and, with her fingertips, touched the woman's breasts with a gentle pressure. This woman had the same problem that had plagued Elda before Moses came to her: breasts that were hard and lumpy and hot with fever. This was likely the "problem with her females" the jailer's wife had found. It happened to women who stopped nursing their babies without weaning them gradually. It happened to women whose babies died, which was why Judah Daniel had had Elda express her milk. A woman could die of it. But she had found Moses's mother, and she was not going to let her die.

Narcissa held the candle as Judah Daniel continued her examination. At last Judah Daniel straightened the sheet over the woman they had called Tabitha and stood next to Narcissa.

"Can you help her?" Narcissa asked in a low tone.

"I can try."

Narcissa nodded. "Well, then. I'll fix it so we can come back."

"If you can—" Judah Daniel hesitated, but Narcissa nodded again, encouraging her to speak her mind. "If you can, fix it so I can come alone, if need be."

Narcissa led the way out of the room and down the hall. Outside the door they saw Murphy leaning back in his chair, his hat slanted low over his eyes.

"Mr. Murphy!" Narcissa's voice cracked like a whip. The jailer pulled off his hat and got to his feet.

"I can't tell if that girl is Tabitha or not. She's too sick to answer questions. But if she doesn't belong to my brother, she belongs to someone. You ought to be ashamed of yourself, treating folks' valuable property like that. I'm sending Judith back here with some medicine. And I'll be coming back myself when the girl can talk sense."

"Yes, ma'am," seemed to be all the stunned jailer could say.

From the jail, they went their separate ways, Narcissa back up to Church Hill and Judah Daniel down to the bakeshop on Main Street. She'd decided not to tell John Chapman just yet that she thought she had found Moses's mother. Instead she asked about the parcel she'd had Darcy make up for her. John, who was busy rolling out piecrust, pointed across the room to a folded-up piece of brown paper.

Judah Daniel took up the paper and spread it out on the clean-scrubbed plank table. John walked over to see. As Judah Daniel had asked her to do, Darcy had drawn the pattern of the quilt taken by Selah from the Chapman house—the quilt that had wrapped Moses. Darcy had done her work with careful strokes of charcoal on the back of a piece of wallpaper that looked roughly as large as the quilt itself had been. The drawing showed a distinctive pattern—a Wagon Wheel with the corners rounded off so the area between the narrow "spokes" of the wheel looked like the petals of a flower. The pattern was repeated three times in row. Under it ran a thick line drawn in charcoal. Then the pattern began again, repeated for half a dozen rows.

"Did Darcy recollect if the pieces was stitched or tied?" Judah Daniel asked.

"Stitched," John answered.

"Hmm. What's this remind you of—this shape?"

John shrugged. "A flower? We got more than a dozen quilts at the house. I don't think I could tell you what any one of 'em look like."

With her forefinger, Judah Daniel traced the outline. "Try to see *this* as the thing"—she said, indicating the spokes—"and *this* as what you see around it, and through it." She poked her finger at the petals, each in turn. "Then what's it look like?"

"Well, now that you mention it, it do put me in mind of something. Hold it up." Darcy did so. John squinted at the shapes drawn on the paper. "It look like that wrought-iron gate at Miss Ferncliff's place."

Judah Daniel nodded.

John was interested now. "Know who made that gate, back about twenty year ago? Web Clark."

Web was an old man, but still strong and vigorous. Judah Daniel knew him well.

John went on. "Ferncliff paid him a pretty penny. Web was a fine blacksmith; you can see his work all over town."

Caught up in the memory, John had lost interest in the quilt. Judah Daniel didn't call him back to it. It wasn't surprising he didn't see anything of meaning there. After all,

John had been born and raised free. And Darcy could scarcely remember her first few years, spent among slaves. But Selah, or Louisa at least, must have known what the quilt meant, since she had gone to some trouble to get possession of it.

Web Clark was an old man, but his years of blacksmithing had left him strong, and he had been pressed into helping put up more hospital barracks at Chimborazo. John Chapman agreed to slight the hotels some of their biscuits, and when his deliveries in town were finished, he and Judah Daniel carried them up to where Web was working. He and two dozen other men—a motley collection of free blacks, slaves, and wharf-rat whites—put down their saws and hammers to join in the feast. Even the foremen were happy enough to stop work at the prospect of fresh biscuits.

Judah Daniel took the opportunity to slip over to Web.

"I sure do miss John Chapman's biscuits," Web told her, his bass voice fairly lilting with the pleasure of the moment.

"You made the wrought-iron gate at the Ferncliff house, that right?"

Web raised his eyebrows in surprise. He finished chewing, wiped crumbs and butter from his mouth, and said, "That right. But that was a good twenty year ago."

"Cast iron been fashionable for quite some time. The fence rails is cast iron, right? So why have the gate made special?"

"Miss Louisa Ferncliff wanted it," he answered.

"Did she suggest that design to you?"

Was it her imagination, or was Web looking uneasy? His eyes were fixed on the second biscuit, which he held like a little jewel in his huge, work-roughened hand. "Miss Ferncliff," he answered. "She were a young lady then. Had her father wrapped around her finger. She drawed it out for me on a piece of paper." He put the rest of the biscuit in his mouth and chewed the mouthful.

Judah Daniel looked up into his eyes. He had to know that it was the truth she needed. "Did it strike you that it looked like a quilt design called the Wagon Wheel? One of the quilts the slaves hang out to let folks know to get ready to run?"

Web looked at her a long time, chewing slowly. At last he swallowed and said quietly, "That was what she wanted." He looked around to where the foremen were finishing their biscuits and ordering the men back to work. "I know Miss Ferncliff ain't the easiest person to get along with. But by their works shall you know them. She done a lot of good for folks in need." He turned again, answering the foreman's shout, "Yes, sir, I'm coming.

"Thank you for the biscuits, Judah Daniel. If Miss Ferncliff need any help, you let me know." There was kindness in his face and voice, but also a warning. The Loyal Brethren—the loose connection of individuals who for years had moved slaves out from the South to freedom in Canada—were protective of each other's secrets.

Narcissa passed through the regiment of whitewashed buildings, row upon row of them, that made up Chimborazo. Some of those who had been wounded the day before in the fighting around Mechanicsville were sitting in the buildings' shadows, speculating about the battle taking place only a few miles away. They, she knew, were the fortunate ones. Others had been left where they'd fallen, because there were not enough men to go and get them, to treat the wounded, to bury the dead.

Where is the glory in this? she thought. Nothing is what it seems. Everything is ugly and depraved and rotten at its core. . . .

"Mrs. Powers!"

The voice she had never heard before, but the face was familiar, though the smile was that of a man, no longer the mocking grin of a skull. It was Sergeant Smith. His flesh was wasted to nearly nothing, but he was sitting propped up in the shade of Ward 27, squinting into the sun, calling to her in a voice hoarse from disuse. He took her hand in both of his. They were the hands she remembered, callused from hard use, but now they could return the pressure of her own. Sergeant Smith had wrestled with death just as Jacob wrestled with the angel, and death had let him go—one man among so many thousands gone.

She knelt beside him and looked into his eyes, bright with life now and not with fever.

"They say I'm going to live." Smith's voice was low, shy as his smile. "My wife's coming for me. I'll be going home. If"—he glanced down at the place where his leg had been—"if she'll still have me."

"Of course she will! She will be proud of you. I know it. Here—take this rose for her." Narcissa took the rosebud out of her waistband and held it out to Smith.

"I'm much obliged," he told her. "I'll press it in my Bible. She was always partial to roses." His fingers touched the petals of a white rose that had opened just beyond the bud. "She carried white roses as a bride. It's been thirteen years last month." He stuck the rose through his buttonhole. Narcissa glimpsed for a moment the young bridegroom he had been, brown-haired, slight but strong. It was a miracle he had lived. Surely good would come of it.

She stood up then to go. Smith seemed to want to hold her in conversation a moment longer. "I heard you were sick," he said.

"It's tertian fever. I had a fever yesterday; today, I'm fine. As for tomorrow—" She shrugged. "It's not so terrible. But it made me realize more than ever how much you all suffer here, being away from your loved ones."

"It was you," Smith said softly, "that saved my life. Not the medicine. Not the doctors. You reminded me why I wanted to live. It's hard to remember sometimes, when flies and rats are crawling over you, and you can't move a muscle to brush 'em off. When you're lying there, there's folks that treat you like a human being, read the Bible and such, even just brush the flies away. The men appreciate it, whether they can ever say so or not. Then there's folks that talk like we can't hear, like we were animals or dead men already."

"They are not all so callous as they seem," Narcissa told him, remembering Cameron Archer. "It's just that they concentrate on the wound, or the disease, so completely that they may lose sight of the person. It might help them not to feel too deeply," she added, "because, so many times, their efforts are in vain."

"Maybe so," Smith answered. "But still it meant a lot for me to have you come by, even for a little while. And the older woman, too—she was good to that man with the bandaged head, and the other men. Then that Wright—I won't use the word that comes to mind for him—he drove her off, said she was stealing drugs."

He must mean Annie, Narcissa realized. And so the man with the bandaged head was Devlin. "What happened to him—the man with the head injury?"

"He woke up. I'm glad it happened before Wright drove her off. I think it'd be some consolation to her."

"He woke up . . . and she knew it?" Narcissa hesitated, choosing her words carefully.

Smith nodded. "I saw them talking. He looked like he wanted to jump right out of that bed." He chuckled. "I reckon I know how he felt. Anyway, she got him calmed down."

"Who else saw them?"

Smith shrugged. "Don't know if anyone did."

"I heard he had to be carried out," Narcissa commented, trying to sound offhand. "You didn't see the men who took him away?"

"No. I didn't see that."

"Well . . . thank you. You rest now. You have a long journey ahead of you. If the rose doesn't last until your wife gets here, don't worry. There will be more at home."

Back at Marshall Street, Narcissa hesitated. Oakwood Cemetery received most of the dead from Chimborazo. James Yates's father was buried there, and Annie had said she went there often. She could go there first and see if she could find Annie. It was out of her way; but she would prefer to meet Annie there rather than return to that decaying ruin of a house at the edge of Bloody Run.

Devlin was alive, and Annie, who'd nursed him, probably knew it. Maybe Annie had felt sorry for him, just as Narcissa had. She might know something about him that would give a clue as to why he had stayed, why he was watching Louisa's house.

No musicians had turned out to play the Dead March—not today. The drummers and buglers were in the field, relaying the officers' commands to their troops. But the other observances went on in force. At least a dozen men were digging graves and lowering the coffins into them. Close by, other men were putting up rough wooden crosses. Here and there, one or a group of black-dressed figures were gathered, many of them women. One of those lone women might be Annie. Her husband had been dead only a few weeks; there was no need to look for his grave among those covered with luxuriant grass or marked with substantial stones.

There, she thought, singling out the thin figure of a

woman whose black dress gave off no silken sheen. Or there, she added, seeing another. Half a dozen women, at least, could be Annie. She decided to begin with the one closest to her. Before she reached her, though, she could tell she had made a mistake, and she took the path that branched to the right, to the next closest mourner.

She knew before the woman turned around that it was Annie—knew by the peculiar tint of her dress and the way she held her shoulders. She was kneeling in front of the wooden cross marking a grave.

Narcissa came up behind her. "Annie," she said gently.

Annie spun around. Her eyes had the dazed look of one whom the mesmerist has just awakened. She scrambled to her feet and turned to face Narcissa, almost as if she were defending the grave against this interloper. Over Annie's shoulder, she read the largest of the few words printed on the marker's crosspiece—JOHN YATES.

"I'm sorry to bother you. There's something I want to ask you. The man you were taking care of in Ward 27, the day we met?" Annie made no sign of having heard. "Why didn't you tell me he was alive? You knew it. You talked with him."

"Who?" Annie seemed so inert, Narcissa wondered if she were ill.

"Devlin," Narcissa answered, trying to keep the impatience she felt out of her voice. "That was what they called him; no one seems to know who he is, or was, really. You must remember. His head was bandaged. You talked to him; I knew that. I didn't know he answered you. Didn't it surprise you, when I told you he had died?"

"Well . . . ," Annie said slowly, "I reckon he's dead by now."

"Why?" Narcissa couldn't keep her voice from rising. "Why should he be?"

Annie made a small gesture with her hands. "Look around you."

"But he got away," Narcissa told her, near to weeping with frustration. "I know he's alive. I've seen him."

Annie looked frightened now. "Seen him where?"

"In the churchyard at St. John's Church."

Annie shook her head. "He ain't buried at St. John's Church. He laying someplace with the dirt over him."

Narcissa stooped a little, trying to look into Annie's eyes. "Annie . . . *Devlin is alive.*"

Annie shook her head. "I don't know what you talking about. My boy named Jimmy. Jimmy Yates."

Annie waited, deferential, while Narcissa tried to think of some words to say to bring Annie out of her confusion. At last Narcissa gave up. At another time, maybe, in another place than this graveyard, she could talk to Annie and get some sort of sensible answer. "Good-bye, Annie," she said at last. "Go home, rest; try not to take it all so much to your heart. We'll talk another day."

The fight raged on under a burning sun, across a field of trampled corn and broken men. Again and again the Confederates started out across the field, then down into the creek. From the higher ground on the other side the Federals rained down a withering fire. On the crest of that ground Brit could see the flash and smoke of cannons, the dark-clad men. But of the hundreds, thousands, of gray-clad soldiers who ran out, none made it to the top of the rise. Some fell back, but what had happened to the others? The ditch must be filling with bodies. Yet somehow, against all reason, the Confederates kept up their onslaught.

Brit was working with a Negro man, the servant of an officer, combing the ground for men whose lives could be saved. When they found one, they would get him back to the wagon. Then, when there was no more room in the wagon, they would drive it back to the field hospital. What made a hospital, Brit discovered, was the presence of a surgeon—no more, no less. This "hospital" had been set up under the shade of some oak trees. Archer and Coster were there, fastening tourniquets and bandaging wounds, amputating if it seemed necessary to save a life. At some point, Brit realized that the voice he heard always in his head—the voice of the reporter, the recorder, putting what he saw and heard into words—had fallen silent.

Up at the Negro Jail, the guard named Murphy grunted, stretched, and led Judah Daniel back inside to where the woman, whoever she was—Tabitha was the name Narcissa had come up with—was locked up. Then he shambled off, not bothering to relock the door behind him. He must have thought Tabitha was too feeble or too frightened to make trouble. But Judah Daniel had seen something else in the woman. Even weak with fever, grieving for her husband, separated from a son she might never see again, Tabitha had held firm to her story—her baby was dead. Just the bad luck of saying it would make a weaker woman quail. Judah Daniel knew that, if she were ever in the position of being this woman's jailer, she would see to it that the door was locked.

Judah Daniel lowered herself onto the floor close to the pallet where Tabitha lay. "You recollect who I am?"

Tabitha shrugged. "You saved my life." She did not sound grateful.

Judah Daniel sighed. "I hope you ain't going to hold that against me." She took hold of Tabitha's left forearm and put her fingers on the inside of the wrist. Tabitha's skin was cooler to the touch than it had been, and her pulse beat slow and steady. Judah Daniel pulled a stoppered pipkin out of the wicker basket she had carried in over her arm. She poured beef tea into a tin cup. Tabitha turned on her side, took the cup, and drank. Her green-gold eyes, set with a little tilt like a Chinaman's, watched Judah Daniel over the edge of the cup.

"If I'd of known how to save your baby without you having to draw another breath, I reckon I'd of let you go like you wanted me to."

Tabitha set the cup down. A slight smile curved the corners of her mouth, and her eyelids drooped—a look that an exacting mistress would have punished with a slap. "I told you, my baby dead."

"Moses safe. We call him Moses. Want to tell me the name you give to him?" She waited a moment; getting no reaction, she went on. "I talked to the blacksmith, Web Clark. Maybe you know his name. I know the Loyal Brethren don't give their names most times."

Tabitha stared straight ahead, giving no sign she had heard.

Judah Daniel shook her head slowly and sighed again. "He's safe, for the time being. But might be there's a danger hanging over him and his new momma and his new brother. What-all's going on, it look like a crazy quilt, but they's a pattern to it. Like this one." She thrust her hand into her apron pocket and pulled out the charcoal drawing Darcy had done of the quilt found with Moses. She held it out in front of Tabitha. The young woman's eyes widened, but she made no move to take the paper.

"When I seen this quilt, I knowed you got the signal to run. You come up here to a big house—one with an iron gate made in the Wagon Wheel pattern. You, and your man, and your baby—thinking you was going to freedom.

"Something gone wrong. Your man got shot dead. You was afraid you'd get caught. So you left your baby where he'd most likely be safe, in the churchyard. And you run, I reckon, till you couldn't run no more."

The girl was listening, Judah Daniel thought, but she was holding herself still like an animal whose only defense is not to be seen. Judah Daniel regretted not having the quilt itself for Tabitha; seeing the quilt that she'd last seen wrapped around her baby would have more of an effect. Too much effect, might be. Judah Daniel wondered whether, if it came down to it, she'd have to break the girl's heart to get at her secret.

"Did she give y'all something—the lady in that house, or her servant? A piece of paper, to take with you to the Yankees?"

The girl drew in a breath and let it out. Other than that, she didn't move. She didn't look at Judah Daniel. She didn't appear to have heard. Judah Daniel studied her face in profile. She was a beautiful girl, the color of milky coffee, with thick curling eyelashes and full lips that curved apart like the petals of a flower. Her baby would be a handsome man—strong-spirited, too, if he took after his mother. And his father, who gave his life for the hope of freedom.

Judah Daniel wanted to say, You got to help us. If John Chapman and his family lose their freedom, all you done to make your son a free man will be in vain. But what came out was, "Don't fret about your son. He ain't gone be no slave. I don't know every last thing God intend on this earth, but I know that." The words came straight from God out of her mouth without her even thinking about them. How it would work out, how long it would take or what troubles would come between, He didn't see fit to tell her.

Judah Daniel walked back up to Church Hill. The fighting was still intense, and the looks on people's faces were anxious for the most part. Things were bad, no doubt about it; but if the Yankees triumphed, it would be like living through a tornado, having everything thrown upside down. Would the city burn? Would the slaves rise up and take revenge on their owners, as some of the whites feared? Would the whites, maddened by their own fears, turn on their slaves first? No . . . likely none of this would happen. From what they'd heard, it hadn't happened in New Orleans. But to be living in times like these, it was hard to know what to pray for. *Thy will be done, Lord; and when it is, give me the strength to accept it.*

→>—<←

Narcissa stood at the window of her bedroom, looking out into the darkness. The house built by Louisa's father stood tall above the homes of lesser merchants; over their roofs, Narcissa could glimpse the procession that was moving up Marshall Street, two blocks away, to the hospitals at Chimborazo. Through the open window she could hear the jingle and creak of the wagons, the cries of the teamsters, the groaned prayers and curses of the wounded for whom every jolt was agony.

To stand here wringing her useless hands was its own sort of torture. Even here, no breeze came to lift the damp hair from her face. How those men must be suffering, in their sweat-soaked wool uniforms, with no drink of water maybe since yesterday morning. . . .

She could take water from Louisa's well and help at least a few of them to drink it. She knew where to find a cup and a bucket; she need not tell anyone or seek anyone's permission.

Out on the street, every kind of conveyance—farm wagons, two-wheeled and four-wheeled army ambulances, private carriages and carts—was crammed to overflowing with the wounded from yesterday's battle at Mechanicsville . . . and with those who had died along the way.

Most had had no medical care at all, so that their wounds
bled openly, or were stanched with a makeshift bandage
torn off someone's shirt. Some held their heads or supported their ruptured limbs, arms, and legs that the doctors would soon cut away in hopes of preserving life. The
luckiest of them had fainted. The vehicles creaked along,
slowed by the heat, the work of climbing, and the conges-
tion of the street. Some of the wounded came on foot,
supported by comrades or sympathetic strangers—old
men, young boys, servants, women. And others like herself, with ghostly pale, set faces, moved among them, offering sips of water to those whom they could reach. In
the light of torches, the street fairly ran with blood.

There was some kind of disturbance up ahead—voices
raised, questions and cries of anger. The line slowed to a
crawl as angry drivers cursed and threatened the ones in
front of them. Then the shout came down the line to
where Narcissa was standing, steadying a young boy's
trembling hands around the cup: "Doctors say there's no
more room! Take 'em back down the hill!" No room at
Chimborazo, with its three thousand beds?

"Damned if I will!" growled the wagon's driver, raising
himself to stand in his seat. "Come on! They'll just have to
find the room." He whipped his horses, and they strained
forward. Narcissa squeezed the hand of the boy she'd
given water to and saw his lips mouth the word *Thanks.*

"Mrs. Powers!"

It was Brit Wallace's voice, calling to her from somewhere
back in the line. She stepped back onto the curb and
searched the faces of the crowd. There he was, driving a
wagon containing four—no, five wounded men, on her side
of the road. She hurried over to him, passed the cup into the
hands of an eager soldier, then walked alongside Brit.

Brit called out to her over the din, "I've been helping
Archer with the wounded. He went on ahead on horse-

back; I expect he's there now." Brit nodded in the direction of Chimborazo.

"They say there's no more room," Narcissa called back, her voice roughened by the knot in her throat.

"And that's one reason," Brit yelled back, "that I'm not going there. These men are bound for the Ferncliff Receiving Hospital. Don't worry—they're not the worst off by any means. But they're from the First Maryland Artillery, so they won't have the comfort of their own people around them, or loved ones searching for them, since their families are behind the lines on the other side."

Narcissa looked again at the wagon. The men's faces were grimed black with powder, but the expressions of most were animated. They were talking among each other and looking around, though a couple sat propped up against their fellows, and bandages were evident on most. One caught her eye and handed her the now-empty cup. She refilled it and handed it back to him. He held it for the man next to him, who had both hands bandaged and seemed to be in considerable pain.

Narcissa jogged to keep up with Brit. "I don't think Louisa Ferncliff will allow these men to be brought into her house."

"Oh, I think she will," Brit replied quite coolly, though the set of his jaw told a different story. "Most of the large homes in town are taking in wounded. Dr. Lester suggested it, and I don't think she will oppose him."

When he drew near to the high wall of St. John's Church, Brit turned the horses. The driver behind him closed the gap: there would be no second chance for Brit to take that route to Chimborazo. Narcissa walked alongside the wagon, her bucket now empty; there was nothing she could do for the present, but her heart rose at the thought of being able to care for these men. The question was, what would Louisa Ferncliff do?

"I had better go and tell Miss Ferncliff," she called up to Brit, quickening her pace to get there ahead of him. "And get the house ready."

As she hurried away, she was dimly aware that a figure on horseback had turned down Grace Street and was coming up behind Brit's wagon. Was one of the surgeons coming to overrule Brit's decision? Well, she couldn't fret about it. She had more than enough to handle with Louisa and Selah.

"I absolutely forbid it."

Louisa's reaction fell nothing short of Narcissa's expectation. Louisa had come to the door of her bedchamber, roused by Narcissa's knocking and Selah's protests of "Miss Ferncliff can't be disturbed," and stood there, dark eyes bright in her pale face, holding herself to the full extent of her five-foot height. "Confederate soldiers, in *my home.* There is no power on Earth that can make me accept it."

"Bend to the power of heaven, then, Louisa," Narcissa answered, "because I do not believe that you can prevent it. Now, Selah," she went on, turning to the servant, "help me move the furniture, so that it does not get bloody."

Selah looked to her mistress for guidance; but Louisa, after a moment of staring, speechless, at Narcissa, slammed the door in both their faces. A moment later they heard the key turn in the lock.

"You can't do this." Selah followed Narcissa, protesting with every step. "Miss Ferncliff—it'll kill her."

"I think Miss Ferncliff is stronger than that," Narcissa responded mildly.

Selah went from pleading to threats. "She's got powerful friends in this city. She can get you all arrested."

Narcissa turned and faced her. "Listen to me, Selah. Miss Ferncliff cannot afford to refuse. And don't you see?

To have wounded soldiers in the house, and surgeons coming by, will make us all safer."

Narcissa led the way into the front parlor, grabbed a little rosewood chair, carried it to the far end of the room, and placed it behind the piano. She went back and grabbed one end of a long settee. Selah waved her hands, shook her head, and seemed to be calling for divine retribution to strike Narcissa down—but at last she took the other end of the settee, and the two of them carried it also to a place of safety behind the piano. They did this with lamps, vases, chairs, a walnut card table, a stuffed cassock, and several spindly tables loaded with bric-a-brac. At last Narcissa stood surveying the open floor. "Good. . . . It's fortunate the carpets are up for the summer, this matting is so much cooler. . . . Oh! Here they are."

Narcissa ran to the front door and down the steps to the street, where the wagon had drawn up. A little crowd of people—it was too dark to tell how many—was gathering, offering themselves to help the wounded.

A moment later Louisa came out behind her and stepped up to the edge of the porch. Louisa had caught up a candle mounted in a hurricane globe and was holding it out from her toward the group that had gathered, but its light was too faint to illumine their faces. Now she spoke up, her voice shaking a little with fear, anger, or both. "Sir!" Brit looked up. Narcissa saw the look of grim determination on his face.

"This is my house! My father was an important person in this town for many years. I insist on my rights!"

A woman's voice—Narcissa could not see the speaker—shot back: "She's nothing but a traitor!"

"I expect she'd rather take in *Yankee* soldiers!" a man yelled.

"I have my rights," Louisa said again. "There is sickness

in this house already. You can't force me to open my house to—"

Louisa took a step back. A small, thin woman had come out of the shadows into the lantern light. She was running straight at Louisa, as if she meant to throw herself on her. It was Annie Yates.

Narcissa stepped forward to intercept her. "Have you come to help with the wounded, Annie? Thank you." Narcissa put her hand on Annie's arm. Her voice and touch seemed to call the woman back from someplace far away.

"I—" There was a long pause, but at last Annie said, "I reckon so."

"Well, then, let's see what we can do." Narcissa kept her hand on Annie's shoulder, steering her back toward the wagon.

Louisa seemed to realize she'd lost the battle. "They're not to be allowed near the basement," she called after Narcissa. "I keep spirits down there. If those men were to get into it—" Louisa turned and swept into the house, queenly even in defeat. Narcissa thought she was probably on her way to lock up the liquor.

Another figure appeared out of the darkness—Dr. Lester. His uniform was so blood-spattered that he could have been wounded himself. Narcissa left Annie under Brit's direction and went to meet Lester. What could have induced such a man to sign a false death certificate for a deserter? It must have been a mistake—so many wounded men, one paper in a sheaf to be signed. . . . Seeing him now, she couldn't suspect him of treachery.

"Mrs. Powers." Lester saluted her. "I'm glad to see you looking well. We shall all have our hands full. I'm on my way up there. But first, let me see what needs doing here. Bring them in, gently, now." They watched as the first of the wounded men were placed onto an improvised stretcher and carried into the house. Then Lester turned back to Narcissa. "I'd be a little careful of Annie Yates if I were you. She looks on the verge of a nervous collapse."

"And who could blame her if she were," Narcissa answered, "considering what she's been through." It isn't only soldiers who are wounded, she thought; and all wounds do not show on the outside.

Brit went back to the empty wagon. He realized he couldn't take it the way he had come—the street was full of traffic, all moving toward Chimborazo if it was moving at all. He could drive around St. John's Church and try a different route. So he led the horses down the street and around the corner, away from the noise and the wavering light from the torches. They were walking past St. John's Church, moving into a cooler, quieter, darker place than the hectic scene they had left behind. Although he was eager to fetch more wounded men, Brit couldn't resist slowing his pace, just for a moment, so he could take in the otherworldly comfort of the church on the hill above him. Then, in the shadows at the edge of the churchyard, he caught sight of a figure beckoning to him. He stepped closer.

"Wallace! Over here." The voice sounded muffled.

Brit stepped closer. From the corner of his eye, he saw something move, so quick it was just a blur. Before he could react, the thing caught him on the side of the head and drove him to the ground.

Back in Louisa Ferncliff's parlor-turned-hospital, the men had had their wounds bandaged. Some had managed to eat something, while others had been dosed fairly heavily with morphine. Brit had left long ago to go to the aid of more wounded men. Judah Daniel was at work in the kitchen. After several hours of tending to them, Narcissa felt the men were old acquaintances: Arthur Gilman, shot through the shoulder; James Trimble, deafened and headachy from a shell exploded near his head; Edward Hardegree, wounded in the upper arm; Abram Winters, bruised and lacerated from spent shell fragments; and Richard Cashion, burned on both hands by the heat of the cannon he was loading.

Selah came into the room from somewhere in the back of the house, carrying two squat bottles coated with dust and cobwebs. These Selah placed on the sideboard. She then opened a little door in the sideboard and took out a wineglass, holding its delicate stem between her thumb and forefinger. She set it carefully on the sideboard's marble top, then brought out another, and another, until there were eight of them.

"Miss Ferncliff told me to open some of her father's brandy for the soldiers—and for you, Miss Powers and Mrs. Powers." Selah's back was stiff, and she spoke the words as if she'd memorized phrases in a foreign language.

"Please tell Miss Ferncliff we are much obliged to her," responded Narcissa, echoing Selah's formality.

Selah filled the first glass, and Narcissa watched as the etched design, delicate as frost on a windowpane, took on the dark-honey glow of the brandy. Gravely she took the glass from Selah and took it over to Hardegree. He was already drowsy from the morphine administered by the surgeons, but he smiled and sipped down the liquid from the glass she held to his lips. "That's mighty good," he murmured, drew the back of his hand across his mouth, and closed his eyes.

Selah finished filling the glasses, then helped Gilman to drink; she was patient, Narcissa noted. Narcissa saw him speak to her, and saw Selah shrug in response—dismissing his thanks, Narcissa imagined. Narcissa helped Winters while Selah moved briskly on to Trimble. Mirrie, who had been reading to him, accepted a glass as well. Friday, lying next to her, looked up expectantly. "You can't have any," Mirrie joked, drawing a laugh from Trimble.

Narcissa picked up a glass and took it to Cashion. She held him to sit up and held the glass for him, since his hands were burned. Cashion sipped, shuddered at the strength of it, then drained the glass in a draft. He nodded toward the remaining glasses on the sideboard. "One of them's for you, Mrs. Powers, remember," he jested, "by order of Miss Ferncliff."

Selah must have heard him, for she picked up a glass and brought it to Narcissa. "Take it."

"All right." Narcissa turned and took the glass from Selah. It looked as fragile as a soap bubble. But if the glass was delicate, the brandy was as strong as she imagined the soldiers' stump-brewed alcohol might be. She took one sip; the liquid burned her lips and tongue and seemed to run like fire through her veins. Before she could take another sip, her hand began to shake. The glass fell from her fingers and smashed on the floor. "Oh! I'm sorry!" She looked over at Selah, who glanced away, a tight little smile on her face. Selah had the last glass in her hand. No doubt she planned to take it up to Louisa. How Selah would enjoy telling Louisa that Narcissa had broken one of her precious wineglasses. As she watched, Selah started slowly up the stairs, carrying the wineglass as if it were the Holy Grail.

The medicine had not worked. The fever was coming again. She would have to tell Mirrie to take over as matron of the Ferncliff Receiving Hospital. Mirrie wouldn't welcome the appointment, but there was nothing she could do about that.

+>-<-

Narcissa lay shivering in the dark, wishing someone would come and fetch the blankets and quilts from the little trunk across the room and add them to the two that were already on the bed. She wished she could do it herself, but she was too cold to uncurl her back, stretch out her legs, get up. . . . The very thought of the air striking her skin sent another, stronger wave of shivers through her.

She lay there a long time, too miserable to think. At last she heard the door creak open. The light from the hall silhouetted a figure who slipped in, then pushed the door almost closed. She licked her dry lips and whispered, "Mirrie?"

Her visitor—Mirrie, Judah Daniel, whoever it was— must not have heard her, must not know she was awake. Careful, padding footsteps brought the visitor to stand over her. She turned her head to see the face, but the little bit of light was in her eyes, and she could see nothing.

Her movement brought a reaction. The shadow receded, moving back toward the door. The light streamed in from the hall, just for a moment, and was blotted out again as the door closed. But she had seen enough this time to tell it was a man—and one who, by his actions, had no business in her room. She told herself it was a mistake: one of the wounded men, or a doctor perhaps, had gotten lost. It couldn't be Devlin; he'd not have dared to come here. Still she lay for a long time, shivering with fear as well as cold. Nothing happened; no one came. At last she fell asleep.

CHAPTER SEVEN

JUNE 28

Early in the morning, more soldiers began to arrive at Louisa Ferncliff's—not patients, but some who were well enough to come down from Chimborazo as orderlies, or simply as visitors in search of their comrades. Dr. Coster stopped in to take a look at the wounded. "McClellan's in retreat," he announced, his tired face bright with pride and relief. The men cheered him, then began to talk with one another, as if the words themselves had gone a long way toward curing them. Coster went up to see Narcissa, and came back down shaking his head. "Her fever is quite high," he told Mirrie.

A few minutes later Selah slipped down the stairs into the parlor. She went up to Mirrie and said, "I've come for Miss Ferncliff's breakfast."

Mirrie glanced around to see if Judah Daniel were near. They had been waiting for this moment and planned together what they would say. "All right, Selah, but it won't be much. We have to divide what little food there is in the house among all these men."

Selah frowned. "There ought to be plenty of ham."

"Not enough," Mirrie answered. "And there's hardly anything to be had in the market, for any amount of money. If we run out of food, Louisa will just have to bear the hunger pains like the rest of us."

Selah seemed to be debating how to respond. Mirrie

went on. "Louisa's farm. . . . Could we not get food from there? Thank goodness it's west of town, and so not likely to be much affected by the fighting."

Selah nodded. "There's plenty of food over to the farm. Salted ham and beef, chickens, eggs, milk, produce from the garden—"

"That's good; then we'll just send—oh. There's no one *to* send, and no vehicles either."

Judah Daniel came over to them. "John Chapman got the bakery wagon. He must be about done with the day's deliveries. I can drive it out there."

Mirrie turned to Judah Daniel. "Oh, do you think you could? That would be wonderful."

"I got to show a pass through the defenses," Judah Daniel reminded her.

Selah nodded.

"Really, Selah," Mirrie urged. "Louisa must give her approval. These men are weak, exhausted. If they don't receive good care, the authorities will know about it. I don't think Louisa wants that. I'll go talk to her, if you like."

Selah sighed. "No need to bother Miss Ferncliff. Just go, like you said. I reckon there's no help for it."

"Meanwhile," Mirrie said to Judah Daniel, "let's see what's on hand that we can give these men for breakfast."

The two women busied themselves searching the shelves and cupboards, the cooling cabinets and root cellar. They fished the butter crock out of the well where it had been keeping cool in the water. They found the hambone with some meat clinging to it; some biscuits that were hard, but edible when warmed; and an assortment of preserved fruits that would make the bits seem more appetizing. Best of all, Louisa had coffee beans, already roasted, ready to grind and boil. The smell would breathe hope into all but the sickest of men. Mirrie had to admit that there was satisfaction in providing for the needs of the body—and her own hunger made the work especially appealing.

Soon after Mirrie and Judah Daniel finished giving breakfast to the men, Selah came down with the pass, along with money for Judah Daniel to bribe her way out of any difficulties that couldn't be overcome by the pass. Selah went back upstairs, and Mirrie turned to Judah Daniel. "Are you sure you'll be all right?"

Judah Daniel put the pass and notes into her apron pocket. "Midwives get used to traveling alone."

Mirrie wanted to say, Don't leave me, but she kept her mouth shut and let Judah Daniel go. She didn't want anyone, least of all the soldiers themselves, to see how strained she felt, left on her own among them—how close to breaking down. She hoped one of the doctors, or someone, would come again soon. What did it mean that McClellan was retreating? Was it over, then? That seemed too much to hope for.

"Miss?" It was Abram Winters; he was motioning to her. She went over to him and saw he was holding in his hand a piece of metal about three inches long and an inch wide. She touched it; the edges were sharp. "It didn't go deep," he told her; "must have been about spent. Just made a cut under my arm and stuck in my shirt. Another piece of the same shell hit the man next to me. Caught him in the neck. Killed him like *that*." Winters snapped his fingers.

What quirk of fate, she wondered, had steered this evil-looking thing a few inches shy of Winters's heart? "Keep it to show your grandchildren," she told him with a smile of reassurance that felt like a lie. If he should be so fortunate this time as to escape infection or illness, he would have to go back and risk it all again.

Mirrie had known dozens, hundreds, of young men over the years her father had taught ancient languages at

Hampden-Sydney College. She'd not been in awe of them; quite the opposite. She'd wondered often enough why the job of ruling the world—this piece of it, at least— should have fallen to them. But she'd grown fond of some of them, enjoyed the company of most, never doubted they would live their lives in the prosperity and security that seemed their birthright. Now the boys she had known, grown into men, were lying in hospitals, or in graves—or fighting still, pretending that something so worthless as the shrapnel Winters held in his hand could not, in an instant, snuff out their lives.

Not long after Judah Daniel left—perhaps a half hour—a woman came up to the door asking for Mrs. Powers.

"I'm Mirrie Powers. Mrs. Powers is my brother's widow."

The woman nodded as if the explanation suited her well enough. "I'm Annie Yates."

"Oh—Annie. You brought Narcissa back here the other evening when she fell ill. I never had a chance to thank you properly."

"I come to help take care of the soldiers."

Mirrie thought she had never seen a living person who looked more like the *Harper's Weekly* caricatures of starving Confederates. Hunger had sharpened the woman's cheekbones and shadowed her eyes. Hard work and unremitting sorrow had all but used up Annie Yates. Mirrie considered for a moment that it might be kinder to reject her offer of help. But if she were to stay, at least she could have a share of the food that Judah Daniel would eventually bring.

"Come in, Mrs. Yates. I'm glad to have your help."

Watching Annie moving among the men, feeding them and finding little ways to make them comfortable, Mirrie felt ashamed of her own protected life. Annie, who from the look of her had always worked hard just to survive, was braver and stronger in this situation than she was. So was Narcissa, come to that . . . and Judah Daniel.

Judah Daniel drove John Chapman's wagon west, following a country road that roughly paralleled the course of the river. Louisa Ferncliff's farm was only a few miles out of town, closer in than the big plantations. Louisa's father might have planned to build a big house on this property and rub shoulders with the Virginia bluebloods. If so, he never got around to it. The old farmhouse put on no airs, and the land around it was planted for the homely purpose of growing food.

The servant who came to meet her looked like he'd have been more at home on an estate. He was a youngish man whose underslung jaw made him look graver than maybe he really was. Despite the heat, Claud Parry wore a black formal coat that proclaimed his standing as a house servant. He didn't look like he'd choose to spend his time at a run-down old farmhouse in the company of field hands who—unless she missed her guess—he despised as beneath him.

She told him her errand. He listened without comment. Then she began to push in the direction of the information she had come after, which she wanted more than food. "Miss Ferncliff send you out here to stay?"

The question got him talking. "Just for a few days," he answered stiffly. "I reckon things be settling down before long, and I be heading back. She can't keep me out here. This ain't what I been hired to do. If she try to keep me out here, I'll just quit. I can get back into town on my own; leave her to whistle for her carriage. I had a good job in a livery stable before this. She don't own me, you know. I got my freedom papers."

"She said she trying to keep you from being impressed to drive ambulances."

Claud's mouth twisted. "She trying to save her coach more than me. She ain't got no feelings for me, more than what I got for her."

"So you ain't worked for her long?"

"Not long, no; about six months. About six months too long," Claud added moodily.

"You from around here?"

"Here?" Claud looked around him. "Naw. I come down from Alexandria just in front of the army. The man I worked for brung me down. He run low on horses after the army took a few of the best ones. Sent me to work for Ferncliff."

"Well," Judah Daniel remarked in the tone of one determined to see a good side in bad news, "at least you be out of it if the Yankees ride into town."

Claud shrugged. "What do I care who I drive for? Let 'em come. They got more horses, more money too. Might bring more business to the livery stable. I want to buy my own someday."

Judah Daniel raised her eyebrows. "Think they let you do that?"

Claud shrugged again. "Times is changing. Ain't nothing 'Old Massa' can do about it."

This might be as good an opening as she was going to get. "I heard Miss Ferncliff's father sold a bunch of his slaves to a neighbor down here. She tried to buy them back, and he wouldn't sell."

"If you want to talk about old times, Isom out there picking snap beans. Go ask him about it."

Well. She'd been wasting her time on Claud Parry. But there was still a question she had to ask. "Miss Ferncliff got the reputation of helping slaves get free. You ever help her with that?"

"That's all talk, far as I know. Her and that Selah get all secretive now and then, but I ain't never seen nothing come of it."

That was that, thought Judah Daniel. Claud might have spent his six months at the bottom of a well for all he knew about Louisa Ferncliff. There was nothing to do but walk out under the hot sun and talk to Isom.

Even from a distance, the rows of neatly planted vegetables warmed her toward the man. There he was, at work in what looked like a little Indian village of bright green tepees. She picked her way carefully through the young squash plants and drew closer to him. Now she could see that what looked like tepees were many bundles of a half-dozen poles, longer than she was tall, spaced a foot or so apart at the bottom and bound together at the top. The bark was left on, giving purchase to the blindly groping tendrils of bean plants. Isom was picking the mature beans and dropping them onto a piece of sacking that lay next to him on the ground. He was a small, wiry man who looked about forty years old. When she saw him full-on, she noticed his left ear was missing, as if it had been cut off flat against his head. She introduced herself. Isom nodded and handed her a bean he'd just picked. She crunched it between her teeth, savoring the sweet raw taste.

"You been with Miss Ferncliff long?" she asked him, hoping for a better answer than she'd had from Claud.

Isom turned the right side of his head to her; probably he was deaf in what remained of his left ear. "Almost twenty years, I reckon." There was a quiet pride in his voice.

"She got the reputation of a good mistress."

Isom's brown eyes met hers. "She been that to me."

"Lots of folks—'specially young folks—wouldn't think much of being stuck out here. I reckon you was about twenty when you come?"

She saw Isom glance over her shoulder in the direction of the house. Claud must have complained to him, too— or shown his resentment in other ways. Isom smiled a little and dropped another bean pod onto the sack. "I don't mind."

Judah Daniel made up her mind to tell a lie. "Web Clark told me to talk to you." *He would have*, she added to herself.

Isom's fingers, suddenly clumsy, snapped the stem he'd been holding. "I ain't heard that name in years."

"Did Web Clark and Miss Ferncliff help you, back when?"

He turned again to look her in the face. "Yes, they did. Most folks, they brung into town, slipped them in and out. With my ear missing, I was too easy to spot. I run away from a place down in South Carolina. I'd be in hell by now, if I'd stayed. I was bound to kill the man who done this to me."

"How many runaways you get coming through here?"

Isom shrugged. "Used to be a lot. Maybe a hundred a year. When the war broke out, I reckon Miss Ferncliff decide to be cautious."

"How about just recently? A man, a woman, and a little baby?"

Isom looked her full in the face. His eyes were troubled. "I don't know about that. What happened to them?"

"The man's dead. The woman's in jail. The baby's safe."

Isom stood, head down, arms loose at his sides—praying, maybe. Judah Daniel moved a step closer to him. "I got to find out what went wrong. To do that, I got to know how they got the word to run to Ferncliff's." She reached into her apron pocket and took out Darcy's drawing of the quilt. "Was it this?"

Isom looked at the piece of paper. At last he said, "I seen something like that. Years ago."

"It was the signal, wasn't it, for a group of slaves to get ready to run. You sure you don't know who got the signal this time?"

Isom shook his head and turned back to his work. She didn't know whether or not to believe him, but she knew he wouldn't say any more. "I'm much obliged to you, Isom," she told him. He looked up; his gaze held hers for a second, then he nodded, giving her leave to do what she had to do.

Isom and the peevish Claud helped load the wagon, and Judah Daniel started back for Richmond. Raven had a heavier load now and was moving slowly in the heat.

For years—until war broke out—Louisa Ferncliff had helped the Underground Railroad in smuggling slaves to freedom. She'd given the kind of love she had to give: love not for a person, but for a people. And she'd gotten in return the kind of love she wanted: not hugging-and-kissing, Christmas-gift-giving love, but respect bordering on awe. Yet a few days ago a slave man had been shot dead and a baby left to God's mercy, all within a couple hundred feet of Louisa's house. For Louisa to do something so contrary to her own nature, she had to be looking toward some other goal—something so important that these three lives weighed light in the balance. Louisa feared the quilt might be found and give her away, so she'd sent Selah for it. The other possibility was, Louisa hadn't known the slaves were coming. Selah wanted the quilt so Louisa would never see it and figure out that the signal had been given without her say-so. In that case, was someone else giving the orders Selah was so used to taking from Louisa Ferncliff?

It didn't seem like what had happened up in the graveyard had just been bad luck for the slave family. Someone had known they were coming, and betrayed them. *Be-*

trayed. A strong word, but not too strong, given what had happened. The hungry folks at Louisa's house would have to wait a little while longer for her delivery. She had to go talk to Tabitha one more time.

At the Negro Jail, Judah Daniel was met by a scowling Murphy. She didn't know the cause for his grumpiness, but that didn't keep him from discharging some of it at her. "We don't need you coming around no more. You can tell your mistress to look someplace else for her sister's slave. The wench's owners done claimed her. Soon as the Yankees gone, they'll be coming to take her back. 'Course, they'd like to know what happened to her baby. You don't know nothing about that, do you?"

"No, sir," Judah Daniel answered, eyes down. "It's just, she been getting better from the medicine I brung her. I got some more with me." She held out the bottle for his inspection.

"Well, I reckon that won't hurt nothing." Murphy rose from his seat and picked up the ring of keys. He moved slowly, showing her he wasn't obliged to do anything she asked. But the fact that he responded at all proved that her medicine had worked in bringing the young woman back to health.

Judah Daniel ventured a question. "If she ain't Tabitha, what's she called?"

"Lettie," he answered. "Lettie McRae."

The young woman was lying on her back on the straw pallet, staring at the ceiling. When she saw Judah Daniel, she sat up, but she said nothing.

"Lettie," Judah Daniel said softly. "We ain't got much time. Let me tell you what I think happened. You one of the McRaes, or your man was. You both knew the stories about Louisa Ferncliff and how she wanted to free your folks years ago. Time by time, over the years, this signal would come—a quilt with a Wagon Wheel design. That was how Louisa sent the signal to run. Then about a year back, when the war broke out, she didn't send it no more. You about give up hope, till just a few days back. A quilt showed up—a new one, but with the same pattern. Weren't but one man supposed to go—your husband. But you done lived all your life in the hope of that signal, and you was bound and determined to go with him, and take your baby."

Judah Daniel was talking as fast as she could, fearing Murphy would return before she could get the answer she needed. Lettie was looking down at the floor, listening but still saying nothing.

"You was waiting, the three of you, up in the churchyard. Something gone wrong. Your husband got shot. You left the baby and run, thinking they'd chase you. Turned out nobody did—you wasn't caught till the next day. But you hoped Louisa—or somebody—would find your baby so he could be free."

Lettie still didn't say anything, didn't even move her head yea or nay, but it seemed to Judah Daniel that she was listening with her whole body. Now she opened her mouth and began to speak, haltingly, as if she weren't used to it. "The Lord is my shepherd," Lettie said in a singsong voice. "He preparest a table before me in the presence of mine enemies. He maketh me to lie down in green pastures. Though I walk through the valley of death, I will fear no evil." Then she looked into Judah Daniel's eyes and said, "Go now. I ain't saying no more."

Lettie shut her mouth and looked away. Judah Daniel wanted to question her further, but at that moment Murphy came in. "You had long enough," he said.

———

Judah Daniel left the jail feeling just a little short of despair. The Twenty-third Psalm—not all of it, and fractured—what did it mean? *The Lord is my shepherd....* Words to strengthen the heart, but no answer to the questions she'd asked. *A table ... the valley of death....*

Narcissa thought perhaps the medicine was beginning to have some effect—or maybe the disease was abating. Surely her fever had not been so high this time, or lasted quite so long. It was still light outside when she got out of bed. She bathed and dressed, then hurried downstairs to find Mirrie and Judah Daniel dishing up supper for the wounded men.

"Narcissa!" Mirrie greeted her with a hug and a kiss on the cheek. "How are you feeling?"

"Well enough to serve as your replacement," Narcissa answered. "Have you and Judah Daniel been holding the fort all day?"

"No. Judah Daniel went out to Louisa's farm and brought back all this delicious food. Annie Yates came to help for a few hours, earlier in the day."

"What about Selah—and Louisa? Have they come around?"

Mirrie pushed her gold-rimmed spectacles higher on her nose. "I've hardly seen them. Louisa won't leave her room. Selah's passed through every now and then, silent and disapproving, like Banquo's ghost. She did bring another bottle of brandy. We'll wait until the last thing to hand the glasses around. Now that you are here, Narcissa, would you mind if I took a few minutes—just to clean up a bit, and clear my head?"

Narcissa helped Judah Daniel carry the dishes back to the kitchen for washing. As soon as they were out of earshot of the soldiers, she asked Judah Daniel about her visit to Louisa's farm.

"Miss Ferncliff's driver just come here a few months back—about the time Susy come, I reckon. He don't know nothing about how things was done in the old days. But the servant living there on the farm, he recognized the pattern in the quilt. The slaves used to use a quilt like that to signal when it was time to run. Miss Ferncliff don't seem to be housing runaways much no more. Could be the war . . . could be she don't want the risk, what with having Susy in the Davis house and all. . . . But the quilt Moses wrapped in, it had the patterns that used to be the signal. Might be it don't mean nothing no more. But Selah gone to a lot of trouble to get the quilt back—why, if it don't mean nothing?"

Narcissa wondered guiltily if Devlin held the key to what happened that night up at St. John's Church. He claimed to know who'd murdered the slave man; maybe he had seen something that could help Judah Daniel. But she couldn't tell Judah Daniel about Devlin. She couldn't dispel her own suspicion that Judah Daniel might be helping Louisa—or Selah, if the two of them could be considered as having separate wills. And even if she did tell, she reasoned, she could hardly go looking for him to ask questions about what he'd seen that night.

It was midnight when Mirrie started to make her way back downstairs. When she found herself outside Louisa's door, she stopped. Something outside of herself, like a strong wind, was moving her. She raised her fist and knocked on Louisa's door. "Louisa! It's me, Mirrie. Let me in." She waited; then, "Louisa! Open the door!"

She was about to knock again when she heard the key turn. The door opened; it was Selah, who took one look at

Mirrie's face and slid away down the hall. Mirrie went in and shut the door behind her.

Louisa was sitting up in bed. "I told Selah to send you away."

Mirrie went over to the bed and looked down at Louisa, who stared back at her, eyes wide with alarm. "Selah couldn't do it. Neither can you. Louisa, if you really have a letter that can end this war, you have to send it—now, right away. Soon it will be too late."

Louisa shifted away from her. "I won't do that."

"You mean to tell me you could stop this, and you won't? They say fifteen thousand men may be dead or wounded on both sides. *Fifteen thousand men.* That's as many men as there were living in Richmond before the war. Fathers, sons, brothers, husbands. This isn't a city anymore. It's a hospital, and a graveyard. I know you want to end slavery. Once the madness is over, people will see . . . will see that it can't—"

"You look quite wild-eyed, Mirrie Powers." Louisa's tone was light, almost teasing.

"Louisa, I can't help but feel I influenced you in this. I told you it was too early to end the war, before Lincoln freed the slaves. I was wrong. No one who is safe at home has the right to say this war should go on so much as another minute. Please, if what I said carried any weight with you, listen to me now: I take back what I said. This has to stop. You have to stop it."

Mirrie stared at Louisa, unable to believe what she was seeing. Louisa's smile was back—not a smile at all, but a tightening of the face that showed a tightening of the heart. "You think what you said changed my mind? I told you the letter is in a safe place, and it will stay there—till the Day of Judgment, at least."

Mirrie felt the wind that had been carrying her die away. She was falling. She put out her hand to steady herself and saw Louisa flinch. The sight stirred an ugly roiling in her heart. Ashamed, frightened, Mirrie ran out the door, past Selah, who was lurking there, and down the steps to the parlor. Mirrie stood in the doorway until the shaking stopped. *I could have killed Louisa.*

→>—<←

"Mrs. Powers."

Narcissa woke with a start. It was Cashion, whose hands had been burned. He had raised himself on his elbow so that he could call to her. His face was pale and running with sweat. She got up and went over to him, picking her way among the pallets of the other men.

"I'm sorry, Mrs. Powers, but the pain . . . I can't stand it anymore. Haven't you got any more morphine?"

Narcissa hesitated. "There's no doctor here. I—" She glanced at the clock on the mantel. It was almost midnight—hours before they could hope for a doctor to come by.

Cashion's voice, low with urgency, cut her off. "Please. You've worked in the hospital. You know what to do, how much to give."

I do, Narcissa thought. I could. Then, looking at the lines of pain in his face: I will.

Narcissa went over to the oil lamp and picked it up. Both Mirrie and Judah Daniel were asleep. "All right," Narcissa whispered. "I'll get it for you." Narcissa went on, stepping carefully, to the sideboard where Dr. Lester had left the medicines. There should be a full bottle of morphine there. Where was it? She picked up each bottle and read the label, then opened each one and smelled the contents. There was a little morphine left in one bottle, but the last full bottle of morphine was gone. Who might have taken it? She thought of all the people who'd come in and out during the day. Then she remembered: Annie Yates. It

was strange—she thought now—that Annie, who'd
been accused of stealing morphine from Chimborazo,
had come here to the home of a woman she appeared to
hate. Narcissa had not wanted to believe the accusation
against Annie; had sought to excuse it if it were true.
But now, any sympathy she might have had for Annie's
terrible loss dropped away from her. Only anger was
left, that Annie could have let these men suffer with no
hope of relief.

She gave the morphine remaining in the bottle to Private Cashion. Then she told him, "I'm going to the hospital for more."

Judah Daniel came to stand next to her. "I can go."

Narcissa thought, then answered, "Thank you. But I
had better do it. They may be more likely to give it to me
than to you."

Narcissa drew her shawl around her and set out. She hurried down up Twenty-fourth Street, crossed Grace and
Broad, and turned right onto Marshall. She passed houses
that, for grief or fear or for the business of nursing, would
not sleep this night. Wounded men were moving through
the city, seeking help—more of them, it seemed, than the
city had help to give. She crossed over the little plank
bridge that spanned Bloody Run. Chimborazo's brick
bakery glowed like a smithy's shop, its ovens blasting
yeast-scented heat into the night. She turned into the hospital grounds, keeping the bakery on her right. Across the
way were the dead houses. She guessed they were already
full, for men were stacking bodies like cordwood on the
ground outside. The flickering light of pine-knot torches
gave hideous animation to the stiffened forms of the
dead. She hurried, almost running, to the headquarters
building. Uniformed men were coming in and out, grim-
faced and bloody . . . surgeons, assistants, stewards, or-

derlies. She went in through the door, then crossed to the far side of the parlor.

"I'm sorry, ma'am, we haven't any names yet."

The speaker was an elderly civilian. He looked as if he'd been through hell himself, his skin was gray and loose, as if he'd lost weight from sickness or grief or sheer exhaustion.

"That's not why I'm here. There are wounded men, back at—back at my house." She did not want to waste time explaining about Louisa Ferncliff, whose name might dry up a loyal Confederate's sympathy. "I've got to get some morphine for them."

The gray-faced man shook his head slowly. "I can't help you with that. You'll have to find a doctor."

"Yes—all right," Narcissa answered. She called out her thanks—he had already turned from her to confront the demands of another petitioner. She had wasted time coming to the headquarters building. And the wards of the Sixth Division—the place where she was most likely to find someone she knew—were at the far end of the grounds, still a long walk away.

As she came close, she saw blood on the ground, and looked to see where it had come from. There, near the door, lay a pile of amputated limbs, raw red meat and splintered bone. Holding her skirts up off the ground, she went to the door and looked in. At least three sets of surgeons and assistants were operating. She recognized none of them at first—all were bareheaded, unshaven, streaked with blood and sweat. Then she saw that one of them was Cameron Archer. He and two other men were amputating a soldier's leg above the knee. She could see the ragged tear in the flesh, and above it the encircling bruise where the tourniquet had been. A few inches higher up on the leg Archer had peeled back the skin and sliced through the flesh, probably with the knife he now held in his teeth, and was sawing. Narcissa knew the sound, that awful rasping of serrated metal on bone. His assistant—she recognized Coster—held a length of silk thread ready to tie off a blood vessel. The patient lay limp as death, thanks to the ministrations of the third man, who had given the chloroform. By the time the patient came to again, his leg would be off; indeed, the whole operation would last only a few minutes. Speed was vital—not only to keep this man from bleeding to death, but to reach as many men as possible before infection poisoned their blood.

A little farther down, Lester and Wright were laboring over another patient. A curtain improvised from bed linens hung on a rope separated this operating room from the rest of the ward.

A familiar pounding came into her head: Do something, it prompted, do something, and if you can do nothing, then run, get away. Narcissa knew she had to keep moving toward her goal, else her concern for Cashion's pain would founder in this ocean of suffering. These men were far worse off than Cashion—but he too deserved relief, and she would obtain it for him if she could. She hurried on to the next door, to the part of the building curtained off from the surgery. Those who had survived their amputations had been brought here. Their wounds were bandaged, and several women moved among the beds, fanning away the flies, bathing faces, giving sips of water.

Ah! There was Rosalie Stedman, dressed with such uncharacteristic simplicity that Narcissa had not known her at first. Narcissa went up to where the doctor's wife was gently sponging caked blood from the beard of a man whose forehead and eyes were bandaged.

"Hello, my dear. I'm glad to see you." Mrs. Stedman spoke as calmly as if Narcissa had just slid into her pew at St. Paul's. "Mr. Mayhew," she said to the bandaged man, "here is a lovely young woman I wish you could see. Shall I ask her to return and visit you when your eyes are better?"

The soldier bared his teeth in a brave grin. "Yes, ma'am."

Narcissa took Mayhew's rough hand and spoke a few words to him. Then, turning back to Mrs. Stedman, she whispered, "I'm sorry. I can't stay. There are wounded men at Miss Ferncliff's."

"My goodness! How is Louisa taking it?"

"She'll survive. But Dr. Lester left two full bottles of morphine, and now they're gone. One of the patients is in pain, and I have nothing to give him."

"Ask him." Mrs. Stedman nodded toward a middle-aged man in a steward's uniform who was walking up the aisle, a bottle and spoon in his hand. "I have to tell you, though, dear, that I doubt you will get it."

Narcissa hurried after the steward and caught up with him.

"Excuse me. Where can I get morphine for some patients?"

The steward glanced at her. "Who sent you?"

"No one sent me," Narcissa replied. "I'm tending to a half-dozen wounded soldiers in a private house." She stepped closer, ready to plead her case.

"Amputees?"

"No, but—"

The steward shook his head, left-right, wasting no motion. "Give them some brandy, whatever you have. We can't spare morphine." His attention was back on his patients.

Narcissa knew there was no point arguing. She had been naive in thinking that the men in charge of the hospital would give the morphine to a woman to administer. Still, even without morphine, she could not help thinking that Cashion and the others were better off at Ferncliff's than they would have been here, where the battle raged on long after the guns had fallen silent.

As she passed by the surgeons once more, she searched

again for Cameron Archer's face. He looked up then—in her direction, though she did not think he saw her. She wanted his help—wanted to lean on his strength. She felt sure that he would want to help her, support her. But he could not do it, could not leave his station among these men; and she could not ask. So she walked on, placing her feet carefully on the blood-slicked path.

Cameron Archer was waiting for the chloroform to take effect on the next patient. He looked over at the steward. "Was that Mrs. Powers? What did she want?"

"Morphine," the steward replied tersely. "There's some wounded men in a house near here."

"Did you give it to her?"

The steward shook his head. "Couldn't. We may need all we have, and more."

"Yes," Archer agreed. His voice was firm, but his eyes searched the darkness beyond the glare of the torches, hoping for one last sight of her. Then the patient on the table, a splintered femur, ceased to struggle and went limp. At that, Archer's training took over, driving all other thoughts from his mind.

A single blast of sound jerked Judah Daniel from restless sleep. It took her a few seconds to put a name to the noise—a shot, somewhere close. She saw Mirrie sit up and reach for her spectacles. The wounded men stirred, with fear or with the impulse to fight back. "It's all right," Judah Daniel told them. She was on her feet when the second shot came. This time she could tell it came from upstairs.

Mirrie grabbed her arm. "Wait—whoever it is may come down the stairs." They waited, straining to hear, but there was no sound of running footsteps, voices, anything.

Judah Daniel picked up the candlestick. "I'll go," she told Mirrie. But Mirrie shook her head. Together they moved to the staircase and up it. All was silent, peaceful. Judah Daniel wondered if their ears had tricked them, if the sounds had really come from somewhere outside the house. But the silence itself was odd. Louisa Ferncliff and Selah had to have heard those shots. . . .

Louisa's door was closed. "Stay here," Judah Daniel whispered to Mirrie. She pushed the door open an inch at a time, expecting every moment to hear Louisa's voice raised in protest. At last she took a step through the door. She could see that Louisa's bed was empty, the covers pushed back. She took another step. There, just beyond the bed, she could see something on the floor. She moved closer. Louisa was lying on the floor, on her back, but twisted a little, so that her left leg was drawn up a little over her right. Her feet were bare. She must be dead, or blacked out at least, she was lying so limp. There was blood on the rose-patterned carpet, and on Louisa's nightdress. The blood had come from a hole in Louisa's chest. There wasn't much blood. Louisa had died quickly.

The candle's flame danced with some silent motion of the air. Judah Daniel felt the hair on the back of her neck stirred by the same slight breeze. She turned. Selah was there, propping herself up against a table, her hand to her throat. Blood soaked the front of her dress. The pistol was on the floor near her feet. Behind her, near the table, lay a pile of broken glass and splintered wood, and the fireplace poker that must have reduced something to this rubble.

For a moment, Judah Daniel couldn't move or speak. She could only watch as Selah took a step forward, swaying as if she were about to fall. Selah's mouth was moving, and terrible sounds were coming out, a gurgling noise, as if Selah were trying to breathe in her own blood. Just as Judah Daniel stepped forward to catch her, Selah swayed, jerked, and collapsed onto the floor. She lay in a heap, eyes open, and still the horrible noise came from her.

Judah Daniel put the candle down and knelt beside Selah. She felt Selah stiffen, her muscles contract. Then Selah went limp. The struggling breaths ceased. It was over. She'd been shot through the lung, Judah Daniel supposed. She'd lived for a few moments. Long enough to take revenge on her killer.

Selah must have shot Louisa right through the heart. Of the two, it was the more merciful death. Selah had died in agony. And her hands were claws, tearing at the carpet. Judah Daniel looked again at Selah's right hand. Her fingers clasped something. Judah Daniel gently opened Selah's hand. It was a little leather case.

"I hoped it was the letter." Mirrie spoke from the doorway. Her voice was flat, as if shock had driven out feeling. "That little case holds a pair of daguerreotypes—Selah and her sister, Susannah. It was on that table." She pointed to the table behind Selah.

Judah Daniel opened the case. She examined the pictures, moving them so that they caught the light: first Susy, then Selah, then Susy again. The little pictures looked like reflections in a soap bubble. Yet there they were, Susy and Selah, caught in a piece of glass. As long as the glass didn't break, she supposed, or suffer some other damage, that moment would be fixed forever.

"Do you know when these pictures were made?" she asked Mirrie.

"Let's see . . . four or five years ago, I think Louisa told me. Selah and Louisa visited Susy in Philadelphia. What is this?" Mirrie turned, her attention caught by something behind Judah Daniel. She was looking at the little pile of broken glass and splintered wood. "Oh!" Mirrie exclaimed. "The hair wreath. Do you think the letter could have been hidden inside the base?"

Judah Daniel picked up the poker and probed the broken globe, the wooden base, and the hair, now crushed into a sad little tangle. "If it was there, it ain't there now."

Mirrie stood up. "Try to find the letter. I'll reassure the men as best I can."

Judah Daniel put the leather case in her pocket. She locked the door behind Mirrie, then stopped to survey the room once more. Drops of blood made a path on the floor between Louisa and Selah. She hadn't noticed them when she first came in. Selah's shot had been made at close range, after she'd gotten the revolver away from Louisa. Then Selah had gone across the floor to the little table—gone to get the daguerreotypes. Did she love her sister so much that she wanted to look at her face one last time? Was it some kind of rebuke to Louisa?

Judah Daniel stepped around the blood and knelt by Louisa. She pulled the nightdress open and saw the hole in Louisa's chest. The slave man, Moses's father, had a hole like that in his chest. *Maybe this is justice.* Then another thought came to her. *I could have done this—to save John Chapman and his family, I would have done it.* Nothing in Louisa's hands, or under her, or concealed under her nightdress. . . . Judah Daniel knew she might not have much time to look before someone came. Where would Louisa have hidden the letter?

She felt under the pillows and under the mattress. Nothing. She went around the room, searching, keeping pace with the quick beat of her heart—*that desk; that table, there's a drawer in it; a loose brick, maybe, in the hearth; that bench, the top might open*—At last she stopped to look more closely at the heavy wardrobe opposite Louisa's bed. *In there, maybe.* It was at least three feet taller than Judah Daniel herself and as broad as her outstretched arms. Two doors opened out from the middle, like window shutters. Each door was fitted with a fancy brass lock—easy enough to force, probably, but there was no need: the keys were in the holes.

Judah Daniel turned the key in the lock on the left-hand door and opened it. The scent of lavender wafted out. The wardrobe was filled with clothing, hung on hooks or folded. On the right-hand side were more clothes, and a stack of little drawers down one side. She opened each one of the half-dozen little drawers and thrust her hand in, but found no papers. Well—the letter could be anywhere, sewn into the lining of a bodice or rolled up into a stocking. She would have to go through everything. One by one she took out each piece of clothing and crushed the fabric between her fingers, feeling for suspicious stiffness, then putting it to one side and taking the next piece. When the wardrobe was empty, she pulled each drawer out and looked into it, and then behind it, feeling with her fingers where the candle's light would not reach. But she found nothing.

Judah Daniel stepped back, surveying the room again. The drops of blood caught her eye. She bent down and examined the droplets. Some of them were smeared— from Selah's struggling steps, or her own careless haste entering the room? No—the smearing was too regular, each drop given a sort of tail like a comet, extending from the wardrobe toward the bed. She stared until she saw the pattern. The pile of the carpet had been brushed against the grain in an arc that extended at least two feet from the wardrobe. It looked as if the wardrobe itself had swung away from the wall, and swung back. And this had happened after Selah had struggled across the room, dripping a trail of blood.

Yes; it was possible. . . . She felt the hair stand up on the back of her neck. Someone else had been in the room with Selah and Louisa, and had disappeared into the wall. That person must be there still, crouching behind the wall, in the little space where Louisa used to hide escaping slaves. Judah Daniel had figured there was a secret room somewhere in the house. But to have the way in be through Louisa's bedroom!—That came, she supposed, from Louisa's wish to have everything done under her eyes. No one would hide in her house without her knowing it. Except maybe, this time, someone had.

The only thing to do was to move the wardrobe. She would need Mirrie's help—maybe not for the moving itself, but for meeting whoever was inside.

Mirrie had picked up the poker and held it at the ready. Judah Daniel gripped the wardrobe and pulled. It didn't budge. She pulled harder, straining her muscles—nothing. She motioned for Mirrie to help her, and they both pulled. Still no movement.

"It can't be that heavy," said Judah Daniel, wiping back hair that had come from beneath the scarf she wore. "Something's holding it."

She turned her attention to the space between the wardrobe and the wall. She could see nothing. Then with her right hand she felt along the back corner of the wardrobe's deep-stained mahogany. About eight inches before her hand reached the floor she felt it, a notch—and then, about four inches lower, a metal knob, cooler than the wood. She knew what it was.

"A dead bolt," she said, turning to Mirrie. "Just like you would put on a door. Only you push this one into the floor—here, just past the edge of the carpet—so the wardrobe don't move."

Mirrie went to the other side of the wardrobe and felt on the other side. "There's another one here," she said. "No wonder we couldn't budge it, even with both of us trying."

Judah Daniel twisted the metal bolt on her side, slid it up out of the hole in the floor, and rested the knob in its wooden notch. "Somebody made that so you would never see it, even if you was scrubbing the floor." Now she pulled at the wardrobe again, and this time she didn't need Mirrie's help. The big piece of furniture pivoted almost noiselessly across the carpet, right across the bloodstains. Judah Daniel squatted on her haunches where the wardrobe had sat. She started to ask Mirrie to come, but Mirrie was already there, holding the lantern. Judah Daniel ran her hand along the wainscoting until she found what she was looking for. She felt the wood give just above the floor molding. She had nudged a panel, about two feet across and a yard high. Once it was out of the way, it would leave a hole big enough for a grown man to crawl through. And it was cut so carefully that it could be fitted back into place from the other side of the wall and would not be noticed until somebody moved the wardrobe aside, as Judah Daniel had just done.

So this was where Louisa had hidden runaway slaves. Judah Daniel wondered how many had stayed there over the years, and why little Moses and Lettie and her husband never made it this far. And who was behind that panel now? Judah Daniel reckoned it was somebody who knew what had happened in this room, somebody who might have killed one or both of the women lying dead on the floor behind them. Judah Daniel listened for a moment, but heard nothing, not even the scuffling of mice. She looked at Mirrie. "We got to see what's there," she said, "and who's there." She pushed hard against the door panel.

The hole opened up into a small room, about ten feet long and six feet wide. The smell of human waste was so strong it was a wonder she hadn't smelled it in Louisa's room. She heard Mirrie behind her and moved over to let her into the space. The room received a little air and a very little light through a hole about ten inches square, straight through the wall of the house. Looking at it, Judah Daniel figured it was probably concealed from the outside by the shutter of one of the windows. Judah Daniel went over to it and probed with her fingers between the plaster and the timber framing. She touched a piece of cloth. Just something a mouse had dragged there for its nest, probably. She tugged at it, finding it bigger than she'd expected. At last she had it out. It was the quilt, cut almost to shreds.

Judah Daniel stared at the quilt as if she could force it to reveal its secrets. Something . . . that clay-red calico with a design of three-leafed sprigs. . . . She reached into her pocket, took out the leather case, and opened it. The quilt piece had the same pattern as the dress in the picture. Susy's dress.

The pieces were coming together now, forming a pattern. Judah Daniel paced the floor. At last she found it— the floorboards had been sawed across. A little cutout place in the wood gave a handhold. She hooked her fingers into it and pulled it up, inch by inch. No one was hiding there. It was just a hole leading down into the first floor of the house. Boards fastened crossways on the wall formed a ladder.

It wouldn't work for her to follow the same route. But if she could get to the other side where this passageway came out. . . . She had a notion where that place was.

CHAPTER EIGHT

Sometime in the small hours of the morning, Brit woke up. Like a soldier summoned by the long roll, he came to immediate wakefulness. But he did not start to his feet. The first movement of his head froze him into immobility; so he lay still and reviewed his situation. He was in a hospital ward: he could tell that much just by the smell of sickness and turpentine. The unfinished rafters over his head indicated that this was Chimborazo. He was lying on a straw-filled tick such as they gave the patients—that was a clue; the intense pain in his head was another. He could recall being knocked down by the force of a cannonball landing near his feet, but nothing after that—nothing about being brought here, which probably was a mercy. He tried to bring his hand up to touch the sore spot in his head, but his limbs felt weak as water. Best just to lie here and wait for the dawn. If he could help it, he would not go back to sleep. The rats here in the hospital were big as cats, and bold enough even in the day.

Narcissa crossed back over Bloody Run at Marshall Street. She thought it must be about one o'clock in the morning. She was thinking of Cashion's burned hands. It galled her that she had nothing to offer him save the liquor grudgingly given by Louisa Ferncliff.

Then she stopped. There might be another way to get what she needed. If Annie Yates had stolen the morphine, she must have taken it back to the house on Franklin Street. The house was only a few blocks from here, only a few steps out of the way back to Louisa's. Annie must be there now—asleep, maybe, her grief dulled by the drug. But even if she had dosed herself liberally, she would not have emptied the bottle. There should be more than enough to ease the pain of the men at Ferncliff's, at least for the few hours until morning, when the doctors would return.

Heartened by the prospect, Narcissa hurried down Twenty-ninth Street to Annie's house. It was the last one on Franklin before the street ended, cut off at the deep ravine that bordered Chimborazo's southwest corner. The street would give a quick way into the hospital, were it not for the ravine, which had been cut into the hillside by Bloody Run. And now, in the height of summer, a thick growth of waste trees and vines filled the ravine, choking off the street. Only a determined or desperate man would try to make his way through.

And this looked the kind of place that would give shelter to desperate men, deserters—or women like Annie, who were desperate in their own way. There were no streetlights here, and many of the fine homes on surrounding streets stood empty, their owners having fled the siege. She thought of Devlin, and found herself wishing she could snuff the lamp's flame: its little glow deepened the darkness around her and advertised to anyone who might be hiding in the shadows that she was a woman, alone.

The gate was open a few inches. Narcissa pushed it open and stepped into the yard. "Annie!" she called, more to hear the sound of her own voice than expecting an answer. She climbed up the spongy steps to the porch of the big old clapboard house. The air seemed cooler here, damp and deadened—*mal aria,* she thought; if I didn't have it already, I'd surely get it here. The lantern's flame shrank as the house breathed on it; Narcissa prayed that it would not go out altogether. When she reached the door, she saw that it, like the gate, stood open an inch or two. Still there was no sign of a candle or a lamp, nothing but profound darkness inside the house. Had Annie herself fled? Narcissa knocked and called; at last, receiving no response, she went into the hall.

Annie Yates was standing there, shadowy and silent, so close that Narcissa gasped. Annie didn't move at the sight of her, and Narcissa's planned speech went unspoken, for clutched in Annie's hands—low, just at her waist—was a pistol. The black hole of its barrel pointed straight at Narcissa, who stood frozen, waiting for recognition to come into Annie's face and for her to move the gun away. But Annie's expression did not alter, and her hands holding the pistol kept their aim.

Narcissa found her voice at last. "Annie?"

"You come into my house like a thief." There was an edge of contempt in Annie's voice, which was muted to little more than a whisper. "Couldn't nobody blame me if I shot you like one."

"You're the thief, Annie. But no one needs to know about it." In the empty hallway, Narcissa's voice sounded louder than she intended. "You stole morphine from wounded men. Now they're lying there in pain, and I can do nothing to help them. What if it were your husband, or your son, lying there? Give it back, and I will keep your secret."

Annie moved at last, a sideways motion of her head that shook off the demand. "I didn't take it from the men. I took it from Louisa Ferncliff."

"Annie . . ." Be careful, Narcissa told herself. "How can that be true? From the time the wounded men were brought to the house, Louisa Ferncliff never left her room. How could she have stolen the morphine?"

"Not her. When did *she* ever have to lift a finger for herself? It was that maid of hers. I seen her. She took one of them bottles and hid it in the drawer of the sideboard. I come along when she weren't looking and poured most of it off and put water in to fill it back up."

Narcissa said nothing. She didn't dare challenge Annie's version of what had happened, not with a pistol pointing at her.

But Annie, as if she could see disbelief in Narcissa's eyes, went on. "They said I took morphine from the hospital. Yes, I done that, but I had good reason." Annie stepped away from Narcissa, back and to the side, slowly, carefully, so that the pistol's aim remained true. "I want you to see why I done it. Give me the light."

Should she try to fight Annie for the pistol? No; she had seen what a pistol shot at close range could do.

Annie gestured for Narcissa to walk in front of her. Narcissa complied, walking slowly down the hall toward the back of the house. They passed through an enclosed walkway into the kitchen. Here a low fire was burning in the fireplace. "Come on out here." Annie walked Narcissa ahead of her to the door and down the steps into the yard. "Open it." Narcissa looked down to see a wide door set at an angle—the entrance to the root cellar, no doubt, bolted across with a heavy piece of timber. Narcissa took hold of the timber and slid it back through the iron bands. It felt rough and balky in her hands, but at last it slid out of the iron band that held it on the right. The door, she saw now, was hinged on both sides to open from the middle. She looked at Annie, wondering what she would be asked to do next. "Open it," Annie said again.

Narcissa grabbed the handle and pulled the door open. Annie came up close behind her. The lamplight fell on a set of shallow stairs that led down into the earth. Beyond the lamp's illumination the space was black as a cave. The air it exhaled was cool and raw, the smell of earth overlaid with the reek of filth. Something was alive down there.

Nothing, Narcissa thought, could make her go down there. She turned around, determined to refuse, but Annie's eyes were as dark and empty as the bore of the pistol she pointed at Narcissa's face. There was nothing to do but follow Annie's orders and hope that whatever was down there would be more merciful.

Then she heard something from the dark space—a voice, rough and whispery.

"Mother?"

A child's cry, in a man's voice.

"Get down there," Annie ordered. "I don't want to shoot you, but I will if I have to." Then she called out into the dark space, "It's all right, honey. It's all right."

"Your son . . . is down there?"

Annie nodded. "My son—Jimmy."

"You told me your son was dead."

Annie's smile looked mad in her gray and haggard face. "I told you he was gone to a better place. I got him out of that hospital ward right from under the noses of all them doctors."

At last Narcissa understood. "Jimmy is Devlin."

"He got knocked out at Seven Pines. I told you the truth about that. They had him wrote down as killed. But I found him. When he come to, I told him what to do. But then he got careless. You seen he was awake. I reckon it had to happen sometime. So I brung him out of the hospital. And now it's time—past time—we got away, me and him. But I got something to take care of first. You go on down. I'll come back. Go on, now!"

Mindful of the pistol, Narcissa started down the brick steps into the earthen hole. Then she turned and reached out to Annie. "Please—let me have the lantern."

Annie hesitated, then handed the lantern to her. Holding it so that she could see her way, Narcissa resumed her descent. As soon as Narcissa's feet touched the packed-earth floor, Annie swung the door closed above her. She heard the scrape of the timber moving back into place.

The cellar seemed to extend a good way under the house, beyond the reach of the lantern's light. A few yards away from her, sitting on the dirt floor, was a young man, dressed in a butternut-dyed private's uniform. His brown beard was grown in now, and his head was uncovered. He sat with knees drawn up, arms encircling them. He looked wary—as if he thought he should be afraid of her. "What'd you come here for?" he whispered.

"I came to get the morphine your mother took from Louisa Ferncliff's house."

"Why you helping that bitch?"

"Do you mean Louisa? I'm not helping Louisa. The morphine wasn't for her. It was left at Louisa's house for the wounded men who are there. Your mother's been stealing morphine all along—from the hospital, and now from Louisa's house. She did it to help you, I suppose—it must have been hard for you to pretend so long to be unconscious."

"You don't know nothing about it." Jimmy sounded sad now, rather than angry. "It weren't my idea. Well, maybe at first. I woke up, and I didn't say nothing. I was scared they'd send me back. But when Mother found me, she started giving me morphine. Then I had to go on faking. They'd send me back, and they'd send her to jail for stealing the morphine."

"Your mother didn't carry you out by herself. Whom did she get to help her?" Narcissa prompted.

"She went to Louisa Ferncliff first. Mother thought Louisa might do it to spite the Confederates—like her taking food to the Yankee prisoners and such. If she hated the Confederates so much, why not help one of their soldiers get away from them? But Louisa said no. Mother hated Louisa after that."

"But someone must have helped her," Narcissa prompted him. "And when I saw you in the graveyard, you said Louisa and Selah killed the slave who was buried there."

"Most likely it was them that killed him," Jimmy asserted stubbornly. "But the one who helped me get out was Dr. Lester."

Narcissa made no reply. Jimmy Yates must be as mad as his mother; it wouldn't do to argue with either of them. Of course, what he said was impossible. Lester was respected, Cameron Archer respected him. . . . Archer had used his name as proof that Devlin was really dead. Dr. Lester signed the death certificate, he'd told her, as if that meant an end to all doubt.

But Devlin was alive. Could he—Devlin, Jimmy—be telling the truth?

Jimmy was explaining. "Lester got a servant of his to help Mother carry me out. And he signed the paper saying what I died of and all. But then we had to do what he said, both Mother and me, else he'd accuse her of stealing the morphine and have her arrested, as well as me. Mother told me he wanted me to take something to the Yankees. Mother was going to go with me."

A servant of Lester's. Susy Reynolds? She had worked for Lester's family before going to the Davises. So Lester could have known that Susy was a spy—in fact, he could have been involved in Louisa's plot from the beginning. After Susy fled the Davises, Lester could have helped Louisa by finding someone else—Jimmy—to take the letter to the Federal camp. Of course, if what Mirrie said about Louisa was true, Lester might have been working against Louisa, trying to get the letter away from her and out to the Federals. In either case, Jimmy was still here: that might mean Lester hadn't yet succeeded in getting the letter out.

"Mother and I had a big fight about it," Jimmy went on. "I told her I wasn't going to betray my country. She pleaded with me. She said we could lie to Dr. Lester, pretend to take the letter. I told her I just wanted to go back to my regiment. I was sick to death of all the lies, sick to death of laying here in the dirt. Four days I been here. Faugh! I rather stand up with the boys and take my chances." Jimmy sighed and shifted, raising a cloud of choking dust. "Finally she said she'd tell Lester we wasn't going to wait any longer, we was taking off back to Floyd County. People there, they don't care too much if you go to fight or not."

"Did you tell your mother you would go with her to Floyd County? You said you wanted to go back to your regiment," Narcissa reminded him.

"I do. But she don't hear me when I talk about going to fight the Yankees again." Jimmy shrugged his shoulders. Despite his beard, he was more boy than man—and it seemed he was more afraid of his mother than of anything either army could do to him.

Jimmy turned his gaze full on Narcissa. His eyes were deeply shadowed, weary-looking. "She didn't used to be like this. She been out of her head since she heard me and Father was both killed. But once she tells Lester we ain't going to help him, I reckon we can take off back home. I just got to see her safe back home. Then I'm going to come back and do my duty."

There was a creak of the floorboards, not directly overhead but somewhere in the main part of the house. Jimmy made a shushing noise. "That's him now."

There were more noises—muted footfalls, boards creaking. Then it grew quiet. Is it over? Narcissa wondered; will Annie be coming to let us out? Then she heard voices, so muffled by distance that it was impossible to tell what they were saying or who the speakers were.

"Jimmy," Narcissa whispered, "your mother may need our help. Is there any other way out of here?" How sincere her concern for Annie was, she couldn't tell. But she knew she couldn't stand much more of being locked in this cellar, left to the mercies of whoever won the argument going on above their heads.

"Just through that door." Jimmy gestured toward the door through which Narcissa had come.

"It's bolted," she told him, fighting back panic.

"I worked out the bolt before. There's a little crack between the doors, big enough to put a nail through. You can stick it into the bolt and drag the bolt across, a bit at a time. I almost got out that way once. But she caught me and took the nail away."

Narcissa looked around. The bare-dirt space was roofed by the timbers undergirding the house. There were plenty of nails, but it would take time to work one loose. Then she noticed the wire handle of the lantern. "What about this?"

"I reckon that would do." Jimmy came forward on his hands and knees to look at the lantern more closely. In a few moments he had the wire off and was threading it through the space between the doors. Narcissa crouched next to him, holding the lantern by the base to give him light to see what he was aiming for.

A noise from overhead froze them both. The boards of the kitchen floor thumped and creaked. Then they heard a woman's voice—Annie's, Narcissa thought. "I tell you, he ain't here. I sent him away. I'm sick of you. First you tell me you going to help me, then you—" Annie's voice faded; Narcissa couldn't make out the words. Suddenly Annie's voice grew stronger, as clear as if they were in the room together. "He's safe. And you ain't going after him." There was more creaking of floorboards, feet scuffling, the sounds of crockery breaking, of something large—a chair, maybe—clattering to the floor. *They're fighting up there.* Then the loud clap of a pistol shot, and a strangled cry that lasted only a second. Then silence.

"Jesus!" Jimmy cursed under his breath, or prayed maybe. The wire fell from his shaking hands. Narcissa picked up the lantern to help him find it. The silence above was kindling a new fear in her—that they would be left here, that no one would come to let them out. *God, please help him get us out of here.*

Jimmy worked for perhaps ten more minutes, stopping at intervals to shake the blood back into his fingers. Still there was no sound save the agonizingly slow scraping of the bolt as it moved, quarter-inch by quarter-inch. At last she heard the wooden bar fall away. Jimmy lunged up at the doors and threw them open. Fresh air came in.

Narcissa stood up, feeling pins and needles in her legs. She hurried after Jimmy, who was running up the steps into the kitchen. He stopped and dropped to his knees. Annie was lying on the floor, the pistol next to her. The shot had caught her in the middle of the chest. Her black dress was soaked with blood.

Jimmy looked up at Narcissa. "Lester did this. I swear to God, I'm going to kill him."

Narcissa picked up the pistol. It looked like the one Annie had been holding. Its single round had been fired, and recently, for it smelled of burned powder. Annie had been killed with her own gun, after the struggle they had heard. Maybe Lester had acted in self-defense.

Narcissa stood listening for sounds in the rest of the house. Surely Lester had fled. He might be hurrying back to Chimborazo. She waited, unsure of what to do. Jimmy seemed unstrung. But sometime—minutes or hours or days from now—he might make good his threat to go after Matthew Lester.

Lester had wealth, power, brilliance, all the things that Annie lacked. But Annie had the determination to kill or be killed for the sake of her son. Whether she'd intended to kill Lester or simply to drive him away, she must have pointed the pistol at him, just as she had at Narcissa. But she'd failed to kill him, and wound up getting shot with her own pistol. Still, though Annie had paid with her life, she had won— Lester had gone off believing Jimmy was safe, beyond his reach. And that he, Lester, was safe from Jimmy.

And now what? If she and Jimmy could catch Lester unawares, perhaps they could surprise him into revealing the truth. But they would have to be careful. Lester had his own pistol, after all; Annie's was no use anymore, unless Jimmy knew where his mother kept the powder and shot. Should she ask him, so that they could be armed when they approached Lester? No, she decided. Jimmy was still Devlin, after all; even though he was kneeling near his mother's body, sobbing as if his heart would break, she was far from sure she could trust him.

She took Jimmy by the arm. "You've got to find someplace to hide. Don't you see? That's what your mother was telling you—that's why she was talking so loud, when she said you were far away from here. She gave her life to save you. You owe it to her to save yourself. The truth will come out, and justice will be done."

Jimmy looked up at her. "He got her blood on his hands, and I'm going after him. You can't stop me."

"No! Jimmy, you can't do that. Your mother gave her life to save yours. If we are careful, we may be able to get Lester to admit what he's done—or at least to show his guilt in front of witnesses."

Jimmy put his chin up. "How?"

"Well—he may go straight back to the Sixth Division and cover his absence with some excuse or other. But it's only about a half mile, and he may be there already."

"We're just a few hundred feet from there." Jimmy's voice was eager now. "We can get through the ravine, cross Bloody Run. I know the way. It's rough," he added, looking a question at her.

"All right," Narcissa answered.

Then a shadow crossed Jimmy's face. "I hate to leave Mother."

"It will only be for a little while. I promise."

Jimmy held the lantern and led the way into the thicket. Narcissa followed, wondering if she had made the wrong choice in letting him take her across the ravine. She knew that their path lay straight down the steep bank of Bloody Run, and then up on the other side. Brambles were catching at her dress, raking her skin. She was afraid to stop, lest she be caught fast. *Is there really a way through?* But Jimmy seemed heedless of the difficulty. He pushed aside thin branches that sprang back, whiplike, to catch her in the face if her forearm wasn't ready to catch them. After a few minutes, though, he stopped, and she stepped out beside him onto the bank of the stream. Jimmy jumped down and reached his hand up to help her. Narcissa scrambled down the bank into the water—it wasn't deep, not even up to her knees—and, lifting her skirts, waded across. At the opposite bank she followed his lead, catching hold of a sapling and pulling herself up the steep incline. The thicket was less dense here, and she could see, ahead and above them, the hospital buildings and men moving about. Jimmy slowed down. She knew he must be wondering what he was letting himself in for, coming back to this place.

"Wait here," she told him. "Let me see if Lester has returned." He didn't protest.

Narcissa took the lantern and started up the rutted hill toward the hospital buildings. With Jimmy now behind her in the shadows, she felt her resolution ebb away. There's something wrong, she thought. It's false, staged. Annie, an unlettered mountain woman, already had proved an adept stage manager when she spirited her son out of the hospital from under the surgeons' noses. But Annie was dead. Jimmy was certain it had been Dr. Lester who killed her. Lester had blackmailed them both, mother and son: he'd told Annie he would have Jimmy arrested for desertion, and he'd told Jimmy he would have Annie arrested for stealing drugs. No—that wasn't right: Jimmy never said Lester spoke to him directly. Annie had told her son the threat came from Lester.

Narcissa was coming close now to the hospitals of the Sixth Division. Where had she seen the doctors when last she was here? How long had it been—a couple of hours? What if they had finished operating? Maybe, she thought, she could find Rosalie Stedman. She walked into the ward building. There at the end of the long room, standing at the washbasin, was Cameron Archer. He was splashing his face with water from the basin. His bloodied sleeves were rolled up above his elbows, and the water in the basin was red from the blood on his hands. She felt her heart lift for a second, but told herself she could not put her burden on him—he had more than enough to do.

He looked up then and saw her. "Narcissa—what in the world?" He came over to her and touched a lock of hair that straggled onto her shoulders.

"I'm all right," she assured him. "I came through the ravine. Where is Dr. Lester?" She was surprised at how calm her voice sounded. She was too exhausted, she supposed, for excitement. And Archer must have been similarly worn down. He simply gestured behind him toward the curtained-off space where she had seen the surgeons at work before. "There. Where I just came from."

"Has he been there all night?"

"Yes. But why—"

"Are you certain he didn't leave, not even for a half hour?" She stepped close to him, her eyes searching his face. She could see the lines around his mouth growing tight.

"Of course I'm certain. We've not been out of one another's sight for more than a few minutes at a time. I thought I saw you earlier. But now—you look like you've strayed out of Screamersville. What is the matter? Did you hear about Brit Wallace?"

"Mr. Wallace? No—is something wrong?"

"He's all right. He's come around. Doesn't remember what happened. Seems he got kicked in the head by a horse or something."

"Where is he?"

"Next door." Archer nodded sideways at the hospital building. "But if that's not what brought you here—"

"I have to speak with Dr. Lester—just for a moment. Can you ask him?" She thought for a moment he was going to refuse. Archer stared at some spot over her head, frowning to himself. The worst of it for him, she thought, would be the embarrassment of admitting to Dr. Lester he had no idea why Narcissa wanted to speak with him. She cast around for a lie that would serve. "Miss Ferncliff has fallen ill. They are close neighbors, you know. He may have attended her, or at least know her medical history."

"I'll tell him," Archer said. "I don't know whether he'll have time to talk with you."

He turned and began walking down the aisle, and she followed. As they came to the curtained-off area, she told him, "I'll be just outside," and slipped out the door.

———————

In a few minutes Lester came out, walking stiff-legged as if his feet hurt him. Blood and sweat streaked his face and soaked his clothing. A vein had burst in his left eye so that the iris seemed to float in a pool of blood.

"What is it, Mrs. Powers? What's happened to Miss Ferncliff?"

When he came close, Narcissa looked up into his face. "James Yates is alive." She watched for signs of guilty knowledge. She saw only incomprehension.

"Well, is he wounded? Is he one of mine?"

"James Yates is Annie Yates's son. She took him out of the hospital. You helped her to do it."

Lester continued to look blank.

"Devlin," she prompted. "James Yates was Devlin."

"Oh—the *sopor caroticus?* Why do you say I helped him?"

"You signed his death certificate, when you knew he wasn't dead."

Lester stared at her. "I did no such thing."

"Your servant—Susy Reynolds—helped his mother carry him out."

"Reynolds? My wife hired her. I don't concern myself with the household."

"You sent the wounded soldiers to Miss Ferncliff's. Why?"

Lester shrugged. "Archer suggested that. He thought you might be safer if you had some loyal Confederates around you. What is it you're getting at? Is there anything wrong with Miss Ferncliff, or not?"

Resolve drained away as confusion flooded in. No one could be so cool as to play that scene. Now none of her conclusions were making sense. As she tried to think what she could say to him, the scene of Annie's death replayed itself in her mind: the shouted words, the pistol shot, the crashing furniture. . . . If it hadn't been Lester, who could it have been? There must be something—a voice, a set of footsteps—why had she never heard the other person speak, or heard the sound of someone running away? Then it came to her what Annie must have done. Annie herself had made the sounds of a struggle, breaking crockery and knocking over a chair. Then she had shot herself with her own pistol. That was why, after the shot, there hadn't been the sound of running footsteps, or any sign that another person had been there.

The story Annie had told Jimmy, about Lester blackmailing her, must have been an attempt to frighten Jimmy into doing what she wanted. She'd told Jimmy that she herself was in danger, and she'd given him the name of someone he would respect as a threat: Dr. Matthew Lester. The fear that Lester would charge Annie with stealing drugs had kept Jimmy quiet for a time. But Jimmy had grown sick of hiding; he'd wanted to go back and face whatever penalty awaited him. Suicide was Annie's final, desperate attempt to force her son to leave the army—to go home—back to the hills where neighbors were only too happy to hide deserters. She'd meant to dose her son with morphine so that he would sleep through her suicide and wake up believing a powerful enemy, a Confederate surgeon, had killed his mother—and would be coming after him. Narcissa's unexpected arrival at Annie's house in the dead of night must have forced her to move more quickly than she'd intended.

"I'm sorry," Narcissa told Lester. "I got it all wrong. Annie must have forged your signature on the death certificate." Annie was clever enough to have done it, even if she couldn't read or write.

Lester straightened his shoulders and looked around. She knew she would not have his attention for very much longer. At last he said, "If Annie Yates is dead, there's nothing I can do, is there?"

"No. I'm sorry," Narcissa said again. She looked after him as he walked back to the curtained-off space where the surgeons were still working. She believed him; but now she had to convince Jimmy Yates that Annie had killed herself, that Lester had not been involved. Otherwise, Jimmy was likely to reload Annie's gun and go after Lester himself.

The best—maybe the only—way to do that was to find out the true source of Annie's fear. For she had been afraid. She'd been so desperate to get Jimmy away that she'd given her own life to do it. But get him away from what? If she'd made up the threat from Lester, there had to be a real threat—a more tangible threat than the Confederate army, which had shown no signs of coming after the young man. A black woman had helped Annie carry out her son. Maybe the woman had worked, not for Dr. Lester, as Annie claimed, but for Louisa Ferncliff. Not Susy, then, but Selah. And Selah could have attacked Brit, too, after he left Louisa's house. But why? All at once it came to her: the newspaper notice, asking for information concerning James Yates. When Brit had shown up at Ferncliff's, Selah had heard his name spoken. Selah was as bold and cunning in her own way as her sister Susy had been. She'd gone after Brit and dealt him a blow so hard the doctors thought he'd been kicked by a horse.

What was Selah doing now? She'd stolen the morphine, so Annie had said, that the doctors had left for the soldiers. What did she plan to do with it? Narcissa remembered the glasses of brandy Selah had so carefully poured the night before. Suppose, tonight, Selah had put morphine in the brandy to make the household sleep? But Annie had watered down the morphine. What would happen when Selah found they weren't asleep after all?

→>-<←

On the way to Louisa Ferncliff's, Narcissa tried to explain to Jimmy what his mother had done. He was very quiet, either accepting her account of what had happened or at least working through it in his own mind. At the door, Narcissa told Jimmy to wait again, then went in. The first person she saw was Mirrie, who was standing, white-lipped, at the bottom of the stairs.

Mirrie came up to Narcissa and whispered, "Louisa and Selah are both dead."

"Oh, God—how?"

"They may have killed each other. There were two shots. We ran upstairs and found them. Selah was . . . still alive."

Narcissa put her arm around Mirrie, who seemed to collect herself and went on. "Someone was hiding in a secret room in the wall of Louisa's bedroom. Judah Daniel thinks that person may have taken the letter and left the house through a secret passage. Judah Daniel's gone after whoever it was."

"Gone—alone? Where?"

"I don't know. But it can't be far."

"I'd better see if she needs help. Annie Yates is dead too. I think she killed herself. Her son is outside. Can you make a place for him here?"

Narcissa went out the door again and came back with a soldier. His uniform, his face, his hands, were all covered in powdery dirt. Tears had washed rivulets in the dirt on his cheeks. Mirrie stepped up to him and took his arm. "Come in. You look exhausted." Then she turned and mouthed over her shoulder to Narcissa, "Be careful."

Louisa Ferncliff's house occupied some of the highest land on Church Hill. But St. John's Church, just across the street, sat on top of a little knob of land that looked down on Louisa's mansion. It was too dark now to make out the details, but in another two or three hours the sun would be rising, and Judah Daniel knew what the dawn would reveal up at St. John's. The lush grass offered rich grazing for cows and sheep. *Green pastures.* The gated brick wall kept them out, though. This land was sacred to the dead—the wealthy and important dead. Their tombstones, like the clothes they had worn in life, had once been fashionable, but now just seemed odd. Why make a tombstone shaped like a table, a slab on four legs with a couple feet of empty space between it and the grass? *Thou preparest a table before me.* The familiar words echoed in her head. *Lie down in green pastures. . . .* It was all here, all around her. The words, like the quilt, held their secret in plain sight, but she had not taken their meaning because she'd heard them so many times before. Lettie had sent her right back to where Moses had been found. Ferncliff's secret was here, under her feet, or very close by.

She stepped carefully among the tombstones, touching first one and then another. She was moving toward the corner of the churchyard closest to Louisa Ferncliff's, walking down from the high ground. *The valley of death.* Here were more odd monuments. They were like the tables in shape and size, but—with brick on all four sides and a slab of granite for a lid—they looked more like boxes, suggesting they were made to hold a coffin. They didn't serve that purpose, she knew. To avoid contagion, or to foil grave robbers, the law required that the dead be buried six feet under the ground. So these bone houses were, she supposed, empty.

She went up to the tomb at the corner of the cemetery nearest to Louisa's. Catty-corner across the street, less than twenty yards away, stood the iron fence that bordered Louisa's property. There had to be an underground passage linking this grave to Louisa's house. Lettie's husband had torn the flesh off his fingers trying to shift the stone atop this grave—trying to get to safety inside Louisa's house. There must be a hidden mechanism, maybe worked from inside. Susy would have to use it to get out. Had she done it already, or was she in there now? There was nothing to do but wait and see.

Judah Daniel was settling herself, resting her back against another boxlike tomb, when she saw someone come out of the door of Louisa Ferncliff's and step into the street—a woman, she could tell that much, holding a lantern. Had Susy outfoxed her? The figure stopped in the street, undecided, it seemed, which way to go. Not Susy; she would be moving quickly. Judah Daniel stepped slowly, cautiously, up to the fence. The woman was only fifteen or twenty feet away from her now.

"Judah Daniel." The woman was calling her name, just above a whisper. It was Narcissa. For a moment Judah Daniel hesitated, wondering if she ought to trust her. Then Narcissa turned, as if she'd felt Judah Daniel's eyes on her, or heard her thought. It was too late now to wish things could be different. Judah Daniel called out, *"Here."*

Narcissa and Judah Daniel crouched close together, eyes fixed on the brick tomb. They whispered, though there seemed to be no one around to hear them. The lantern had been put out so as not to give warning of their presence.

"So you mean," Narcissa was saying, "Susy's been hiding in the house all along, waiting for a chance to get the letter?"

"Don't it make sense? Susy must have brung the quilt with her from up north, thinking she might use it for a signal. When Louisa refused to act, Susy dressed up in men's clothes and took the quilt out to the slaves on the farm, to the McRaes—her own cousins, though she hadn't seen them in more than twenty years. When they got here, Lettie and her husband and baby, something gone wrong. Susy had to find somebody else to take the letter. With what you told me about Annie Yates and Jimmy, I reckon it was them she went to next."

"Yes," Narcissa whispered excitedly. "Susy helped Annie carry him out of the hospital. Annie couldn't read or write, but Susy could, and she'd worked as a servant in Lester's house; she knew how to write his name. It must have been Susy who signed the death certificate. And tonight, Annie stole the morphine left for the wounded men. She took the bottle that Selah had hidden, poured off most of the morphine, and refilled it with water."

"Yes." Judah Daniel thought about what she had seen up in Louisa's room. "I reckon it—" She hushed, listening for that sound again: a little noise, a scrape of stone on brick. . . . It came again. "Give me the lantern, and stay hid," she whispered to Narcissa. "If she got another pistol, best you don't give her nothing to aim at."

Judah Daniel crouched next to the tomb, hiding the lantern, and waited. Little by little, the stone top moved sideways. Judah Daniel strained her eyes to see the dark figure slip out—wearing men's clothes. She waited until the stone top scraped back into place, then brought out the lantern. Susy stood, braced to run, but she seemed to relax a bit at the sight of Judah Daniel.

"Susy, it's Judah Daniel. John Chapman's friend."

"I know who you are. Stay away from me." Susy's voice was low, firm—surprisingly strong, considering the shock she must have received. "I have a pistol."

Judah Daniel kept talking. "You was hiding, there in the house. I followed you at Louisa's, after the fire. I seen you in the hall, hunched over like you was crying. I thought you was Selah."

Susy's smile widened. She looked strangely elated. "I'm

taking the letter out to the Union camp, tonight. Now. You can't stop me."

Judah Daniel put her hand in her apron pocket. "You left your revolver next to Louisa's body."

"I left it there. And I'm sure you did the same. You're not a fool. You knew it had to be found there, so that everyone would know Louisa and Selah killed each other. That way, the story has an ending. No one goes looking for a killer. No one asks questions that could turn up the story of a stolen letter."

"There's other ways I can stop you, without shooting you."

Susy shook her head. "I can't think of any. If you come too close, I'll scream, I'll fight you. People will come running. I'll tell them John Chapman stole the letter, and I went after him to get it. Even if you kill me, how long will it take you to find the letter? Maybe I have it on my person—but where? Maybe it's back there, in the tunnel. Can you find it before the police come and find it themselves? You won't take that chance, not when you know the trail leads back to John Chapman."

"You think you're mighty smart. But it was Selah outwitted you, in the end. Did you know Selah lived for a while, after you shot her? She left a message: a daguerreotype picture of you. She had it in her hand when she died. I found the quilt too, where you hid it. When I saw it up next to the picture of you, the pattern of the quilt piece look just like the dress you was wearing in the picture. Selah couldn't read or write. But you taught her something about the meaning of quilts. She wanted someone to know you was to blame for the killings.

"It was the baby that made the whole thing fall to pieces. When you got scared about the quilt giving away the secret, you had Selah come after the baby. She took him, but she didn't trust you with him, so she brung him back, but she kept the quilt. That give it away—it was the quilt, not the baby, you wanted."

"Selah was weak," Susy protested. She didn't seem so happy now.

"Not so weak," Judah Daniel answered, "till you broke her. You forced her to choose between you and Louisa. She couldn't do that. She tried to help you without hurting Louisa, without Louisa even knowing. Selah snuck you into the house, didn't she? She set that fire to get everybody out so you could get into Louisa's secret room. Then the wounded soldiers was brung into the house and Louisa made her mind up not to leave her room until they was gone. You was on the other side of the wall from that letter, but you couldn't get it. That liked to kill you, I reckon. . . . When did you figure out it was in the hair wreath?"

Susy's expression sharpened. Then her smile returned. "Having those soldiers brought in proved to be a blessing in disguise. It upset Mirrie Powers so, she tried to make Louisa use the letter. From my hiding place, I heard Louisa tell her it would stay hidden until the Day of Judgment—when the dead will be reunited with their hair, I suppose! But I didn't figure that out at first. Last night, Selah put morphine in Louisa's brandy so we could search the room. She drugged Louisa again tonight—and I found the letter, but Louisa woke up."

"What Louisa got tonight was mostly water."

Susy's eyes widened as she took this in. She obviously hadn't known why the morphine failed to work the second time.

Judah Daniel went on. "It weren't smart of you to drag Annie Yates and her son into this. Annie took most of the morphine and refilled the bottle with water. When Selah let you out of the hiding hole, she thought Louisa would sleep through till morning. But Louisa woke up and tried to stop you. So you killed her."

"It wasn't my fault!" Susy fired back. "I was already out in the room when Louisa woke up. I couldn't hide. And I wouldn't put it past her to have me arrested, even if it meant prison for her as well."

"After you killed Louisa, Selah come after you. So you shot her too."

"Selah jumped on me like a fury. I had to stop her. She would have ripped my eyes out. I killed them, and I'm sorry about it, but I'd do it again if I had to." Susy must have seen something in Judah Daniel's face, some resistance to her reasoning. "I disturb your comfortable world, don't I, Judah Daniel? You're like John Chapman. You've got your own freedom; you don't care about all the others. Don't you see? Personal feelings can't be allowed to interfere. I am a soldier, as much as any man wearing blue. In that moment, they were the enemy."

Judah Daniel nodded in mock agreement. "Un-huh. I reckon that's what you told Selah, to drive the wedge between her and Louisa."

Susy scowled. "Louisa toyed with us all; even Selah and me, and she'd known us since we were children—raised us, really. Not that it was so extraordinarily generous of her. We were her half-sisters, after all, got by her father on one of his slaves. When I stole the letter from Davis's house, it was what Louisa wanted; what she'd brought me here to do. Then she changed her mind. She couldn't see past her own grand theories. None of the ones I turned to for help could see past their own petty interests. Now it's up to me to take the letter. It isn't my choice to leave Richmond. I could still work here, in secret—or even in the open, no one much notices a servant. But there's no one else I can trust to take it now."

"Annie Yates dead. That seem to be the fate of people you *trust*."

After a moment, though, Susy answered. "Annie came

to Louisa for help smuggling her son out of the hospital. She said he was willing to go over to the Yankees. Selah overheard them talking. Louisa sent Annie away, but Selah went after her and told her there was another way. Selah was thinking of me—thinking that Annie's son could take the letter. It would have worked, only we couldn't find the letter at Louisa's. Annie got tired of waiting, I suppose. I don't know what happened to her. I didn't kill her."

"She killed herself to save her son from you. But the worst one, maybe, was the McRaes: father dead, mother in jail, baby left to his fate—why, Susy?"

Susy sighed, whether from sorrow or impatience Judah Daniel couldn't tell. "I told you—Louisa backed out of our agreement. She refused to send the letter. Given that, I couldn't very well ask her to hide the slave who would take the letter out to the Union camp. But I'd already sent the quilt, with the message about when and where to meet. I was here at the appointed time, but the slave, Jack McRae, got here before me. I told him he would have to hide in the woods and wait, that I didn't have the letter yet. He went mad. He jumped me. I shot him to save my own life. I didn't even know he'd brought a woman and a baby with him. He was supposed to come alone."

Judah Daniel felt cold with anger. "I seen his hands. He tried to claw his way into that grave there. He knowed that was the table prepared for him, to save him from his enemies, just like in the Psalm—the way in to Louisa's. And Louisa would of done right by him and his family; but you was only interested in the letter. That's why Selah tried to keep Louisa from finding out about what you done. She didn't want Louisa to hate you."

"I never intended for any of this to happen. I wouldn't have hurt the child—certainly I wouldn't have been worse to him than his own mother, who left him in the church-yard. But I would do it all again, and more, for a Union victory. Isn't there anything in the world that's worth that much to you?" Susy stared at Judah Daniel for a long moment, then shrugged. "It doesn't matter. I'm taking the letter to McClellan. There's nothing you can do to stop me—nothing you'd be willing to do."

Narcissa spoke out of the shadows. "It's too late, Susy. Haven't you heard? McClellan has sounded retreat." She stepped forward into the light of Judah Daniel's lantern.

Susy took a step back, put off balance, it seemed, by the sudden appearance of Narcissa. In an instant she had composed herself again. "I'll take my chances," she answered back, almost gaily. Then she turned and ran.

Narcissa started to follow her, but it was a halfhearted effort; after a few yards, she slowed and stopped. Judah Daniel came up beside her. "If we caught her," Narcissa explained, "we'd have to kill her—wouldn't we? There wouldn't be any other way to keep her quiet."

Judah Daniel understood. "She rather die famous than hide out till the war over. Anyway—if she get out, she ain't likely to talk about John Chapman. She don't want to share her glory."

"If I'd had that pistol in my hand," said Narcissa, "I think I would have used it. And then I would have been no different from Susy herself."

Judah Daniel was thinking the same thing: how easy it would have been over the past few days to kill any one of them—Selah, Louisa, now Susy—and to do so believing it would bring an end to it all. But if she'd killed any one of them, she would have wound up having to kill all of them—so bound together had the three of them been. "If you fix your eyes on the sun," she said at last, "it make you blind to everything that's not so bright. You wind up not seeing nothing but the sun."

"Yes," Narcissa said slowly. "Yes, I know what you mean."

→>—<←

Cameron Archer stood looking down at the bodies of Louisa and Selah. "You say Selah was still alive when you found them?"

"Just for a little while. Yes."

"Well, it's clear enough what happened. Louisa shot at Selah. The ball went through Selah's right lung. The recoil might have put Louisa off balance—I'm sure she wasn't used to firing a pistol. And she may have been shocked by what she had done. She may not have meant to shoot her, just to threaten her." Archer was smiling as he proposed solutions to the puzzle. "It may be that Louisa fired by mistake, not realizing it was Selah. She probably kept the pistol by her bed. Many ladies do—though most of them are afraid of the Yankees," he added dryly, "and I don't suppose Louisa Ferncliff anticipated trouble from that quarter.

"Selah," he continued, "was much stronger than Louisa, more accustomed to physical labor. She had enough strength left to get the pistol away from Louisa. She must have been holding on to Louisa, grappling with her. From fear, anger, or just by accident, Selah fired. It was point-blank range, right through Louisa's heart. Then Selah staggered to the door—see the blood on the floor there? But she couldn't make it. It must have been just a few moments later that you came in."

Archer straightened, folded his arms across his chest, and looked at Narcissa. He seemed to be waiting for her to express her admiration, but she couldn't think of anything to say. He was wrong, of course, but she couldn't tell him that. She could never let Cameron Archer know about the stolen letter that might have been an invitation to a Union victory.

"Thank you," she said at last. It wasn't much, but it was said warmly, and she saw him blush.

Archer turned to go, then turned back. "I'm sending an ambulance for the men downstairs. We'll find a place for them at Chimborazo, or somewhere. I don't imagine you'll want to be staying here any longer."

-+>-<+-

Brit's forehead was bandaged, and his smile when he saw her did nothing to ease Narcissa's guilt. She leaned over and gave him a kiss on the cheek.

"Forgive me for not getting up," he said wryly.

"What happened to you?"

Brit made a face. "It's a bit foggy."

"Is there anything you remember?"

"I remember being bowled over by a cannonball. But they tell me that was three days ago, at Mechanicsville, and that I was walking and talking and driving a wagon full of wounded men in between. I don't remember any of that. The next thing I remember is waking up here."

Narcissa spoke close to his ear. "Well—I'm afraid I have to ask your forgiveness. I think I know why you are here. I put a notice in the paper, you see, advertising for information about a young soldier, a private named James Yates. I only wanted to find out where he was buried, so that I could tell his mother, Annie. I asked for replies to be directed to you, at the Exchange Hotel."

"That doesn't seem dangerous," Brit remarked lightly.

Narcissa gave a sigh. She was wondering what kind of an explanation she could give for what had happened without touching on the stolen letter. That secret was not hers to tell. At last she said, "It shouldn't have been. But it was all false. James Yates hadn't died of injuries received at Seven Pines. His mother knew he was alive, that he'd recovered from his wounds. She'd been tending to him in the hospital. She'd forged a death certificate and gotten him out. I don't know why she made up the story about his body being lost, unless it was to cover a little slip she made. She said she went to Oakwood Cemetery every day to visit her husband's grave. Then she must have remembered she'd told me her son was dead as well. It would sound too strange to say, 'and my son's grave too, of course,' as an afterthought. So, when I asked where her son was buried, she panicked and told me she didn't know."

Narcissa paused, wondering if her lie would give her away as Annie's had done. Had she mentioned Annie couldn't read? No; she didn't think so; forge ahead, then. "When she saw the notice in the paper giving your name, she had no way to connect it with me. She thought someone else had found out the truth, or was on the verge of finding it out. Since you weren't at the Exchange any longer, she couldn't find you. But then when you brought the wounded men to Louisa's, she must have heard someone—me again, probably—say your name. She went after you and—"

"And had her gang of ruffians attack me," Brit interjected. "Please, Mrs. Powers, don't tell me an elderly widow fetched me a blow that left me unconscious for two days."

Narcissa smiled. "Not so elderly. And those mountain women are strong."

"I'm still not certain," Brit argued. "I really thought this was Ownby's doing."

It was Narcissa's turn to be puzzled. "Who is Ownby?"

"Lieutenant Ownby seemed to take a dislike to me. But now that I think of it, ransacking my room wasn't really the kind of thing he would do. He would have been afraid of spilling ink on his trousers. And if he'd had some underlings do it, he certainly would have stayed around to see the look on my face when I saw the damage. I'd been trying to figure out how he managed to get in here and steal a dispatch I wrote, until *your friend* Dr. Archer told me he took it out of my pocket after I was brought in."

"Oh. . . ." Narcissa wondered what this might mean. Archer could get on his high horse, especially where Brit was concerned.

"Don't worry," Brit reassured her. "He gave it back. I promptly put it into the fire, which I should have done myself as soon as the ink was dry on the blasted thing—if not before."

Brit fell silent a moment, staring into space. Then he looked into her eyes. "In any case, if you're right about what happened, I'm very glad you did use my name. If you'd given your own, it might have been *you* waking up with a dreadful headache, and days of your life missing."

Or worse, Narcissa thought, remembering how she'd been at Annie's mercy on more than one occasion. Instead, since Narcissa had not turned in Jimmy as a malingerer, Annie had returned kindness for kindness. Maybe it would have been better if she had turned him in—maybe these deeds of violence and despair would never have happened. But she would never know; and at the least it seemed she'd likely saved her own life.

CHAPTER NINE

JUNE 30

For Narcissa, the fever's siege was ending—just as the siege was ending for the city. She felt only the warmth of the morning sun as she walked with Mirrie down Franklin Street, both women carrying white roses for Annie's grave. On the street in front of the house that had been Annie's, a wagon waited. Annie's coffin had already been lifted into it. Jimmy Yates was waiting, wearing his uniform, a forage cap clutched in his two hands. He was a skinny young man, with skin as pale as cheese, and he blinked against the glare of the sun.

"Soon as we bury her," he said, "I'm going to report to my regiment. I just don't feel right about going back home, when the other fellows ain't. Maybe by winter we can all go home."

"I hope so," Narcissa told him.

They walked behind the wagon to Oakwood Cemetery. Narcissa had paid for a small plot there. She hadn't mentioned this to Jimmy, figuring he couldn't repay her, and he didn't seem to wonder how it had come about. He was in a kind of shock from everything that had happened to him; or maybe his mother had protected him from the hard realities of life so that he didn't think about how things had to be paid for. It wasn't only young princes who were coddled, it seemed. Annie, who'd had next to nothing, had willingly given it all up for her son. What would happen to Jimmy? She hated to think.

Over the past year, so many mothers had taken long and dangerous journeys—journeys that cost the little money they had—to this city of hospitals and graves. When hurt, when dying, soldiers called for their mothers, just as they had done years before in childhood troubles.

The grave had been dug. Jimmy and the Negro driver of the wagon lifted down the pine box. The hot sun beat down on them.

Narcissa took out the little black-bound prayer book she had taken from the shelf at Louisa Ferncliff's. "I'll read the service, if you like. That's what Mrs. Brockenbrough did for Colonel Stuart's Captain Latané."

"I'd be much obliged to you," Jimmy answered.

Jimmy, Mirrie, and the Negro driver bowed their heads as Narcissa read the familiar passage from Second Corinthians concerning the resurrection of the dead. Then she turned to the prayer to be said at the grave. "Man, that is born of a woman, hath but a short time to live, and is full of misery. He cometh up, and is cut down, like a flower; he fleeth as it were a shadow . . ." She thought again of the son that she had lost, hours after his birth. Would she have given her life to save him, even if it was a sin? Of course she would. God, forgive Annie Yates, she prayed. Forgive us all.

Lettie was well enough now to have no more need of doctoring, so Judah Daniel had to think of another way into the Negro Jail. She took the last of the whiskey Mirrie had given her to make the medicine for Narcissa. Bearing this gift, she went to see the guard named Murphy.

"How do I know it ain't poisoned?" Murphy asked her. In answer, she took the bottle and swallowed a mouthful.

He watched with narrowed eyes for a few moments, as if half expecting her to drop dead, but at last he took the bottle. "All right," he told her. "Five minutes. Her owners is coming soon, and I don't want to be thinking you in there maybe damaging their property."

As usual, Lettie was lying on her straw mat. Judah Daniel walked past her to the little window set high in the wall and beckoned to Lettie. "Come over here, honey."

Lettie got up slowly and stood in front of Judah Daniel.

"Climb on my back," Judah Daniel said. She got down on her hands and knees to make a stepstool of her body. Lettie put one foot on her, gingerly shifted her weight onto it, then brought up the other foot.

"Can you see?" Judah Daniel asked her.

"I see a man and a woman," Lettie whispered, barely loud enough for Judah Daniel to hear. "The woman holding a baby."

"That your son," Judah Daniel whispered back. "We call him Moses. Elda Chapman gon' be his momma, and John Chapman his granddaddy, till you come back for him."

Lettie stayed there for a moment. She must have been holding on to something, the window bars maybe, because she weighed almost nothing. Then she climbed slowly down and put out her hand to help Judah Daniel up.

They heard steps in the hall—Murphy, most likely. In the last bit of time they would have together, Lettie put her head close to Judah Daniel's and murmured, "Thank you."

As Judah Daniel was leaving, Murphy stopped her again. She noted the liquor bottle was almost empty. "You ain't got no call to come down here no more." He eyed her coldly, and she knew she'd better be careful, or he would start asking questions about her.

Judah Daniel shrugged. Her body took on what she thought of as her whipped-dog look—head low, shoulders narrow, eyes turned from the accusing glare. The look said, *I didn't do nothing, don't take your boot to me, lowly as I am.* It was used to disarm, to deflect blame, but it could backfire with men—and women—who liked to hurt those weaker than themselves. "All right, sir. I'll stay away."

"You do that," Murphy snapped, then raised the bottle to his lips to drain the last drops.

Judah Daniel went out to the alley, but stopped dead at the sight of three white men who must have just come up. One of the men was standing just in front of John, his back to Judah Daniel. The man had his hands on his hips and his legs apart—a threatening stance, like a dog with its head down and its hackles raised. She recognized him—a plug-ugly named Fuller. The other two were slouching, joking with each other. She heard Fuller say, "What you got there, Chapman? You come to collect the reward for that there runaway?"

"Oh, no, sir," she heard John reply. "This my grand-baby."

Judah Daniel edged closer to hear what Fuller would say to this. His voice was loud, so his fellows could hear him, probably. "We been looking all over town for a slave baby just a few weeks old."

"Oh! Well—this my grandbaby, born in freedom."

Fuller turned to Elda. "You the mother?"

The dazed look on Elda's face struck fear into Judah Daniel. Elda had never shown much feeling for the baby Moses. Now the baby's safety depended on her caring enough to lie for him, and being sharp enough to tell the right lie.

"I said, you the mother?" the man asked her again, more gruffly.

Elda nodded.

"What's his name?"

"Well, sir . . . we calls him Moses, sometimes," Elda whispered. "But he named Tyler, after his daddy." She shifted the baby closer and rubbed her chin against his head.

"I heard your baby died," Fuller responded.

Elda shuddered and shook her head. "He been sick," she said softly. "He all right now."

"You got his papers?"

"Yes, sir," John Chapman spoke up. "I got them back at the house."

Fuller stood there for a moment longer. Then he shook his head. "Well, you best get him out of here. Somebody might get the wrong notion."

Judah Daniel, who'd been watching this, breathed easy for the first time in a long while. Then she faded back down the alley, keeping out of the way of the three white men.

→>‹←

Narcissa walked up on Chimborazo Heights, out to the farthest extremity to the east overlooking the river. The Federals were in retreat, turning their long supply train like a lumbering beast trapped in a place too small for it, heading southeast to Harrison's Landing on the James well below the city. The audacious General Lee, the city's new hero, pursued them. Perhaps they would go away and never return. But there were so many of them.

She had set her mind to doing something eccentric, or childish at the very least. She had come here to walk among the lines of sheets where they hung clean and white, taking heat out of the air and releasing a subtle vapor. She passed between the rows and stepped up to first one and then another, close as she could without touching, feeling the mist from them cool on her face and hands and even—did she imagine it?—through her layers of clothes.

She could not walk away from the world. These sheets bore stains of blood, and no amount of washing would ever blanch them back to pristine whiteness. And still she felt her heart lift with the memory of a time she had felt safe. Everyone she had ever loved, starting with her mother, whom she had followed to the laundry line as soon as she could walk—it seemed as if they were all there, close by, just out of sight on the other side of these sheets.

"I saw you walking this way. I couldn't imagine where you were going."

She turned and looked down the long white row to see Cameron Archer. His hazel eyes looked tired, his hair and beard overgrown. He stood looking at her, arms crossed, a little smile on his face. It was, Narcissa thought, the warmest look she had ever seen on Cameron Archer's face. "You know," he said, "this brings back memories. I used to play among the clotheslines when I was a boy, pretending the laundry basket was my ship and the sheets were my sails. It was a good escape. Is that what you are doing?"

"I used to do that as well, though for me the sheets were flags flying from the turrets of my castle. Right now I'm trying to get up my nerve to go back into the wards. Do you think Dr. Lester has forgiven me?"

"Forgiven you? I doubt he recollects the whole episode. In fact, he asked me this morning if you were well enough to come back."

She suspected this was a lie. Probably Archer himself had smoothed the way, explained to Lester that she'd been out of her mind with exhaustion and fever—and Narcissa wondered herself if that had, in fact, been true. In any case, it was kind of Archer to ease her way back. "Thank you," she said. "I'm ready now."

She went to him. He waited for her, and she moved close enough so that he gazed down at her. She could see the care etched in his face, but care for what, she wondered. For his patients? For his city? For her, perhaps? When he didn't turn toward the hospital, she felt her heart quicken. Without looking away, she held out her hand to him. She saw his eyes drop to her hand and then come back to her face, and he tilted his head, ever so slightly, as he took her hand, not in a handshake but in a grip that held it tightly in his own.

"Mrs. Powers, I want you to know I admire"—he stopped for an instant with a look that seemed to say, Bear with me—"more than admire you. With this war so much upon us, there is much in our hearts that goes unsaid."

Tell me, she wished. But a moment passed, and another. The breeze freshened, and a sheet swirled up between their faces. When it settled and she could see his eyes again, it was as if he had awakened from a dream. This was no longer a boy's ship or a girl's castle. He was a doctor, she was a nurse, war raged, and duty called. His grip on her hand eased a little, and he folded his arm under hers as he turned to lead her back out of their private world.

Even in men's clothes, Susy Reynolds felt awkward on a horse. Her city upbringing hadn't given her much experience with the animals. But her lack of ease in the saddle did not dim the elation she felt. Soon she would be on board a swift Union ship, heading north to freedom. Soon she would get the recognition she had earned for stealing an important document from the home of the Confederate president. She smiled to herself as she imagined the caricatures in *Harper's*, the *Enquirer*, the *Times*—Davis, scrawny and hollow-eyed, would be sitting at his desk, staring off into space, while she, demure and deferential, slipped an envelope out from under his hand. For dramatic effect, the artist would exaggerate the size of the envelope, make it as big as a tea tray, with an important-looking seal. . . .

The young aide-de-camp, Lieutenant Cummings, had brought her out from the rear-guard outpost at White Oak Swamp. They had ridden hard for a couple of hours, passing mile after mile of supply wagons, the lifeline of the glorious Union army. The covered wagons, pulled by teams of six horses, still seemed heavy with unused supplies. She'd had to fight down bitterness at the sight of this army—better equipped and further from exhaustion than the Confederate forces, yet, unbelievably, in retreat. If not for Louisa Ferncliff's stubborn resistance, the letter might have gotten out in time to prevent this calamity. Still—she had proven what could be done. It was what the three of them—she, Louisa, and Selah—had always wanted, planned for, dreamed of. The other two had fallen away, made weak by circumstances and by their own shortcomings. Susy refused to take their defection to her heart. She was stronger than they were, and she would hold fast.

They rounded the hill at last. The lieutenant pulled up. She tugged on the reins, and the horse slowed obligingly. They came to a halt looking out at the landing below them, and the James River beyond, sparkling under the brilliant sky. The sight took her breath away—Union warships riding at anchor on the smooth-flowing water, the Stars and Stripes flying from them bright as new paint. There was the *Galena*, her armor plating ruptured in the failed attack she had led at Drewry's Bluff six weeks before, but still impressive with her big guns trained on the shore.

In a moment they were moving again, heading for the

little cluster of tents at the landing. Judging by the small size of the encampment, they had not reached the main Union fortifications. Of course, General McClellan would want to stay close to his army. She had insisted on being taken to him. At the sight of the letter she carried, the officers whose job it was to protect the retreat had agreed. Lieutenant Cummings now carried the letter. But that was all right. Military protocol demanded an orderly and cautious approach to such things.

They passed through questioning guards and approached the tents. There they stopped; a young soldier, little more than a boy, ran out to take the horses. She slipped down from the saddle unaided, glad again of her masculine attire. Lieutenant Cummings had gone ahead of her and was talking to a high-ranking officer. After a few moments this officer led Cummings to the largest of the tents. Its flaps were pulled wide open to admit the breeze. Inside she could see another officer sitting at a little wooden table. She waited—all this had to proceed with military decorum, after all—but she could not keep herself from peering at the man sitting there in the shade. She could see straight dark hair, cut short; a square, bold-featured face; an abundant mustache with a thin strip of beard just beneath the lower lip; a fine uniform with bright buttons in sets of three, gilt-edged shoulder straps; knee-high boots. She was standing a mere fifteen feet away from Major General George McClellan, commander of the Army of the Potomac. In an instant those dark eyes would be fixed on her. She felt her heart pound with excitement bordering on pain.

From the aide's hand McClellan took the envelope, noted the charred edge, the stamped red seal and the pencil scrawl, then pulled out the piece of thin blue paper and unfolded it. The date written at the top right-hand corner was June 22.

The lieutenant glanced over his shoulder at Susy. "It's an educated hand," he pointed out. "Not likely the black woman could have forged it, though she speaks well enough."

"No," McClellan agreed. The strong, slanting script covered four pages, growing looser—more hurried, or more vehement—toward the end. The signature was that of a man who'd signed his name often, and who'd put some thought into the impression it should make. *Henry A. Wise*—the three parts of the name were linked together, made with one stroke of the pen, so that the *y* swooped up to the *A*, whose crosspiece slashed down to form the first leg of the *W*.

He turned back to the first page, scanning the letter's contents. "Paucity of men . . . vulnerable to attack . . . McClellan's superior numbers . . . one concerted thrust at this point, and the city will be taken. . . ."

McClellan snorted. Superior numbers! He scowled past the young aide who had brought the letter toward the woman in her ludicrous disguise. Then he spoke, loud enough for her to hear. "Whoever wrote this letter knew nothing of the true state of things. It could be genuine. That hardly matters. If it is, it merely reveals Brigadier General Wise's ignorance. Or it could be a forgery, designed to lead us into a trap. Like so many other attempts, it failed. I am bringing my gallant army out of the snares laid for us."

In Susy Reynolds's eyes, the dazzling day went white. A wordless sound, like wind through a stand of trees, filled her ears. In a moment, though, she had recovered. *I'll go to Lincoln himself,* she vowed silently, and held out her hand for the letter. She stared in disbelief as McClellan crumpled the thin blue paper in his fist. For an instant, their eyes met. Then he turned and addressed Lieutenant

Cummings. "On second thought, put it into the fire. God forbid my enemies should find it and use it against me—as I know they would not scruple to do. They are everywhere," he pronounced solemnly, with the slightest glance in Susy's direction. "Even here."

Another uniformed aide came up. He saluted McClellan and said, "Sir, Commander Rodgers presents his compliments and asks if you are ready to board the *Galena*."

McClellan returned the salute, then turned away into the tent. Lieutenant Cummings followed him a few steps. "Sir, what do you want me to do with her?"

McClellan stopped. "Whatever she was after with this, it need not concern us now. Let her find her own way home."

Students of Richmond history will know that my Louisa Ferncliff is a fictionalized version of Elizabeth Van Lew, the Richmond Unionist who is said to have placed her free black former servant, Mary Elizabeth Bowser, as a servant and spy in the household of Jefferson Davis. Historical works on Van Lew and Bowser include *Cornbread and Maggots, Cloak and Dagger: Union Prisoners and Spies in Civil War Richmond* by David D. Ryan; and *A Yankee Spy in Richmond: The Civil War Diary of "Crazy Bet" Van Lew*, edited by Ryan. Photographs of Elizabeth Van Lew, her Church Hill mansion, and the space under the eaves where she hid escaping slaves and Union prisoners appear in *Shadows in Silver: A Record of Virginia, 1850–1900 in Contemporary Photographs taken by George and Huestis Cook with Additions from the Cook Collection*, by A. Lawrence Kocher and Howard Dearstyne. Wellesley professor Elizabeth Varon is currently at work on a biography of Van Lew. Fact-based fictional accounts of Van Lew and Bowser's story are *Dear Ellen Bee: A Civil War Scrapbook of Two Union Spies*, by Mary E. Lyons and Muriel M. Branch, a fascinating and beautiful book for young adult readers; and *The Secret of the Lion's Head* by Beverly B. Hall, effectively told for younger readers from the point of view of Van Lew's niece Annie.

Individuals may disagree as to whether Van Lew and

Bowser were heroines or traitors. Even the other characters in this book would disagree on that question. What interests me is what might have happened if two strong-willed people in such a relationship had been tried in the crucible of besieged Richmond. The resulting violence, betrayal, and death are no reflection on the historical Van Lew and Bowser, but come simply from the fact that I write murder mysteries.

Elizabeth Van Lew's house was destroyed after her death, but St. John's Church still stands nearby, and Chimborazo is now the site of a museum of Civil War medicine operated by the National Park Service. The most thorough work on Chimborazo Hospital is the 1999 dissertation by Carol Cranmer Green (*Chimborazo Hospital: A Description and Evaluation of the Confederacy's Largest Hospital*), which I understand is being readied for publication. The National Park Service also offers tours of the Seven Days battle sites.

Civil Blood

"This is mystery at its best: strong storytelling, dark secrets, and plenty of startling turns along the way."

—*Roanoke Times*

The third in the series that the *Richmond Times* calls "deeply satisfying" opens in the spring of 1862 as the war escalates and troops move in for battle. But in Richmond an even greater threat looms. Smallpox has broken out. Narcissa, Judah, and their friend, journalist Brit Wallace, suspect this is more than a microbial contagion.   *ISBN 0-14-200124-4*

Chickahominy Fever

"A fascinating story."   —*Civil War Book Review*

It is June 1862, Union forces have the city surrounded, and a crucial letter detailing the weak points of Confederate defenses has been spirited by a black servant into the heart of Richmond's Unionist underground. But amid the confusion and danger of the siege, two women have more immediate concerns; Narcissa Powers attempts to locate the body of a Confederate soldier that has mysteriously gone missing, while Judah Daniel searches for the mother of an abandoned infant.   *ISBN 0-14-200456-1*